junction of earth
and sky

Susan Buttenwieser is the author of the short story collection, *We Were Lucky With the Rain* (Four Way Books) and she has been awarded several fiction fellowships from the Virginia Center for the Creative Arts. Her writing has appeared in numerous publications and she has taught creative writing in New York City schools, libraries, homeless shelters, juvenile detention facilities and at a women's maximum-security prison. *Junction of Earth and Sky* is her first novel.

junction of earth and sky

SUSAN BUTTENWIESER

MANILLA PRESS

First published in the UK in 2024 by
ZAFFRE
An imprint of Zaffre Publishing Group
A Bonnier Books UK company
4th Floor, Victoria House, Bloomsbury Square, London, WC1B 4DA
Owned by Bonnier Books
Sveavägen 56, Stockholm, Sweden

Copyright © Susan Buttenwieser, 2024

All rights reserved.
No part of this publication may be reproduced,
stored or transmitted in any form by any means, electronic,
mechanical, photocopying or otherwise, without the
prior written permission of the publisher.

The right of Susan Buttenwieser to be identified as Author of this
work has been asserted by her in accordance with the
Copyright, Designs and Patents Act, 1988.

This is a work of fiction. Names, places, events and
incidents are either the products of the author's
imagination or used fictitiously. Any resemblance to
actual persons, living or dead, or actual
events is purely coincidental.

A CIP catalogue record for this book is
available from the British Library.

Hardback ISBN: 978-1-78658-346-8
Trade paperback ISBN: 978-1-78658-383-3

Also available as an ebook and an audiobook

1 3 5 7 9 10 8 6 4 2

Typeset by IDSUK (Data Connection) Ltd
Printed and bound in Great Britain by Clays Ltd, Elcograf S.p.A.

Zaffre is an imprint of Zaffre Publishing Group
A Bonnier Books UK company
www.bonnierbooks.co.uk

For Rae, Lola and Andy and in loving memory of my grandmother, Helen

Contents

1. A Minor Movement of Muscles, 1993 — 1
2. This Isn't a Good Idea, 1940 — 8
3. If, 1971 — 21
4. The Distance Already Travelled, 1974 — 26
5. Daddy, 1975 — 36
6. The Miller's Tomb, 1940 — 46
7. Terminal Velocity, 1990 — 54
8. Maybe We'll Go Camping, 1978 — 62
9. Opening Day, 1979 — 79
10. Waiting, 1979 — 90
11. What Remains, 1940 — 97
12. Still Life, 1990 — 105
13. Moms' Night Out, 1980 — 112
14. Summer is Money, 1981 — 122
15. Early Bird Singers, 1982 — 132
16. The Arrival, 1940 — 144
17. Blue Mornings by Cold Storage Beach, 1991 — 153
18. It's Too Late, 1983 — 162
19. Conditional Probability Equations, 1984 — 167
20. Smouldering, 1985 — 179
21. That Kind of Gone, 1941 — 194
22. Force of Your Suck, 1992 — 203

23. Junior Life-Saving, 1986   213
24. Hidden Scars, Invisible Wounds 1988   221
25. Someday, 1989   232
26. Route Two Citgo Station, 1993   236
27. Month of Mondays, 1993   242
28. Apparent Junction of Earth and Sky, 1996   252
29. The Aftermath, 1997   264
30. Descending Lines, 1999   270

Acknowledgements   278

1

A Minor Movement of Muscles

1993

SINCLAIR'S PHARMACY HASN'T EVEN opened yet, but Marnie can already see there are problems with Jimmy's plan to rob it. The drugstore is on the main street of this beach town, and as they park outside and wait for it to open, Jimmy says holding it up will be totally easy, like taking candy from a baby. He says, this early on a Sunday morning, only one person will be working and the place is old-school so there won't be much in the way of security, no video cameras or cash registers behind Plexiglas the way the chains have. All they have to do is wave the gun in front of the cashier, who is probably going to be some little old lady, and the money in the till and the safe and all the prescription pills will be theirs, he tells Marnie.

The first problem with Jimmy's plan occurs only a few minutes later, when a powder-blue Oldsmobile Omega pulls into the parking space in front of them. An elderly woman in sunglasses and a flowered bathing suit cover-up gets out on the passenger side of the car and takes slow, deliberate steps towards the pharmacy. As the woman waits, lights come on inside and Marnie can see two employees walking around the store. Then, the man behind the wheel of the Oldsmobile rolls down all the windows and crooks out his left arm, dangling a cigarette, so he would definitely be able to hear screaming coming from inside the pharmacy. Now there are at least four people to deal with.

Marnie and Jimmy have been living in his Chevy Nova for months, running heroin and cocaine and whatever else their dealer wants moved along the southern New England coastline. Jimmy insists that Marnie stay in the car when they go to the dealer's house. For her own good, Jimmy says. But a lot of what he says isn't actually the truth. Like, it would be easy to rob this drugstore. Or that selling drugs could be profitable even when the proportion of personal ingestion exceeds the amount sold. No matter how the maths is done, no matter what Jimmy says, the numbers never add up. All the money they make dealing goes towards their heroin habit, with barely enough left over for gas, and they have to shoplift or dumpster-dive in order to eat.

Marnie looks over at her boyfriend, his grey sunken eyes, dried-out patchy skin the colour of a spider web. He looks like a corpse when he's asleep and sometimes, in the mornings when she wakes up first, she checks him for a pulse. This is the person she has everything pinned on.

Some of the towns they pass through are named for places in England. Marnie remembers her grandmother, who was English, always pointing out the irony that Americans went to all this trouble to overthrow the British government, and then couldn't think what to call anything. Her grandmother had been Marnie's primary caregiver, and on their weekly trips to the library when she was little, they'd look through the world atlas and invent expeditions they were going to take together *someday*. 'Let's pretend we're going on a safari, just the two of us,' her grandmother would say. 'And we're off to see some lions and zebras and giraffes.'

'How about a gorilla?' Back then, Marnie's tastes tended towards gorillas.

'Oh, most definitely a gorilla. Yes, absolutely. We must see a gorilla.'

The street is starting to wake up after a Saturday night. It's a warm July morning and clusters of vacationers are starting to form outside Vi's Beach Sundries and Supplies, directly across from Sinclair's and Jimmy's Chevy Nova. There's a young couple with a baby in a jogging stroller sitting on a bench with the paper spread out in front of them, holding Styrofoam cups of coffee. A group of moms dole out doughnuts to their kids, while the dads shout out the scores of last night's baseball games. Four guys are even starting in on Bud Tall Boys. Yet more witnesses.

'Jimmy,' Marnie whispers.

'What is it?' His eyes scrunch up with irritation every time Marnie speaks.

'I don't have a good feeling about this,' she says.

He takes a long breath and exhales loudly, his pupils pinpoints of rage. 'Why do you do this?' He slams his hand on the steering wheel. 'You're always bringing your negative energy into everything!' He mimics her in a high-pitched screech. '"Jimmy, I don't have a good feeling about this. Jimmy, I'm scared. Jimmy this, Jimmy that!" I'm so done with your paranoid, fucked-up shit, Marnie!'

She closes her eyes and tries not to cry. What would happen if she grabbed her backpack, opened the passenger door and got out of the car? She has tried before to get away from her boyfriend. But even after a heroin overdose in February, when she almost died, the gravitational pull was too much and she went right back to him. Now she no longer has it in her. The ability to leave Jimmy.

There have been some occasional good moments. In early June, they went out to Block Island, delivering to a musician, and stayed overnight in his house on a cliff overlooking the ocean. It was like being in some sort of dream, sleeping in an actual bed the entire night. This crazy-ass comfortable bed, with like 400-thread-count cotton sheets, and soft down pillows, the waves crashing right outside their bedroom, white curtains – clean, white curtains – blowing in the floor-to-ceiling windows. Amazing coke, the kind that actually makes you feel good, which they did at dinner with wine while watching the sunset and listening to jazz. Just her and Jimmy and the musician and his girlfriend, like all civilised and normal.

Normal is so far away that when Marnie stumbles upon it, she feels like she'll break apart. Last week, they slept outside a campground so they could sneak in to use the bathrooms. Marnie swam at dawn in the salt water pond, floating on her back while nearby a father was fishing with his son in a rowboat. She listened while the man showed his son the way to put a worm on the hook without cutting his fingers and how to cast, the fishing line whipping through the air before landing in the water. The sky became pink and orange and even a hint of purple. Marnie could have stayed there all day listening to the man tell his son fishing stories in his soft, gentle voice. After she had a shower, she saw them at a picnic table with the mom and a baby, eating breakfast by a small campfire. A feeling of total loneliness had come over her and she ran to the car, crying the whole way. 'What's your fucking problem?' Jimmy said when she got into the front seat.

The older woman waiting outside the drugstore pulls out a piece of paper. The man in the Oldsmobile Omega calls out to her. 'What?' she asks him. They are talking loudly, yelling really, and Marnie can hear them as clearly as if they are right in the car with her and Jimmy.

'Can you get me some Tums?' the man shouts.

'I told you not to order that orange juice,' his wife says. 'It doesn't agree with you. I told you.'

'Can you just get the Tums, Rita? You're going in anyway. What's the difference?'

'The difference is I just bought a whole huge pack of them on sale. This place is kinda pricey.'

A young woman around Marnie's age – 21 – unlocks the door from inside Sinclair's and opens it. 'Good morning,' she says. 'Sorry to keep you waiting. What can I help you with today?'

'Oh, it's all right, dear. Just picking up my prescription and some Tums. Now, where would I find those?'

After the woman has gone inside, the man in the Oldsmobile Omega turns on the radio, flipping around from news to the Top 40 until he settles on 'Uptown Girl'.

'There's so many people around, Jimmy,' Marnie says. 'This is too messed up. You don't know shit about holding up stores.'

'Would you just shut the fuck up and stop harshing me with your negative vibes?' Jimmy opens the glove compartment and pulls out the gun, tucks it in between his boxers and his blue jeans, pulls his T-shirt over it.

'I'm not doing it.' Marnie stares straight ahead. 'I'm not going in there with you.'

'Why are you like this?' He twists around until he is up on his knees and puts his hands around Marnie's throat, squeezing hard.

'Please, Jimmy, don't,' she croaks, trying to shove him away.

'Shut the fuck up!' His teeth are clenched, his lips curled into a snarl. 'Just shut the fuck up.'

She starts to cry as his fingers tighten around her windpipe. Finally, he releases her and lies back across the seat. They are both panting, as if they've just had sex. He rubs at his face.

'Fine, I'll do it myself. I have to do everything, don't I?' Jimmy gets out of the car and leans in to talk to her. 'Keep the engine running. Think you can at least do that?' Then he slams the door behind him.

Marnie moves over to the driver's seat. After pulling out of the parking space, she idles there in the street. It would be possible for her to lift her foot off the brake, place it on the gas pedal and drive away. It's only a matter of a few inches, the shifting of her right leg, swivelling her ankle, a minor movement of the muscles in her right foot, her toes. Instead, she adjusts the rear-view mirror and waits for Jimmy, ready to floor it when he comes back outside.

2

This Isn't a Good Idea

1940

IT'S ALICE'S IDEA TO get Pearl swimming. Today. This morning. Right now, here on Sea Place Beach. The little girl turned five at the end of May, and it's July already, but all she can manage are a few doggy-paddle strokes between her older sister, Lou, and Alice. Tomorrow, the army will finish installing barbed wire, mines and concrete blockades, part of the bulwark to protect Spithandle from a Nazi invasion, which people fear could happen now that France has been occupied. Tomorrow, swimming at Sea Place Beach will be banned, and no one will be allowed on it or anywhere else along the south-eastern coast of England.

All week the two friends have been trying to teach Pearl to swim in the sea. Yesterday, she was no longer clinging to them, scared to let go for a brief moment, like she had been. Pearl seemed truly on the verge, and she begged Lou and Alice to promise they would come back in the morning so she could try again. Of course they would, the older girls said. All three knew that if they waited any longer, there might not be another opportunity for a long time. No one knew when the beaches would open up again.

This summer, the weather has been unusually good for days on end, and most have been clear and free from rain. And certainly warm enough for Alice and Lou to take Pearl in the afternoons to Sea Place Beach, which is ten miles to the west of Brighton. As long as it's not pouring, the rocky shore teems with children playing between the wooden pilings when the tide is too far out for swimming, and shouting and splashing about in the water when it comes back in.

Alice woke in the night to a thunderstorm that swept through Spithandle, and its remnants were still palpable earlier in the morning, with the trees shaking and swaying. Now, as she stands at the edge of the water holding Pearl's small hand, the wind churns the water, creating giant, powerful-looking swells. The opposite of yesterday's conditions when the sea was flat, the air still. Only Alice, Pearl and Lou are even wearing swimming costumes. Everyone else is dressed. A few children wade around in the shallows while the rest content themselves with playing on the pebbly beach. No one is swimming.

'This isn't a good idea, Alice,' Lou says. 'Even *I* wouldn't dare go in the sea when it's this rough.'

'But I really, really, really want to,' Pearl says, even though she's shivering. 'Please, Lou. Let me have a go?'

Alice scans the water. She is fourteen, a year older than Lou, and her friend generally looks up to her. If they can just get past where the waves are breaking, it looks calm enough to swim, she tells Lou. 'It will be fine,' Alice says, taking hold of Pearl's hand and leading her out into the rough water.

When the little girl's feet can no longer reach the sand, she grips on to Alice's forearm for support and they make their way into the deeper water. Alice grabs Pearl, tells her to shut her eyes and hold her breath, and attempts to dive through an oncoming wave. But the pull of the tide is too strong, and they end up beneath it instead. Pearl screams just before it comes crashing down on them.

The wave engulfs Alice and she tumbles over and over, losing hold of Pearl. Salt water burns inside her nose. She is lifted up before being slammed onto the shore. The current sucks back hard, and Alice digs at the small rocks and grey sand. Seaweed clings to her arms and legs and there is some around her neck. Pearl is further out, flailing in the waves, and only part of her face is visible. Alice claws through the water, trying to reach her. But she can't break through and loses all control of her body. Once again, she is overcome by the violent surf and bashed back onto the shore. Pearl gets caught in a riptide and dragged out even further. Then a wave washes over her, and she disappears altogether.

Lou dives into the water to try to get to her little sister, crying and swimming at the same time, flailing around in the sea swell. She is not as strong a swimmer as Alice, and she worries that Lou will also drown. That within minutes, she will have lost them both.

JUNCTION OF EARTH AND SKY

The children who had been playing nearby are now all gathered by the water's edge, shouting out encouragement. Alice dives into an oncoming wave, but it's no use. When she's finally got her breath and turns around to try yet again, she catches sight of an older boy in the water, swimming out towards Pearl. Keeping his head down in the water, his arms slice through the large waves and he manages to get past the point where they are breaking. He reaches Pearl and flips her over so her face is up and out of the water. He wraps an arm around her head to keep it upright and swims one-handed, parallel to the shore, until he is out of the riptide. He heads towards the beach, catching a wave and holding on to Pearl at the same time. Some boys call out to him and rush into the water. Alice and Lou make their way towards them and help carry Pearl's limp body onto dry land.

The little girl's face is ashen, her lips a purply-blue. The older boy places his mouth over Pearl's and breathes air into it. A crowd gathers round.

Some girls from Alice and Lou's school suggest fetching the soldiers who are further along the beach, followed quickly by a disagreement over whether they would help or not. Some of the younger boys argue about how to perform mouth-to-mouth, shouting admonishments to the older boy blowing air into Pearl's tiny mouth. 'You're doing it all wrong, you are,' one of boys says.

'Shut your gob, will you.' Another boy pushes him over.

Lou is on her knees, her face covered with her hands, and she rocks back and forth weeping next to her motionless sister. Alice holds on to her friend. *This is my fault. Stupid Alice, stupid, stupid Alice*, she says to herself. She is breathing so fast that she feels light-headed, as if she might pass out, and she focuses on a seagull hovering above to try to steady herself.

Finally, Pearl begins to cough, spewing out seawater onto the rocks, and opens her eyes. The older boy leans back, wipes at his face and smiles. That's when Alice realises who he is: Danny O'Neill, from the Irish family who live over on Pemberton Road.

The three girls are rushed home in an army truck with a medic, who helps carry Pearl into the house and lays her down on the settee in the front room.

How could she have let this happen, Alice thinks once Pearl is upstairs in bed with her mother, Mrs Flight. Lou has been sent to fetch Mrs Smith, the gypsy woman who lives at the end of their road, to come round with her potions to ward off any possible ill effects from the near drowning.

While Lou is her best friend, Pearl is like the little sister Alice never had. She first held Pearl when she was a week old, the only person outside the immediate family who her mother allowed. She remembered still the feel of Pearl's thin, delicate skin, how her head was not even fully attached to her body, her milky smell and the way her face scrunched up right before she cried. Alice helped Lou take care of her infant sister, bringing her out in the pram to the front garden for fresh air in the mornings, bathing her, cuddling her when she was falling asleep. She remembers when Pearl began to smile, could sit up on her own, roll over, and took her first steps. Pearl squealed whenever she saw Alice. 'She's got two big sisters,' Mrs Flight would beam.

And yet she almost died, all because of Alice. 'Your actions are always three steps ahead of reason, young lady,' Miss Milton, the head teacher, would say to her every time she got in trouble for passing notes or disrupting class with snarky remarks. Alice is always pushing Lou to do things they aren't supposed to, like taking Pearl on a bus over to Brighton to see the circus without telling their mother, or racing their bikes down the steep part of Honeysuckle Lane without using the brakes, and even once sneaking out of the house on a hot night to swim in the sea when there was a full moon.

Alice has always loved swimming in the sea. Her mother taught her how before she even started school. They went to the beach every day to swim until the weather turned and it was dark by the middle of the afternoon, resuming the regimen again as soon as the days grew warmer and longer in the spring. Most afternoons, Alice would swim alongside her mother in her pink bathing cap. They used to live across from the beach and slept with the windows open, the smell of the salt water always present in their modest bungalow. The rhythm of the waves crashing onto the rocky beach was a constant, like the beating of a heart, and Alice still finds it the most soothing sound in the whole, entire world.

Her mother died four years ago, when she was ten, and her father couldn't cope without her, and turned to drink.

He didn't know the first thing about raising a daughter, and Alice often arrived at school wearing a dirty uniform, her hair unkempt. They had no family in the area and the mothers in the neighbourhood took it upon themselves to look after her. Soon after her mother's death, Alice began spending more and more time at Lou's house, going home with her best friend most afternoons at the end of the school day, and often staying over. Her father was found unconscious on the streets numerous times and at one point, there was talk of having to place Alice in a children's home. That's when Mrs Flight – Auntie – offered to take in Alice permanently.

What would happen if she decides Alice is more trouble than she's worth? She must try harder to behave, she simply must.

The front room is in a bit of a state from the influx of unexpected visitors, and Alice begins to straighten up. There is a dirty teacup on the floor by the settee, another one on the dining table that separates the small front room from the scullery, and yet another on the shelving unit that runs the length of the back wall in the front room. She gathers them up and washes them off in the sink overlooking the back garden and leaves them to dry on the draining board. The soldiers tramped in dirt, and Alice sweeps it up and takes the rug outside to shake it off.

The day has brightened and the late-morning sun feels warm in the unshaded square of grass bordered by a low cement wall in the Flights' front garden. Their home, a terraced two-up, two-down, is identical to all the other ones along their road. Everyone is outside playing: the four Christie sisters skipping with the two Simms girls; the Mason girls on their bikes; the young Brown children playing hopscotch with the Weavers; and the Farley boys racing up and down the road on their home-made cart, with the other boys chasing along beside them. They start at one end and go all the way to the other, where the dirt road dead-ends at the grassy oval, which is crowded with yet more children up in the oak tree that dominates the middle, playing tag and 'Mother May I?'

Once she's done shaking out the rug, Alice sees Danny O'Neill walking along their road, heading in the direction of the Flights' house. He is seventeen, three years older than Alice, and although they have never spoken to each other before, she knows all about his family. They are the kind of family everyone knows about because of Danny's older brothers, who are involved with a gang of young men running numbers out of the rough pub on Colchester Avenue and getting into fights and picking on anyone who even looks at them. Whenever Alice encounters Danny's brothers, she makes sure to cross over the road. But Danny is said to be the bright spot in the family, a practicing Catholic like his mum, who finished his schooling and avoided getting sucked into his brothers' way of making a living. Instead, he has a proper job at the Turner's farm. The only decent one of Mrs O'Neill's five sons, people say.

Alice had not taken much notice of Danny before. Until now. His black hair, still damp from the sea, and his soft brown eyes, make him look like a film star. Usually, Alice has no trouble making conversation with people she doesn't know, but once he reaches the entrance of the front garden, she struggles even to make eye contact with him.

'Hello there. How's the wee girl, then?' He stuffs his hands in his pockets and kicks at the ground. They are only a few feet apart. 'Thought I'd come round to make sure she's OK. Is she, then?'

'She's fine, yeah. Absolutely fine.' Alice concentrates on her feet.

'Oh, that's something, isn't it? Thought she was a goner for sure when I saw her out there in those waves.' His eyebrows are jagged with worry at the memory. 'I'm Danny, by the way. We didn't actually have time for proper introductions earlier, did we?' He smiles at her and Alice smiles back.

'No, we didn't. I'm Alice, and ... um ... would you like to come in for a cuppa?'

'I'm in a bit of a state, so. Not exactly suitable for calling in on anyone at the moment, now, am I?'

'Don't be stupid. Auntie won't mind, will she? We've got clean towels out the back. You can dry yourself off. Besides, the least we can do is offer you a cup of tea.' She shows him in and he follows her through the front room, to the scullery until they reach the back door. 'See? There, on the line?' Alice points to the towels that have been drying on the clothesline in the small back garden. 'You can sort yourself out while I put the kettle on.'

While she's filling the kettle with water, Alice sneaks looks at him. He has his back to her and doesn't realise she is watching as he takes off his shirt. He shakes his hair dry, rubs the towel over his head, his muscle-toned stomach and smooth chest. She knows she must stop, that she's being rude, but she can't help herself, even when he turns and sees that she's staring right at him.

Like the other girls her age, Alice has never gone steady before. She has been out only the one time with a boy, Harry Miles, who took her to the pictures. They sat in the back of the cinema and he tried to kiss her. But his breath was rancid and she almost gagged. He smelled as if it'd been a long time since he'd had a wash. A few other boys have asked her to get ice cream, go with them to the summer funfair, but she's always turned them down.

She brings the kettle over to the hob, lights it and waits for the water to boil. When Danny comes inside, she keeps her back to him, hoping he won't notice that her hands are quivering.

Danny asks if he can sit down.

''Course you can. Sorry, don't know where my manners have gone to this morning.' Alice blushes and turns to face him.

'It's nothing.' He smiles at her and takes a seat at the table.

While she waits for the water to boil, Alice begins to dry off two teacups. But her hands are still shaking and she ends up dropping one of them. It breaks apart when it hits the floor, scattering porcelain everywhere.

'I can't seem to do anything right today.' Alice kneels down to pick up the pieces of the broken cup. 'And now look what I've done. Auntie will be ever so cross when she sees this.'

Danny crouches beside her to help. 'It's just a cup,' he says. 'It doesn't matter. Here, let me take those. Careful now, don't want to cut yourself on them bits.'

He reaches for the pieces of the broken cup in her hands, which tremble even more at his touch, and the pieces fall onto the floor.

'You're shaking, you are.' Danny takes hold of her wrists to still her shuddering fingers, and holds her gaze. Her heart is beating so hard, she is certain he can hear it and her face flushes. She has read about this feeling in books: swooning. This must be what it means to swoon.

'So I've a confession to make,' Danny says. 'I've seen you before, I have.'

'Yeah?'

'I've noticed you. Been noticing you for quite a while now, actually.'

'You've noticed *me*?'

'I have.' Danny keeps hold of her hands. 'I wouldn't lie to you.'

'I wouldn't think you would. Where have you noticed me, then?'

'Well, let's see. Quite a number of places. But I've mostly noticed you on the beach and that. You're the kind of girl that catches a feller's attention, if you don't mind me saying so.'

'Is that so?' says Alice.

'It is so. You are quite beautiful, Alice, you are.'

He reaches over to touch the side of her face, leans in and kisses her right on the lips. Alice is so startled that she pulls away, even though she wants nothing more than to keep kissing him. They look at each other and smile.

He is bending in for another kiss when there is banging on the front door. Mrs Simms from across the road torpedoes in without waiting for anyone to answer, her usual method of entering the Flights' house. Alice pulls away from Danny quick, hoping the awful woman didn't catch them kissing. Yet another thing to upset Auntie.

'I just heard about Pearlie!' Mrs Simms' voice never goes below a level-ten shriek, which she somehow manages while gripping a cigarette between her lips. 'I can't believe it. Terrible. Where is she?'

'Upstairs.' Alice points at the ceiling.

'Who is this, then?' Her face scowls in disapproval as she leans in for a closer look. 'You're Dolores O'Neill's boy, aren't you? What you doing here?'

'I am indeed. And I'm making a move. That's what I'm doing.' He takes Alice's hand and squeezes it, smiles at her before crossing the room. 'Pleasure to meet you,' he says when he passes Mrs Simms. 'And you as well, Alice.' He makes a slight bowing motion with his head before leaving.

'What was Dolores O'Neill's boy doing here anyway?' Mrs Simms doesn't wait for an answer before starting up the narrow stairs. Her heavy footsteps cause the whole house to quake.

The water begins to boil in the kettle and when Alice turns off the hob, she has to hold onto it for a moment to catch her balance. She feels as if she's still in the turbulence of the waves, still being tossed around in the strong current. She sits down hard on a chair and closes her eyes, trying to hold onto this sudden, good moment for a little while longer. Then she begins to clear up the remains of the broken cup. Wiping away the traces of everything that has just happened.

3

If

1971

IF SONNY NEVER LAID eyes on the crack of Denise's ass peeking out from her jeans as she bent down to get filler in Martin's Hardware on a drizzling April morning, things might have turned out differently.

Sonny was in there with his buddy, Jackson, helping him out on a dry-walling job.

'Think it's by the stripper,' Denise said when they asked her for help after a fruitless search. 'We're running low, but I'm pretty sure we still have some.'

They followed her as she led them to the back of the store. When they reached the paint section, she squatted down, searching the lower shelf, and Sonny saw it. They waited in line to pay while Denise answered questions from other customers about air compressors, hose reels, Allen wrenches, made pressure washer recommendations. By the time they got to Jackson's truck, Sonny was smitten.

'She was fine,' Sonny said when they drove back to the house on Edgemore Road where they were dry-walling a bathroom.

'Denise?' Jackson considered this for a moment. 'I could see that. But she's got a boyfriend and shit so don't get your hopes up.'

But that's all Sonny had. Hopes. Nothing real. Nothing he could hold in his hands. Helping Jackson on these little gigs was the best thing that had come along in a long time. The pay was decent, and had the added benefit that Jackson didn't say anything when he was late to work and hung-over.

Sonny kept finding reasons to go back to Martin's Hardware over the next few weeks. Jackson was getting all the small side jobs that his uncle, a contractor with a successful, twenty-five-year business, didn't have time for. After the dry-walling job, they painted a dining room on Pineland Ave., replastered and painted the ceilings of the second-floor bedrooms on a Sycamore Drive colonial, which had water stains from a leaky roof. Sonny started coming to work on time, and always volunteered to go on the supply runs.

'Hey, Denise.' He tried to sound casual, as if he hadn't spent the whole drive thinking of things to say to her. It seemed to be having some sort of effect, her face lighting up just a little when he walked in, stopping whatever she was doing to see what he needed.

April became May, and one day after work while they were folding up the dust sheets, rinsing off brushes, Jackson's uncle offered them another job, painting one of those large houses on Cedar Hill. The entire exterior, plus the kitchen and the dining room. It had to be done quickly, and without any mistakes. 'These are long-time clients. Very important people to me, but the wife is picky, so I'm going out on a limb here and trusting you guys with this one.' He gave Sonny a hard look. 'They want the whole thing done in a week while they're away on vacation.'

It was going to be a push to finish it on time, so Sonny and Jackson needed to work through the weekend and be at the house every morning by seven, he explained. The both of them. He'd be there to let them in, and if they were even five minutes late, that was it. He knew plenty of guys who'd like the job. He would come back at the end of the day to check on their progress, lock up the house.

Jackson listened carefully while his uncle explained the outlines of the job. But Sonny was distracted, thinking about Denise's ass. He imagined grabbing hold of it while they were fucking.

'My uncle's gonna hire me for real at the beginning of the summer. He gets a lot of work then. That is, if this goes OK,' Jackson told him later at the Parkside Lounge, sucking on a lime after a tequila shot, washing it down with a beer chaser. Someone was playing the two Doors' songs on the jukebox.

Jackson moving on to permanent employment meant the end of these jobs, this money, and Sonny would have to figure something else out, all on his own. Which he wasn't good at, his mother, Alice, often reminded him. He was still living at home, though he avoided her as much as possible, so he didn't have to hear her lecturing him about his drinking and lack of a 'proper job'. How when she was growing up back in England, all the men his age would have had a family and been out fighting in the war, not just lolling about at home. It was shameful, it was, having a 'front row seat' to Sonny's life. He just wanted enough money so he could move out and away from her.

Sonny wasn't late even once to the Cedar Hill job, and Jackson's uncle was happy, so happy that he was thinking of giving them a bonus when they finished at the end of the week. The days were becoming warmer and longer and Sonny felt something verging on OK-ness. The flirting with Denise was finally paying off, and she agreed to go have a drink with him on Friday at the Parkside. Her boyfriend would be out with his buddies anyway, she said, and besides, he'd been a real dick lately.

They met at nine and sat at one of those small tables by the front window. She didn't have her hair up in a tight ponytail, the way she wore it at the hardware store. Instead, it swirled around her shoulders and she kept sweeping it back when she lifted her Jack and Coke or smoked. It was brown and silky, and Sonny wanted it to fall all over him. By the time the Parkside was closing up, they were still enjoying each other's company. Sonny walked Denise to her car in the parking lot out back and he kissed her. Pressing up against her, fingers working their way inside her jeans, he finally got to touch her ass. Then Sonny had an idea.

He couldn't bring her back to his place, to his childhood bedroom, with his mother right there in the next room.

He knew the Cedar Hill house well by that point. There was a spare key in the garage. No one would know.

So he squeezed her ass in the master bedroom, and the sex was even better than he had fantasised about all those many weeks. Afterwards, instead of going home, they both fell asleep. They slept through the rest of the night and into the next morning, when the family returned home early because their youngest had a fever and the forecast was for rain. When they saw the unfamiliar car in the driveway, they thought it was a break-in and called the police.

There was no bonus. All the dry-walling and painting and replastering gigs ended, as did his friendship with Jackson, who spent the next few months trying to win back his uncle's trust. After she bailed him out the next morning, Sonny's mother said it was time for him to move out and learn to live on his own. But Denise was going to break up with her boyfriend – she told him last night – so at least there was that. At least he got Denise, he thought as his mother drove him home from the police station. What he didn't realise, sitting in the passenger seat of his mother's car, was just how long he would get Denise for.

If Denise had been on her break that day at Martin's Hardware when Sonny first came in ... If Sonny and Jackson had found the filler on their own ... If Sonny hadn't seen the crack of Denise's ass ... he wouldn't have become a father in someone else's bedroom on a late spring evening. And Marnie would have never been born.

4

The Distance Already Travelled

1974

SONNY IS SO DRUNK he can barely get his key in the lock, cursing with each failed turn until finally it's open. He hits the wall of the narrow hallway hard, like a boulder, before ricocheting along it towards the living room where Denise is asleep on the couch. She doesn't hear her husband coming home until he is right over her.

'You slut! You fucking slut!' He pulls her onto the floor by her hair with his large, meaty bear-paw hands. There is a ripping sound as a huge wad of it tears away from her scalp. Once she hits the floor, he starts kicking her with his steel toe Carhartt's, a tyre iron against her ribcage. 'Eddie said he saw you with George. He saw you. In George's car, giving him a blow job.'

Denise curls up in a foetal position to shield her body from her husband's boots, and covers her face with her arms. There is a cracking sound as the boots connect with the left side of her torso, her face, again and again. *Stop it*, she screams as loud as she can, hoping someone in their apartment building will hear her and call the police, like they did last week. Not that the police did anything when they arrived, but at least it disrupted the beating long enough for Denise to grab Marnie and get out of there.

She crawls on all fours to get away from him, pleading with him to stop. Sonny throws the bottle of half-drunk red wine that Denise had been making her way through before passing out. She ducks in time and it smashes against the wall, glass and red wine splattering everywhere. Marnie begins to cry in the bedroom, calling out, *Mum-mum, Mum-mum.*

Denise gets behind the sofa. 'Please, Sonny,' she whimpers.

He takes a swaying step towards her, his breath coming in pants. 'You humiliate me one more time, Denise, I swear I'm gonna fucking kill you.' He clomps off to the bedroom, slamming the door behind him.

Everything hurts – her face, her left side, the back of her skull – and blood streams from her nose. She grabs tissues from a box on the side table, holds them gently to her face, and takes slow, careful steps towards Marnie's bedroom, but she has fallen back to sleep in a corner of her toddler bed. Her stuffed dog is wedged tight in her arms, and Denise places her open palm on Marnie's warm back. The little girl seems to know to avoid her father when he's been drinking, which is most of the time. 'Mum-Mum?' she calls out when Sonny starts yelling. Once, after he'd thrown all the dirty dishes in the kitchen sink onto the floor, she'd found Marnie in her bed, a blanket over her head, rocking back and forth.

The Kleenex is soaked through with blood, so she goes to the bathroom, sits on the toilet and wads up balls of toilet paper, tilts her head back. There's a stabbing sensation when she breathes in, similar to the pain she felt after a beating a few months ago which resulted in broken ribs.

She's not sure when Sonny started snorting speed, or freebasing, but the combination with the alcohol has made him constantly angry and paranoid that she is cheating on him. A few weeks ago, she got two black eyes because he was convinced she was having an affair with the downstairs neighbour. The broken ribs were about one of her co-workers. She doesn't want to be here when he wakes up, but where could she and Marnie go? There's no way to explain her bruises and emergency room visits to her girlfriends. Most of them still live at home with their parents, and don't know anything about marriage or being a mom. And everyone told her it was a bad idea to marry Sonny. He's crazy, a fucking psycho, her friends said. If only she had listened to them.

She manages to stem the bleeding and avoids looking at herself in the mirror while searching the medicine cabinet for the bottle of aspirin. She swallows a couple of pills with water from the tap. In the end, she decides on going to her older brother's house, just outside Boston. Even though it means driving for almost two hours, Mike always knows what to do, and things seem more solvable in his presence. Their parents died when they were kids, and although their Aunt Shirley took them in, it was her big brother who actually looked after her. If she could just talk to him in his kitchen over a cup of coffee, Denise is certain she could figure this out. She throws a few of Marnie's things in a plastic bag, and carries her out to the car, the little girl's stuffed dog in her arms. Somehow Marnie stays asleep during the transfer.

Once they reach the interstate, it starts raining so hard, Denise can barely see out of the windscreen, the highway a blurry mixture of reds and whites from the car lights up ahead and on the other side of the median. She swerves hard, just missing a skidding tractor-trailer, and her hands tremble, slick with sweat as she grips the steering wheel. Fuck, fuck, fuck, fuck, fuck, fuck, fuck, she sings in her head to the tune of 'Twinkle, Twinkle, Little Star', in an attempt to stay focused on the road.

She passes a sign for a rest stop in five miles, so she changes into the slow lane, keeping the car at a steady 40 miles per hour, hoping to avoid hydroplaning through the immense puddles extending out from the breakdown lane. Finally, she reaches the exit and follows the off-ramp as it curves around to a Howard Johnson's.

Denise pulls into the parking lot, fishes around in her purse for her pack of Kools, lights one up and takes a long, slow drag, leaning back against the headrest. It hurts on the inhale, and she can taste blood in her mouth. Beside her, Marnie is stretched out across the front seat, asleep, still clutching the stuffed grey dog held together with masking tape. She can't fall asleep without it. Her bare feet stick out from her blanket, her small toes warm in Denise's hand. She tucks a strand of hair behind

Marnie's ear. It's soft, almost golden hair when the sunlight hits it just right.

The rain shotguns the roof of the car, the wipers flap back and forth, back and forth. It's just beginning to get light. This early in the morning, there shouldn't be much traffic, so they could make it to her brother's from here in about an hour.

Denise left so fast, she didn't even think to call and let them know she and Marnie were on their way. If they show up unannounced, Mike's bitchy wife, Cath, won't like it and everything will start off on the wrong foot. Cath always makes jokes that aren't really jokes about Sonny and his drinking, gives Denise unsolicited parenting advice, makes facial expressions at Mike to show her disapproval of them both. Denise always feels judged in her presence. Sonny and Denise weren't the only ones who'd been drunk at Thanksgiving last year, but Cath had acted as if they were.

Marnie stirs slightly and her stuffed dog rolls onto the car floor. Denise picks it up and carefully places it between her daughter's arms, hoping not to wake her. A bus pulls up in front of the Howard Johnson's. Denise stabs out her cigarette in the ashtray and lights up another one as the passengers descend the stairs, legs stiff after long hours in the cramped seats. The driver rolls up the door on the underbelly of the bus and they shuffle forward to get their bags, before heading off to waiting cars. A woman from the bus and her little girl hurry to get into a red station wagon. The man inside kisses and hugs them both, the little girl climbing over into the back seat before they drive away.

Maybe after a few nights at Mike's, she could take Marnie and drive across the country. She has a friend from school who lives in Los Angeles. They could start all over again, put some serious miles between her and Sonny.

Denise opens the car door and takes careful steps towards the phone booth. After putting in the dime, she holds the phone a few inches away from her face, so the receiver doesn't touch it, and dials the familiar number. It rings for a long time before Mike finally answers it.

'Yeah?' he croaks.

'Hiya.' Denise begins to cry at the sound of her brother's voice.

'Dee!' She can hear him shifting around in the bed, and Cath's rumbling. 'Jeez, what time is it? Dee, it's five o'clock in the morning. What's going on, Denise? What did Sonny do now?'

Denise swallows a sob. 'It's kind of a long story, but I'll tell you when I get there. I was calling 'cause I'm on my way with Marnie and I thought I should let you know.'

'Today, Dee? Jesus. Of all the days.' He puts his hand over the receiver and she can hear his muffled voice, then Cath's, back and forth, getting louder and louder. She can picture them in bed, the phone pulled between them, arguing. 'Mikey,' she shouts, but he doesn't respond.

'Hey, Denise, are you OK?' Now it's Cath, talking in the same tone she uses for her three small children. 'What do you need, hon?'

Denise swallows and tries to imagine she is talking to a difficult customer at the Big Hoss Steak House where she works. 'Oh, hey, Cath. Sorry to be calling so early like this. I was just . . . I was just wondering if we could come stay with you tonight – Marnie and me, that is. We . . . We need somewhere to stay.'

There is a long silence before Cath replies. 'We really got a day, Denise. It's Teresa's birthday party.'

'Oh my God. Did I miss her birthday? Oh fuck, I'm really sorry, Cath. Shit.' Denise thinks it's possible she has never remembered Teresa's birthday or those of her two older brothers, Sean and Pat, has never called any of them to say happy birthday or sent them presents, the way Mike and Cath always do for Marnie.

'No, no, her birthday is Tuesday, Denise, the seventeenth, right? We're just having the party today. Mike found this clown guy who's gonna come and do some magic tricks. Anyway, so—'

'Marnie will love that.'

'The thing is, I'm thinking if you guys came later this afternoon, that would make more sense. I mean, it's gonna be bananas. Can you believe this weather? I was counting on them being outside. No such luck. But, of course you're welcome to come stay here. Any time after three should be safe, and our house will hopefully no longer be an insane asylum.'

'Thanks, Cath, appreciate it. Can I talk to Mikey?' Denise looks out at the rain, wondering what she and Marnie could possibly do for the next ten hours while they wait for her niece's birthday party to end.

'OK, see you later this afternoon? That will be great, Denise. To see you both. Looking forward to it. Here's your brother. Ba-bye.'

Denise can hear their voices, though they are barely audible through someone's palm stretched across the phone receiver.

'I guess Cath doesn't want us coming,' Denise says when her brother gets back on.

'Of course you should come. That's not what we're saying. Just like, later. This afternoon, like Cath explained. 'Cause of the party and all.'

'Forget it, Mikey, OK? Forget I even called.'

'Wait, hold on, Dee. Don't be like that. We're not saying don't come, just that we got this party which will be crazy 'cause of the rain and we can't really like ... We can't really deal with whatever you got going on right now.' His voice gets quieter. 'It's Teresa's day, Denise. Today's not about you.'

'Sorry my problems are so inconvenient for you. Next time, I'll try to schedule things better. Hope everyone *really* enjoys the party!' Denise throws the receiver against the wall in the booth, and it swings around on its thick silver chain, bouncing off the walls, with Mike calling out, *Denise, Denise, come on now.*

It's raining harder now, soaking her canvas sneakers as she hurries to her car. Once inside, she lights up another cigarette and cries some more. She doesn't have enough money for even one night at the Howard Johnson's. And she needs to go to the hospital. That leaves only one option: Sonny's mother.

She didn't like his mother at first, and the feeling was mutual. When Sonny told her they were having a baby together, Alice strongly disapproved. 'With that girl?' she said, wrinkling up her face in disgust at Denise. 'You are joking. Is she even twenty-one?'

'Almost,' Sonny had said. 'Aren't you, babe?'

Alice shook her head. 'What do you two know about taking care of a baby?'

But the night Marnie was born, Alice came to the hospital and held her new granddaughter for as long as the maternity ward nurses would allow. Once they were back home, she was there every day to help Denise take care of her newborn. She taught Denise all the things that no one in the hospital had bothered with: how to get the tiny infant to latch on so she could nurse without getting engorged; to burp her halfway through feeding her and again when she finished, so she'd be less fussy; and to swaddle her tight in a blanket. Alice explained that the black shrivelled piece of umbilical cord needed to be cleaned every day with rubbing alcohol until it fell off, which would take about two weeks. She brought over dinners that only needed to be heated up, did the laundry, cleaned their apartment. Took the baby on walks along Crane's Beach so Denise could rest. But mostly she held Marnie. Whenever she first arrived at Sonny and Denise's apartment, she rushed to pick up the baby, cradling her, singing to her.

When Denise started waitressing again, she only took shifts that aligned with Alice's work schedule. Even from the very beginning, she could never count on Sonny. She dropped the baby off in the afternoons when Alice got home from her job at New Jordan Elementary. Alice fixed up the second bedroom in her apartment, Sonny's old room, for the baby, put in a crib, painted it a light purple with white trim around the windows, hung gauzy white curtains, put up pictures of butterflies, puppies and kittens, and Peter Rabbit. She wanted Marnie to have 'a proper nursery' whenever she stayed over. Which became more and more frequent, and Marnie slept more nights at her grandmother's than in her own home.

Denise waits until the rain lets up before crossing over the thruway and heading in the opposite direction. Reversing back on herself, and the distance she already travelled.

5

Daddy

1975

THE LARGE WINDOWS IN the front office of New Jordan Elementary let in blinding sunshine on clear days, and the room is often buzzing with gossip between the school support staff and the teachers. Most days are non-stop but today was brutal. Petie Summers got a bloody nose during the first session of recess. Lucy Whittle threw up during lunch; they were serving Sloppy Joes, so it was especially gruesome, the lunch aides reported. Harry Miller and Joseph Sullivan got into a fistfight and spent the afternoon waiting in the front office to be picked up by their mothers. There'd been a lice outbreak in Mrs Snow's fourth grade class and five children were sent home. Chicken pox was sweeping the school, so an hour before the final bell, Principal Madden requested that a note be sent home with every student explaining yet again the school's sick policy.

And right after dismissal was Alice's 'surprise' leaving party. The school secretary, Dolly Elkins – Mrs Elkins to the students and teachers – had warned Alice about it.

The two women spent every weekday together, more or less, since the autumn of 1948, so Dolly knew Alice hated being the centre of attention, and even more, getting caught off guard.

Alice played along when the teachers streamed in with a cake and cards from their students, then Principal Madden made a speech. He had asked Alice out a few times over the years, but she always turned him down. She needed less complications in her life, not more, which having an affair with her boss would have brought. But Alice had even cried for a few brief moments during his speech before getting herself under control.

Now it's all over, and Alice finishes wiping off the inside of the drawers and the work surface of her desk. Three cardboard boxes are filled, taped shut and ready now to be moved out to her car. It had taken several weeks to pack up the decades she spent in the right-hand corner desk of the front office. Her replacement starts on Monday.

'How you holding up there?' Dolly asks.

'Oh, that was harder than I expected it would be.'

Dolly is usually gone by this time of day, an hour after dismissal, when the school is emptied of students and most teachers. Usually, only the custodians are left, pushing mops across floors, emptying out trash cans, cleaning the bathrooms. But Dolly remains at her desk, fussing around with the mound of papers on top, staying here with Alice until the very end.

Together, the two women have been through six principals, hundreds of teachers, thousands of children and parents, cutbacks, teacher layoffs, teacher walkouts, deaths, births, a custodial strike, the school expanding its catchment area to now include several hamlets, rebuilding the gym, a new library, the Vietnam War, the Civil Rights movement, Woodstock, Stonewall, feminism, athletic victories and scholarly achievements, school plays, concerts, fairs, festivals, graduations, along with the everyday triumphs and defeats of children.

Neither woman is sure how to go on without the other, but it's hard for either of them to put that into words. Alice, however, is certain that had she never met Dolly, she would not have survived raising Sonny all on her own, here in America.

When Alice first arrived, pregnant and alone, relatives of Mrs Flight had taken her in and put her up for a while in Providence. But Alice longed to be closer to the sea, and eventually she and her little boy moved down to New Jordan, a fishing village on the Block Island Sound near the port where the ferries went to and from Block Island. When Mrs Flight had taken in Alice, her father had given her some money, which she never touched. She gave it all to Alice when she left for America. Although it was only a modest amount, there was enough to cover the rent on a two-bedroom apartment on the second floor of a triple-decker, less than a mile away from the water.

Once Sonny was enrolled in school, Alice looked for work. She needed a car and eventually wanted enough financial security so that someday she could afford a house with a garden for her child. But most of all, she wanted to be able to afford university for Sonny. If there was one thing Alice had been certain of in the fall of 1948, it was that her son would not only finish his schooling, but go on to get a university education.

Now, though, the idea that she ever thought higher education was a possibility for her son seems ludicrous. He didn't make it past ninth grade and has been in and out of work ever since, the kind of work available to a violent alcoholic with a burgeoning criminal record.

Sonny was always a handful, even as a baby. He never slept and after he took his first steps, he never stopped moving. He wouldn't mind Alice, caused a scene in the grocery store, the butcher's, the fruit and veg shop, and she dreaded being out in public with him.

Once he was in school and saw the other children with two parents, sisters, brothers, grandparents, he began to wonder about his own family. Why was it just him and Alice?

'How come I don't have a daddy?' Sonny asked his mother one morning. 'Everyone else has one.'

Alice was folding laundry on the sofa, and took a long time to think how to answer the question. 'That's not the case at all. Not everyone has a father, now, do they?' Alice sorted the clean clothes into two neat piles and carried Sonny's into his room and started to put them away, hoping that was the end of the boy's questions.

Sonny followed her. 'I wish I had a daddy. I wish it wasn't only you. Mummies are mean.'

'That's quite enough now.' Alice slammed the drawers on the dresser and went into the kitchen and started in on the dirty cereal bowls from their breakfast.

'Daddies are better than mummies! Daddy! Daddy! Daddy! Daddy, Daddy, Daddy! Daaady!' Sonny wrapped his arms around his mother's legs and bit the back of her left knee.

Alice turned the water off. 'Stop it! Stop messing about!'

'I want a daddy!' he shouted. 'I want a daddy now! I don't want a mummy anymore!'

She grabbed him by his pyjamas and held him close to her face. 'You don't speak to me like that!' She was about to slap him before catching herself. She ran to the bathroom, shut the door, sat on the toilet seat and began to cry. Her hands trembled and she wished that it was later in the day, so she could put Sonny to bed and have a drink.

'Mummy.' Sonny sniffled on the other side of the bathroom door, pressing himself right up against it. 'Am I a bad boy? Is that why I don't have a daddy?'

Alice tried to still her hands. There wasn't an explanation of who Sonny's father was that would make sense to a little boy. It didn't even make sense to Alice. He never said he wanted a father again.

After Sonny's first few weeks at school, Alice had taken a part-time job answering the phones at an insurance agency, which was supposed to let her out at one, in time to get to New Jordan Elementary by dismissal. She had arranged for Sonny to be allowed to eat a packed lunch with his teacher in the classroom, instead of going home like the other children did for their midday meal. But her boss started giving her extra work that needed to be done right away just as she was getting ready to leave. 'It'll be done in a jiffy, doll,' he promised, handing her a large stack of papers that needed to be filed. It took well over an hour, making her late, and she had to collect Sonny from the front office where Dolly waited with him. The school was emptied out of everyone and had the quiet hush of a funeral parlour. All the other children had gone home or were in the playground by the side of the school, their mothers talking to one another in tight circles. Sonny looked so small, sitting by himself on the wooden bench opposite Dolly's desk.

By the middle of October, it was clear that Alice's boss had no intention of sticking to the hours she was hired to work. One day, after apologising to Dolly yet again, Alice broke down in front of her. She didn't know what to do. She couldn't afford not to work, but she couldn't stand being late every day. Dolly gave the little boy a piece of candy from the stash she kept in her desk for emergencies such as this, and told him to wait outside. She passed Alice a box of tissues, the underside of her soft arms wobbling when she moved. 'You're from England, aren't you?'

Alice nodded and blew her nose.

'My father was born there. In Liverpool. Came here in 1919. Where are you from? You been here long?'

'I'm originally from the South Coast, but I was evacuated up north during the war and then I came here.'

'Oh, my! Well, isn't that something? I've always wanted to go to England.'

'Me, too.' Tears slipped down Alice's cheeks. 'I'd do anything to go back. I should never have come here, I should never have left.'

'There, there, now. It's going to be all right.' Dolly came from behind her desk and the two women sat together on the bench. 'We'll figure this out, I'm sure. But we can't have Sonny waiting in here every day. Now do you mind me asking, what exactly is the trouble?'

Alice's voice went up an octave and she explained in a rush of words about her job and the situation with the boss.

'Is there another child that Sonny could go home with?' Dolly asked.

'We don't really know many people,' Alice admitted.

Dolly patted Alice's left arm and thought for a moment. She was a calm, efficient woman and loved nothing more than solving other people's problems.

'Now here's a funny idea for you, so bear with me. Miss Emory, my assistant, died over the summer and I still haven't found a replacement. You wouldn't consider working here in the front office, would you? The pay is probably not as good as what you're making at that insurance agency, but we do have excellent benefits, and the principal is a lovely man. You could be in the same building as your boy all day long. Wouldn't that be nice? And I must say, I do love the long summer breaks.'

And that was that. Alice loved the job, loved working with Dolly, and had remained there ever since. But then

JUNCTION OF EARTH AND SKY

Denise showed up early one Sunday morning a few months ago with Marnie. Sonny had broken her nose, cracked two ribs, and given her two black eyes, so bruised and swollen she could barely open them. Alice knew her son drank too much and wasn't much of a father or a husband, but this was the first time she saw exactly what he was doing to Denise, how badly he was hurting her. She was so upset by it all that she insisted her daughter-in-law and Marnie move in that very day.

Denise took Sonny's old room, and Alice had Marnie share her bedroom. Whenever Marnie woke in the middle of the night, as she often did in those first few weeks, she'd get out of her toddler bed, climb in with her grandmother and fall back asleep. They would wake up curled together as the sun rose, the whole entire sky pink as if they were in the middle of a fairy tale, Alice would say to the little girl. Marnie would grab some story books and sit in Alice's lap while she read to her, the room growing lighter and lighter.

When Alice got back from work, she'd take the little girl to Crane's Beach in the afternoons. They'd look for sea glass, shells, heart-shaped rocks, smooth pebbles, driftwood that they took home and placed along the bookshelves, the bathroom counter, the baseboard above the tub, the side tables in the living room, and the little stool by Marnie's bed: their growing collection of 'souvenirs from the sea'.

But Denise was hoping to go back to the waitressing schedule she had before Marnie was born, and that meant long work days. And all Alice wanted was more time with

Marnie. She wanted the whole day. Every single day. Not just the afternoons and weekends. Only a few years from now, Marnie would start school. Before that happened, Alice wanted to do all the things she missed out on with Sonny when he was little, so she decided to leave her job and look after Marnie full-time. She had never enjoyed Sonny the way she enjoys Marnie. He was so hard to manage and she was overwhelmed, looking after him all by herself, in this strange new country where she didn't know anyone. Sometimes, in darker moments, she wished he had never been born.

She'll never get that time back with Sonny. It's gone forever now. But it could be different with Marnie. She plans to take her to the library for morning story hours and to family swim at the local pool. On rainy days, they can bake and do art projects. She'll read her stories and knit her sweaters, sew her dresses. They'll go to Crane's Beach as much as possible. And Alice will be able to take Marnie back and forth to the school bus when she does start school, and be with her every afternoon. This is her second chance at raising a child.

Bruce Daniels, the head custodian, arrives with a hand truck and straps Alice's three boxes on with bungee cords. 'Ready?' he says, giving her body the once-over like he always does.

'I suppose,' Alice says and looks at Dolly, who has started to cry. 'You're going to get me going again.'

'I'm sorry.' Dolly wipes at her eyes.

Alice hugs her friend, whispers 'Thank you,' and walks beside Bruce and the three boxes. They are filled with two coffee mugs, some children's drawings, tiny clay sculptures, flyers and programmes from the many years of plays, musicals, concerts, graduations, as well as pictures of Marnie as a newborn, on her birthdays, and at Crane's Beach. She doesn't have any photos of Sonny, and the few teachers and staff that are left from his student days never ask how he is doing. Everyone already knows the answer. He appears often enough in the police blotter section of the paper.

A voice pierces through the static of Bruce's walkie-talkie as he loads the boxes into the back seat of Alice's car. A toilet is blocked up in the girls' bathroom on the second floor. He radios in that he'll be there in a few minutes and they say their goodbyes. Alice sits in her car for a moment to have a little weep, and then that's it. She drives a little faster than usual because Marnie is at home waiting for her grandmother. The only thing that matters.

6

The Miller's Tomb

1940

'Tell me again about the beach,' Alice says to Danny.

They are lying on a woollen blanket, facing each other, in the meadow near the Miller's Tomb just before daybreak. He smiles at her and runs his right hand through her hair, his left arm around her. 'I knew you were about to ask me that.'

It is her favourite story: how Danny had been noticing her on Sea Place Beach since the beginning of the summer. Weeks before he saved Pearl. It was hard not to notice Alice, he says, because she is the most beautiful girl he has ever seen. Once he had seen her in the town centre and it felt like his heart had shot up into his throat. Another time, she was on her bike with the wind blowing her hair all around and he had thought, *I must know her, I must know that girl*.

'And now I do.' He traces his index finger around her lips.

'I must be such a disappointment to you then, the real, actual me.'

JUNCTION OF EARTH AND SKY

'That's it exactly. I am hugely disappointed, Alice. I really am.' He pulls her in closer and begins to kiss her, opens his mouth and wraps his tongue around hers. He makes a slight moaning sound. 'Oh Alice, oh Alice,' he whispers in her ear, and holds her even tighter.

The sun has yet to creep up above the Downs, and the meadow is bathed in grey pre-dawn light. It's Danny's idea to meet up here by the Miller's Tomb, the highest point in Spithandle, and watch the sunrise together, before he is due at the Turners' farm, where he works. Before Auntie can ask Alice where exactly she is going, why she is leaving the house so early in the morning. She was still asleep when Alice sneaked out a little while earlier, walked her bike as quietly as possible until she reached the end of the road. Hoping not to draw the attention of any of the neighbourhood mums who would surely tell on her.

Now that she is up here with Danny, she doesn't even care about the consequences. It's all worth it. He's brought a picnic of fruit he scrumped, plums and blackberries, and a sausage roll that he nicked from the Turners. But they haven't touched any of it.

It's just starting to get lighter when they hear a plane engine. Danny is the first to see it, pointing it out to Alice. 'It's a German plane.' He scrambles to his feet, and pulls her up. 'Run!' They are totally exposed, out in the middle of the field. The plane flies closer and closer. Danny grabs hold of Alice's hand and they head towards the hedges and trees, leaving everything behind. When they reach the thicket, the plane is right above them and low enough in the sky that when it banks left and dips down, Alice can see the pilot's goggles. Danny almost pushes her into the hedge, which scrapes her arms and legs. He scrambles in after her and drapes his body over hers as they hide. She shuts her eyes tight and waits. *This is my punishment*, she thinks, *for sneaking out of the house.*

The sound of the plane's engine grows fainter and fainter and then Alice hears another plane. 'It's a Spitfire,' Danny tells her. He's keeping watch on what's happening. 'It's chasing after the German plane. Alice, look.' She sits up and sees off in the distance the Spitfire roaring after it. She clutches on to Danny as the Spitfire gets closer and closer, before shooting it down. Afterwards, the Spitfire pilot does a victory roll and flies away.

Danny bursts out of the hedge and hollers, 'Alice! Alice! Did you see that?'

She inches her way out to join Danny, careful not to cut herself on the way. 'Yes, I see, I see.'

'Oh, that was really something, Alice, that really was.'

The sun is rising up above the Downs, and the sky is clear – hardly any clouds – and the English Channel glistens in the early morning light. On bright days, like this one promises to be, you can see over to Brighton and sometimes, even all the way to the Seven Sisters, the chalk cliffs between Eastbourne and Seaford, miles and miles away.

This early in the morning, Alice and Danny are the only ones up here. If it had been later in the day, this meadow would be filled with children. Since the beaches have been closed off to the public, this is where Alice and Lou bring Pearl most afternoons to get some respite from the August heat. They make hideouts with the girls from their road in the hedges, dig for treasure in the chalk pits, climb the trees, chase each other around the fields, play hide and seek. On particularly hot days, they cool off in bogs filled with rainwater.

The days are starting to get shorter, the grass browner, and summer is slipping away. They haven't much time left together. In two weeks, Danny will be leaving to go fight with the British Army.

He takes Alice's hand and they walk towards their bikes, which they left by the gate near the Miller's Tomb. It contains the body of an eighteenth-century smuggler who built his own grave while he was still alive, requesting to be buried upside down. The raised tomb is surrounded by iron spikes, and it's supposed to be good luck to walk around it three times, and bad luck if you don't. Alice and Danny circle the grey, mossy grave, walking single file in total silence.

Alice closes her eyes as she takes slow, deliberate steps around the Miller's Tomb, wishing hard for Danny to stay here with her, for him not be killed like the German pilot with the goggles, for time to speed up to when the war is over and they can be together again. Once around they go, twice, three times. Then they head for their bikes.

'How come we've never met before?' Danny says. 'You've been right here the whole time.'

'I know. Stupid, isn't it?'

'Alice? Will you still be my girl? Even when I'm away?'

''Course I will.'

'I won't even look at other girls, I promise.'

'You better not.' She slaps his arm. 'I will hunt you down, if you do.'

'I'm serious, Alice. I've never felt this way before. Not ever.' He takes hold of her hand. 'I'm going to save myself for you, Alice. For when I come back.' They kiss one last time before parting.

Even though Alice has only known Danny for six weeks (and two days), it is hard for her to conceive of her life before they met. What did she used to think about? She is consumed with Danny, and the way it feels to lie with him in a field of cow parsley and tall grass, with his arms around her and his soft, delicate fingers running through her hair, stroking her cheeks.

On the way home, Alice thinks of the pilot's goggles. She has seen German planes shot down before, but never one so close. In the aftermath, the army and fire brigade arrive to extinguish the flames, and if a crowd has gathered, they will shoo everyone away so they can remove the body. After the site has been cleared and the army trucks and fire engines have left, boys will swarm the demolished plane like hyenas after a lion's kill, taking equipment, gauges, torches, bullets, bombs, guns ... anything they can rip out with their bare hands and use for their games.

After breakfast, Alice does the washing-up. Pearl and Lou are outside, weeding the back garden. Heat has

JUNCTION OF EARTH AND SKY

descended on Spithandle and all the windows are opened wide in an attempt to cool the stifling house.

Mrs Flight is out by the low wooden fencing that separates their front garden from the Weavers' identical patch next door, with the other mothers from the road. Alice can hear every word they are saying to one another. They gather every morning to drink mugs of tea and smoke cigarettes, huddled together, a whole flock of them. In that brief period of time that they have to themselves, in between breakfasting their children and seeing to the household chores, the mothers worry and gossip. They worry about the possibility of a coastal invasion, discuss who has lost a son, a father, a brother. It is not uncommon for a steady stream of the mothers to spend all day bringing food to the home of a newly bereaved woman. The streets are overrun with an ever-increasing number of Canadian soldiers, and the cricket pitch and grounds at Broadwater Green are covered with army trucks.

Mrs Simms says she was awake all night, waiting for the air-raid sirens to go off. Mrs Weaver says it's so much worse when you are jolted awake by them: gives you the fright of your life being woken like that and having to run out in your nightclothes to the shelter in the back garden. Mrs Brown says it's hardly worth the trouble to sleep anymore. Oh, and did they hear that Jeanie Malview lost her boy and there was a collection going round for her, and people were dropping off food there later on.

And what about that plane this morning? Mrs Simms says. Did they hear? Right up by the Miller's Tomb. Where all the children play. What if it had happened later in the day, if the Spitfire had not come by in time? Oh, it was all just too awful to contemplate.

Mrs Weaver says, *right, I must make a move.* And just like that, it's over, and they all scatter.

Mrs Flight comes inside the house to ready herself for the long day ahead, bustling around, handing out orders. It's Tuesday, washing day, and Alice is to see to that while Lou is sent upstairs to dust and mop the floors, and Pearl is to accompany her to the shops.

'I'm trying to make my eyes shake. Mum, watch me,' Pearl says while Mrs Flight is looking for the ration book and her purse. She presses her back up against the wall. 'Mum, I can do a handstand. Mum, Mummy.'

'Lovey, please,' Mrs Flight says, and tells her to wait outside for her.

Once her daughters have left the room, she calls to Alice. 'Come here, we need to have a talk, my love.' Mrs Flight has taken a seat at the table and indicates that Alice should join her. She keeps her eyes closed while she speaks. 'You've been spending an awful lot of time with Danny O'Neill, I understand.'

Alice blushes, wondering if she knows about this morning before realising that of course she does. She knows everything. 'Yes, Auntie.'

'I know that when you meet a boy for the first time, it can feel like real love. But you're only fourteen and there's still so much time. And I'm sure Danny must seem like the most wonderful boy in the world. And I'm not trying to say he isn't. However, you must know you are like a daughter to me, so I wouldn't feel right about Lou being so serious about a boy. Not yet, that is. I had to say something, that's all.'

She gives Alice's hand a squeeze. 'Has he enlisted, love?'

Alice wells up and nods her head. 'He leaves in two weeks, Auntie.'

'Oh, love.' She holds Alice for a moment. 'You'd better get all the sleep you can now, before he leaves. I've hardly slept at all since my George has gone. I'll add Danny to my nightly prayers, I will.'

'That's kind of you.' Alice swallows and thinks of the pilot's goggles again.

After his plane was hit, he must have known it would crash, that he probably wouldn't survive. But there was a brief moment before, when he was suspended between two realities. With only a stranger, Alice, as his final witness.

7

Terminal Velocity

1990

'Are you going to fuck her?'

Marnie is on the living room floor in a strange house, too wasted to sit up, surrounded by three boys. Three very drunk boys.

'Dude, if you're not gonna fuck her, then I will.'

'Think we can all have a turn.'

This last comment elicits a long, surround-sound laughing jag. Even though these boys are seniors at New Jordan Regional High, just like Marnie, they are on the varsity soccer team and hang out only with the other kids on the varsity sports teams, so Marnie has never talked to any of them before tonight. Earlier this evening, they were all at Mimi Edwards' house party and now, somehow, they are here. Marnie can't think how it happened, how she got to this house, why she is with these three boys. And how come Tim, her friend, isn't saying anything to defend her? 'Tim?' she calls out for him.

'Oh, dude, your homo boyfriend won't give a shit if we have a little fun, will he? Now's his chance. Maybe some gangbanging will straighten that kid out? Where'd that little homo go anyway?'

'"Some gangbanging will straighten him out." Dude, you are so funny.'

'Seriously, dude, where'd the little homo go?'

Marnie and Tim had gone to the party at Mimi Edwards' house together. She lives in one of those big houses that overlook the ocean, and it seemed almost everyone in their entire grade was there. They started off by doing tequila shots with Nikki Fantana and her boyfriend around a kitchen island. Then they smoked a three-pronged joint and danced to the Buzzcocks up on stools. More tequila shots followed, and Marnie and her friends were body slamming, laughing and ricocheting off one another and into some other kids from their class in the large, crowded kitchen. Marnie had to pee, and it took a long time wandering throughout the vast downstairs to locate an available bathroom. On the way back to the kitchen, one of the boys on the soccer team started talking to her, offered her a drink from his red Solo cup, which was something brown and sweet. Marnie polished off the whole thing while they smoked a joint together in the living room. He had some hash in his car, he told Marnie, before leading her outside to the large circular driveway. Two other boys from the soccer team were with him and then they were in a car driving somewhere and she was sitting on a soccer team boy's lap in the front seat, her forehead pressed up against the windscreen. They drove fast along a highway, and she leaned into his neck when they came to a curve because she felt like she might throw up. She could barely walk once they arrived at this house she had never been to before, and needed help getting inside.

Now, as Marnie lies on the living room floor, she can't remember if Tim had been in the car with them or if he stayed at the party. It feels like the room is spinning around and around. She rolls over and tries to get up on all fours, but loses her balance and falls over.

'Look at her arm. Look.' Marnie's left arm is jerked around, her body dragged across the thick carpeting.

'Stop,' she slurs, and tries to yell for help, but she is spiralling faster and faster towards unconsciousness.

'She's like one of those porno blow-up dolls. I'm gonna stick my dick in her mouth.'

'No way, man. She might bite it off. Pull her pants down.'

Marnie slithers along the floor, ending up underneath a side table, tangling herself in the legs, and it topples over.

'Oh my fucking God. She's like my dog. My stupid dog did the same thing. Holy shit, this girl is so fucked up.'

The boys are shrieking, and one of them starts fumbling with the snap at the top of her jeans, undoing the zipper and tugging them down.

'Leave me alone,' Marnie says, drawing her knees up towards her crotch.

'What the fuck, you guys?' It's Tim, but his voice sounds far away, as if he is in a tunnel. 'Jesus Christ!'

Someone picks Marnie up and she struggles to get away. But it's no use. The boys laugh and laugh and laugh.

That was last night. Now Marnie wakes up alone, in a child's trundle bed. Early morning light seeps in through the windows, splashing against the pink walls. Tim is asleep on the floor beside her. They are both fully dressed. And then Marnie remembers. She remembers everything.

It's late January, and a lot of her classmates spent the fall of senior year consumed with their SAT scores and applying to college. Last year, Marnie was on track to do the same thing. She was in Star Achievers, the guidance counsellor's after-school club for the students with good enough grades to be eligible for academic scholarships. But once school started in September, she stopped going to the club meetings and her grades dropped. In class, instead of sitting up front, taking notes and participating like she had always done, Marnie stared out the window or doodled in her notebook to make it look like she was paying attention. Lost inside her head for each 55-minute period, wishing time would go by faster, wishing for it all to end.

Just before Christmas break, the guidance counsellor, Ms Fabian, hauled her into her office after an 'incident' during chemistry involving Sharon Dolin. Ms Fabian had dyed purple and platinum hair, wore calico cat glasses, and decorated her small office with posters of bands in an attempt, it seemed, to come off as cooler than the other teachers. She flipped through the papers in Marnie's file for a while before looking up at her. 'We miss seeing you in Star Achievers,' she said. 'Your grades are really not what they used to be. You've never been in any trouble before. What's going on?'

Marnie stared at the brown shag rug. She thought if she tried counting the strands, it might help to get through this meeting. There was no way to explain to Ms Fabian how Sharon Dolin, who had been her lab partner that day, wouldn't stop going on about the Seaview Motel, and how she couldn't believe Marnie actually lived there. 'That's so weird,' Sharon Dolin had said. 'Who lives in a motel?' Marnie didn't reply, just wrote down observations on a worksheet while they mixed together chemicals for their experiment, like they were supposed to be doing. Sharon Dolin sucked her thumb up until fifth grade and smelled like sour milk, so Marnie didn't care what she thought. But the girl was relentless, kept saying the Seaview was gross and how people said it was haunted. Marnie couldn't take it anymore. She told her to fuck off and shoved her, which caused her to drop the tube filled with chemicals, and then Sharon Dolin had screamed.

'I know you lost your grandmother last summer.' Ms Fabian closed the file and took off her glasses. Marnie hated when people used that phrase, as if somehow, she had misplaced Alice. 'That's really hard. Have you thought about seeing a therapist? I'd really suggest it if you are still feeling this sad. Can I give you a couple of names?'

Marnie swallowed, her jaw tightening. What good would that do? Could a therapist take all the cancer out of her grandmother and bring her back to life? That's what would actually be helpful, Marnie wanted to shout, as Ms Fabian wrote down some numbers and sent Marnie back to class.

After her grandmother died last summer, she went to live with her mother. But in August, Denise visited her boyfriend in Florida and he asked her to marry him and move down there. Uncle Mike and Cath said she could live with them, but that would have meant senior year in a new school in a new state. Instead, she went to live with Dolly, her grandmother's best friend, at the Seaview Motel, where she was the manager. Marnie knew she should be grateful and that her grandmother would have expected that of her. But the only thing Dolly ever wanted to talk about was Marnie's grandmother, and how much she missed her. Sometimes she would start to cry when she was recounting stories about Alice. Marnie couldn't stand it. Although she knew she was being rude, Marnie ended up retreating to her tiny bedroom, where she would draw in her sketchbook and read, or just stare at the walls, the water-stained ceiling. On the weekends, she often stayed at Nikki Fantana's house and spent her free time with Tim, and in general tried to avoid being around Dolly as much as possible.

It was right after Christmas when Tim said he was thinking of leaving New Jordan. His father had found out he was gay and living at home was no longer tenable. He had already got into a few colleges and finished all his high school credits, so he could graduate early. He had a friend in Worcester who was living with a band in an abandoned factory taken over by musicians and artists.

There was plenty of room for them both, Tim told Marnie. She should come, too. By that point, Marnie was staying most nights at Nikki's, and she told Dolly that she didn't want to burden her anymore, that she was just going to finish out the school year at her friend's house. And Nikki's mother assumed she had gone back to living with Dolly full-time. There was no one really tracking what was happening to Marnie, except Uncle Mike, and it was easy to lie to him and Aunt Cath during their weekly Sunday night phone calls.

Everything had finally come together earlier this week. Benny Nichols, the main weed dealer at school, said he would give Tim and Marnie a ride to Worcester if they covered the gas for the two-hour drive. He just needed to make some deliveries on the way. They were supposed to leave Friday, after collecting their things from Tim's house while his father was at work, and Benny would pick them up there. But when they saw him after school, he said to meet at Mimi's party later on instead. He never showed up.

Marnie's mouth is dry, as if she has been sucking on a rock all night. She needs water, cold water. Her insides lurch when she sits up. The hallway landing is filled with closed doors, and she opens one to find the soccer players passed out on bunk beds and the floor. Another door leads to the master bedroom. Finally, Marnie finds a bathroom, scoops in mouthfuls of water using her hands. She brushes her teeth using her index finger before rousing

Tim, and they walk quietly out of the house, hoping to avoid waking the boys.

The area is made up of large houses with manicured lawns where nothing looks amiss, unlike the neighbourhood Marnie grew up in. When they reach a commercial street, they find a payphone and start calling around, trying to find Benny. Once they locate him, a new plan is made to meet at the Friendly's on Longwood in a couple of hours. When they get to Tim's house, he has her wait outside and returns with their bags.

His father had shouted at him, smacked him hard across the face, told him if he left now, that was it, Tim reports once they are seated in a booth at Friendly's a little while later.

A sweaty waiter takes their order, his hair damp beneath his white paper hat. He is wearing a large badge on the front of his uniformed shirt: *If I forget to ask if you want soup, it's on me.*

The food arrives and they eat without talking, each in their own worlds with their fried eggs and bacon, toast and home fries. Marnie checks the clock on the back wall of the restaurant. In an hour, they'll get into Benny's rusted AMC Pacer and head up Route 1. Away from New Jordan, where she has lived her entire life. But without her grandmother, each familiar place only jolts her back to a life that no longer exists. She finishes up her food, pushes the plate away. One more hour, and then she'll be gone.

8

Maybe We'll Go Camping

1978

'MAYBE WE'LL GO CAMPING,' Marnie's daddy suggests every time he drops by. Which is usually around dinnertime, unannounced, with a plastic bag filled with his dirty clothes. Alice has asked her son over and over again to please call her first, so she can be prepared. Not surprise her – or his ex-wife, who has been living here, in Alice's home, with Marnie for the past four years, ever since they split up. But he doesn't listen to his mother, just shows up, without any warning, like he's done this evening.

While his clothes are in the dryer, he tells Marnie how it's possible to see constellations and falling stars when you are camping in the woods, far away from the unnatural light pouring from houses and streetlights. That there is nothing like cooking hot dogs on a stick over an open fire, roasting marshmallows until they are soft and gooey on the inside with a golden-brown crust, squeezing them between two graham crackers with a piece of warmed-up chocolate. Sleeping all night long in a tent. As if she doesn't know what it's like.

Yet, she has been camping only a few months ago, over Memorial Day weekend. Drove in Uncle Mike's orange VW bus down to a beach in Maryland where there were wild horses, with her mother and her cousins and her aunt and uncle. And they did all the things her daddy is talking about. But still, camping with her daddy sounds fun, so she doesn't say anything when he says to her, 'Maybe we'll go camping together and you can see for yourself.'

'Except you've never been,' Sonny's mother says to him without looking up from her knitting – a yellow sweater for Marnie, with a purple rabbit on the front. Her granddaughter's favourite colours. Marnie is on the floor playing with the Fisher-Price parking garage that her father brought her; Alice wondered aloud how he could afford such a big present when it wasn't even her birthday or anything.

'That's because you never let me go camping.' Sonny picks at the tab on the can of his Narragansett and swallows down the last of the beer. 'Dolly was always inviting me to go with them and you always said I couldn't.'

'I don't remember that.' It's a hot evening, and a circular fan shoves thick air around the room. They only have the one fan, and all day, Alice has been plugging and unplugging the thing, carrying it from one room to the next, in a futile attempt to keep the apartment cool.

'It must be nice having your memory.' Her son slides his lower jaw from side to side, which he does when he's angry. 'You can invent a better past for yourself, can't you?'

Alice puts down her knitting needles. 'Being rude to me is not a very persuasive tactic.'

'Sorry.' He blinks hard.

Marnie's daddy is a big man and he has scars on his face. On the rare occasion that she's out in public with him, she can tell people are afraid of him. They move out of his way, avoid looking directly at him, and if he's rude, which he often is, they just let it go. But he doesn't scare her grandmother. In fact, it seems like it might be the other way around.

'What do you know about camping anyway?' Alice considers her son, his large frame slumped over, looking more the way he did as a teenager than a 36-year-old man. She returns to her knitting.

'What's to know? Any idiot can set up a tent.'

'You don't have a tent.'

'I'm gonna borrow one from my buddy. If you must know.'

Alice can feel the beginning of the headache that she often gets when she's around her son. She checks the time. 'It's getting late. I think you should be going home now. It's Marnie's bedtime.'

'It's only 7.30. It's not even dark yet.'

'This is what time six-year-olds go to bed. For your information.'

'Come on, Ma.' He softens his voice. 'I'd just be taking her to Sullivan State Park. It's like ten bleedin' minutes away. Give me a chance, would you? I already got Friday off work.'

'You want to take her camping *this* Friday? In two days' time?'

'Yes, this Friday, Ma!' He slams the beer can onto the side table next to him. Marnie stops playing with the plastic garage, moves towards her grandmother and sits by her fuzzy slippers. 'I'm sorry,' he says.

'You don't talk to me like that,' she says, stroking Marnie's hair. 'And I said that it's time for you to leave. Marnie, love, go and brush your teeth now. There's a good girl.'

Sonny starts to say more, but seems to think better of it. He kisses his daughter goodbye on the top of her head. 'Good night, sweetheart. If we go camping, I'll take you to McDonald's. How does that sound?'

Marnie smiles at her father before glancing at her grandmother, unsure what the right answer is, not wanting to make either one of them mad at her, before heading for the bathroom. Even with the door closed, she can hear her father trying to talk her grandmother into the camping trip. If her grandmother agrees to this, it will be the first time Marnie has ever spent a night alone with her father.

'I'm really trying to be a better dad. Is that so wrong?'

Her grandmother is talking so softly, Marnie can't hear her reply.

'I just want to do something with my little girl. She's all I have, Ma. It's just one night. Is that really too much to ask? I did the anger management class, and I'm watching my drinking, like the judge said I had to. I'm doing everything I can.'

When her grandmother comes in to read her a bedtime story and asks if she wants to go camping with her father, she says that she does. She really, really does.

'Well, that settles that, then,' Alice says.

The morning of the camping trip, her grandmother makes her French toast, which is a special treat breakfast and usually reserved for Sundays only. 'Always good to begin an adventure on a full stomach,' she says when she dishes it out onto a plate.

Marnie's mother has already left for work, like usual on Friday mornings. Denise and Alice had an argument about the camping trip, but in the end, her mother agreed with Alice that it was good Sonny wanted to do something with his daughter, that it signalled a possible change in him. Maybe he'll end up being more involved after all.

Alice takes a seat opposite her granddaughter and sips her tea. She's been up for a while, and long ago had her usual breakfast of banana slices and cereal. 'Now eat up quick, lovey, while it's still hot, and then we can get you ready,' she tells her granddaughter.

Marnie is dressed in her favourite T-shirt, the one with pictures of Wacky Pack decals on the front and jean shorts. She has a flannel shirt tied around her waist. After breakfast, her grandmother helps her pack an overnight bag with pyjamas, long pants, a sweatshirt, a toothbrush, bug spray, a book and a flashlight, a small drawing pad and some coloured pencils, and her stuffed dog that she can't sleep without. Then she puts on the hiking boots that

Uncle Mike gave her earlier in the summer for their camping trip. When she is ready, they sit on the couch in the living room, waiting for her daddy to collect her.

Sonny is over an hour late, and Alice scolds him when he finally arrives. She hugs Marnie extra tight when they say goodbye. He promises to have her home by noon the next day.

They have only gone a few blocks when Sonny stops to use a payphone to call his friend. When he returns, he says he has some exciting news. His buddy suggested they could camp in his backyard. He's got a cottage right on a lake, and it would be much better than going to Sullivan State Park.

'It's kinda crap there really,' Sonny says. 'Pretty crowded and dirty. At my buddy's place, we can have the whole yard to ourselves.'

Marnie remembers her grandmother saying he'd never been camping before, and she wonders if he's ever been to Sullivan State Park. Kids at school have talked about how much fun it is to go camping there, because it has a large pond and a giant playground with a wooden fort in it. A funny feeling in Marnie's stomach starts up. 'Does Nanny know where we're going?'

But the question angers her father, and he gets that scary look on his face. 'What's it to her, where we go? She doesn't need to stick her nose into everything.'

Her father starts the car and Marnie regrets saying anything, and the funny feeling turns into a sharp pain. She puts her hands across her middle and gives it a little pat, like her grandmother does when she's feeling nauseous.

They drive for a while along a busy highway, and her father listens to loud music on the radio, the same kind that Marnie's mommy likes. She can't remember being with both her parents in the same room, or what the apartment where the three of them used to live looks like. There are only photographs to prove that it actually happened: the three of them in front of a Christmas tree when she was a baby; her mother giving her a bath; and Marnie sitting in a high chair and her daddy feeding her with a tiny spoon.

After they have been driving for almost two hours, her father points out a sign advertising a McDonald's at the next exit. Marnie has never been inside one before, but she's seen the television commercials, so she was surprised when her grandmother told her that Ronald McDonald and the Hamburglar wouldn't actually be there. Just the food.

Once they've ordered, her father carries a tray with their lunch to a booth and they sit opposite each other. 'How nice is this?' Sonny smiles at his daughter and they settle into their meal. Her father unwraps his Big Mac, douses the greasy paper with ketchup and takes large bites, alternating fries with the burger in between sucking hard on the yellow and red straw sticking out of his large vanilla milkshake. He ordered the same thing for Marnie, and she copies his eating pattern.

'You know, I'm putting together some money,' her father says. 'Couple more months and I'm gonna have enough to last me the rest of the year.'

Marnie nods, unsure what to say.

'Maybe we could go to Disney World? How does that sound?'

Marnie smiles at the thought of it.

A man and two young boys take a seat in the booth opposite Marnie and her father. 'Wife dump the kid on you as well?' he asks Sonny.

Her daddy doesn't reply, doesn't even look over at the man. He eats quickly and finishes first. Marnie is trying to make her way through the vast amount of food in front of her. She manages a few bites of the Big Mac, which barely fits in her mouth. The French fries are salty and make her fingers oily, and she keeps wiping them on her shorts. She sucks at her milkshake, but it's so thick and cold that it makes her stomach hurt.

'You don't like it?' Sonny asks when Marnie stops eating and leans back, resting her hands once again on her stomach.

'I love it.'

'Well, eat up, then. What's wrong with you?'

'I can't eat any more, Daddy. There's no more room in my tummy.'

Sonny gets the scary look on his face again. 'I spent all that money and you barely ate any of it!'

'Sorry, Daddy.'

'That's a real waste, that is. A real waste of money!'

Marnie looks down into her lap while her father yells at her.

'You think I have that kind of money? Money I can just throw in the garbage? Is that what you think?'

'No, Daddy.' Marnie begins to cry. The man and the two boys in the booth opposite stop eating to look over at them. So does the woman sitting by herself with a cup of coffee at a nearby table, and the three teenage girls sharing a large box of French fries and a soda in the booth diagonal to theirs.

'Well, what do you expect when you buy so much food for such a little girl?' says the man with the two boys.

'Why don't you mind your own damn business?' Sonny moves his jaw from side to side.

'I don't appreciate your tone, sir.'

'Well, *I* don't *appreciate* you being such an asshole,' Marnie's daddy says. His voice is raised, and customers at tables in the front section turn to see what's going on.

'Watch the language there, big guy. Settle down, OK?' the man says.

Sonny gets out of the booth and stands over the man, who looks straight ahead, pushing his glasses on to the bridge of his nose, as if ignoring Sonny will somehow make him go away.

'What did you say to me?' Sonny says.

'Look, we are all just trying to enjoy our lunch with our kids, aren't we? Why don't you just calm down?'

'Oh, I'm calm. I'm fucking calm. I just don't like people interfering with me, you got it?' Sonny pounds his fist on the table top in their booth. The man's sons look terrified and the littler one begins to cry.

Marnie's stomach hurts even more. It feels like the French fries and pieces of the Big Mac are swimming around in the milkshake, the food rising higher and higher until the entire contents of her belly are in the back of her throat. Marnie coughs, and it all comes spilling out onto the table top.

'Oh my God!' the woman with the coffee shouts.

'That is so disgusting!' says one of the teenage girls, and her friends shriek and laugh.

Sonny shoves the man. 'See, look what you did to my little girl!' He shoves him again.

'Cut it out,' the man says.

'No, you cut it out, you piece of shit.' Sonny shoves the man hard enough so that he bumps into one of his sons seated next to him. By this time, both boys are wailing.

Marnie throws up again, but Sonny has his back to her and doesn't notice until the woman with the coffee shouts at him to attend to his daughter.

'What the fuck?' he says when he turns to see the mess at their table.

'Daddy, I want to go home,' Marnie sobs. 'I don't want to go camping. I just want to go home. I want Nanny.'

'Don't be such a baby!'

The woman with the coffee goes to the registers and finds the manager, who approaches their booth. 'What's going on here?'

'Come on, man. Why doesn't everyone just leave us alone? I'm just trying to have lunch with my daughter. Jesus!' Sonny picks up a tray and slams it down on the table top.

'Sir, you need to leave right now or I'm calling the police.'

'Let's go.' Sonny grabs Marnie by the wrists and pulls her out of the booth. She concentrates on her feet as her daddy drags her through the restaurant. Everyone is staring at them, muttering disapproval as they pass by. There's still the taste of vomit in her mouth and she wishes she could get a drink to wash it away. Her grandmother always gives her ginger ale or Coca-Cola when she's been sick to her stomach. And some of the sick got on her T-shirt and there are droplets dotting her flannel shirt as well. But she's never seen her daddy this angry, and is much too frightened to ask if they can get some napkins so she can clean herself up.

Outside, their footsteps echo off the pavement. When they reach the car, he tells her to hurry it up and get in. Marnie could run back inside the McDonald's and ask someone to call her grandmother, but her daddy has already slammed her door shut. 'That guy was such a piece of shit,' her daddy says when he gets in on his side. 'They all were. All of them.'

Marnie doesn't know what to say, and concentrates hard so she doesn't start crying again, because that will definitely anger him. Once they are back on the highway, Sonny drives fast, even faster than he did before. She rests her head against the window. They drive for a long time, getting on and off the highway, and Sonny keeps shouting to himself about the lousy directions his friend gave him. At one point, Marnie asks if they can stop so she can use the bathroom, but that only makes her father lose his temper yet again, so she pinches her fingers to try to forget about it, closes her eyes, and manages to fall asleep.

JUNCTION OF EARTH AND SKY

She wakes up to find they are at another rest stop. Her father is asleep, his head bent at a weird angle, and there's an empty bottle of Wild Turkey by his side. She doesn't know how long she has slept or what time it is, but the sun is low in the sky, the way it is in the late afternoon. It seems they have spent most of the day travelling and still they have not arrived. Marnie is sticky and hot from sleeping in the car, desperate for the toilet. Quietly, so as not to wake her father, she opens her door, crouches down and pees right there in the parking lot, not even bothering to check if anyone can see her.

Finally, her daddy wakes up and they drive some more on the thruway, before taking an exit to a one-lane highway and stopping at a gas station for directions. But the attendant hasn't heard of the road they are looking for, so her daddy calls him a fucking idiot, and they speed away. They drive for a couple more miles before pulling into a bar. Sonny calls his friend, who tells him to just stay where they are and he'll meet them there. They are so close by, Sonny explains to Marnie when he gets off the phone.

Marnie and her daddy take a seat in a booth in the back of the bar. Marnie has brought her backpack inside, and she gets out her drawing pad and her coloured pencils and her stuffed animal and starts to draw while they wait for Sonny's friend to arrive. He turns out to be a big man, even bigger than Sonny. When the two men greet, they pretend to punch each other before embracing. They are messing around so much that they lose their footing and fall onto the floor, taking a chair with them. Once again, everyone is staring at them and Marnie feels tears forming. She looks down at her drawing, hoping the large, loud man won't notice.

'Get a load of this,' the man says. 'Fuckin' Sonny's kid. Look at her, she's so fuckin' sensitive. Aww. That's so cute, Sonny. Look, you got a delicate flower here, don't you?'

The men order shots with beer chasers and the waitress says she'll bring Marnie a soda. She returns with the men's drinks, a 7-Up in a large glass with ice for Marnie, and a bowl of pretzels, which is the only available thing the bar has to eat. The waitress finds some crayons for her. When she gets bored of drawing, she takes out her book and tries to read, but it's dark and hard to see. Sonny and his friend order shot after shot, saying weird things to the waitress and trying to grab her when she delivers each round. They break a glass, and Sonny's friend falls over at one point when he gets up to use the bathroom. A few of the man's friends come over to the booth to talk with them, and one of them pinches Marnie's cheeks, telling her it's never too early for love.

It was almost dark when they got here, so it must be past her bedtime now, Marnie thinks when her daddy and his friend go play darts on the other side of the bar. They don't seem in any hurry to leave. Marnie hasn't had anything to eat since McDonald's, and she wonders if they will still cook hot dogs and roast marshmallows and look at the stars. If they will even end up sleeping in a tent when they get to the house. Whenever that will be. She goes to the bathroom and brushes her teeth in the sink, but decides not to change into her pyjamas because it's really dirty in the toilet stall. When she comes back, her daddy is at the bar talking to a group of men and they are all laughing at something he said. He doesn't even notice when she passes him on the way to their booth in the back, but some of the other customers give her funny looks.

Her daddy bought her a kite for her birthday this year, shaped like a blue butterfly with purple and yellow streamers on the end, and they'd gone to Crane's Beach to fly it. He told Marnie to hold the string while he tried to get it airborne. But the wind ripping off the water kept battering the kite onto the sand. Her daddy tossed it again and again into the air, and each time, it torpedoed straight down. Then, he tried running while he threw it into a gust and the kite stayed up that time. He jogged back to Marnie, showing her how to work the string so the kite remained in the flow of the wind. Soaring higher and higher above them, it became more than just a combination of nylon, sticks, ribbons and a stabilising tail. A blue butterfly sliced through the dull sky with a yellow and purple tail dancing behind. Together, they held tight to the taut piece of string connecting them as the kite dipped and curved with the currents of the wind.

Now she watches her father miming hitting a ball with a baseball bat and making gestures while he tells the crowd at the bar a story. They are laughing, some so hard that they have to bend over. Marnie folds her sweatshirt and puts it on top of her backpack to make a pillow, lies down along the wooden bench with her stuffed animal. The bench vibrates with music blaring from the jukebox.

Someone is gently shaking Marnie's arm. 'Hey, sweetie.' It's the waitress, crouched down beside her. 'Where did your dad go? Is he coming back for you, sweetie? Because it's time to go home. We're closing up now.'

The lights are on in the bar and a man is sweeping the floor with a big broom. All the chairs are upside down on top of the tables, like they are in school at the beginning of the day.

'I don't know.' Marnie sits up.

'What about your mom?' the waitress asks. 'Was she supposed to pick you up here?'

Marnie shakes her head. 'Where's Daddy?'

'Well, I don't know, honey. But don't you worry, we'll find him.' She takes a seat by Marnie and puts her arm around her shoulder, and gives it a squeeze. 'Phil!' she shouts at the man who is wiping a cloth over the bar. 'Phil, can you come over here?'

He crosses the bar. 'We running a day care centre in here now?' he says when he sees Marnie. 'What the hell, Cheryl? How did she get in here?'

'She was with those two shit-faced guys.' The waitress lowers her voice.

'Jesus Christ. Well, why in the world would you let them leave without her?'

'I didn't realise, did I? It was busy, and one minute they were here, the next they were gone. I assumed she went with them.'

'What are we going to do with her?' the bartender asks. 'We're going to have to call the cops or something.'

Marnie starts to cry and puts her hands over her face.

'It's going to be OK, honey,' the waitress says to her. 'Don't be scared. We're going to get you home. Now, where do you live?'

'With Nanny and Mommy,' Marnie sniffles.

'Do you know your address and phone number?' the waitress asks. 'And what are Nanny's and Mommy's names? What do grown-ups call them?'

'Are you crazy? She's not going to know any of that. She's too young.' He starts walking towards the bar. 'I'm calling the cops.'

'I know my number. I do,' Marnie tells the waitress. Alice made her memorise her phone number and her address, and she has it written down on a piece of paper that she keeps with her. Her grandmother made sure she put in the front pocket of her backpack. Marnie finds the slip of paper and gives it to the waitress.

Several months later, Marnie answers the phone when Alice is in the bath. It's the first time Marnie has heard her father's voice since the summer. 'Hi, Daddy,' she says.

It's hard to hear him because there is so much noise in the background – loud music and people laughing – and her daddy has to shout into the phone. He'll be back next summer, she doesn't need to worry, he'll definitely be back. 'Maybe we'll go camping again,' he says.

'Camping?' Marnie asks.

'Who is that?' Her grandmother comes out of the bathroom, wrapped in a robe, dripping a trail of water.

'It's Daddy.'

'I need to talk with Daddy a minute, love. You go and get your pyjamas on.' She takes the phone from Marnie and indicates with her chin that she is to leave the room so her grandmother can talk in private. 'You listen to me,' she says to him once Marnie is in the hallway. 'Don't you ever mention camping again, all right? She was upset for a long time after that trip you took her on. We all were. It's not happening again, you understand me?'

When her grandmother comes in to read her a bedtime story, Marnie curls up onto her lap. She feels so warm in her grandmother's arms and Alice holds her extra tight. It seems possible in this moment, intertwined with her grandmother, that it will always be like this. Then she realises her grandmother has started to cry, silent sobs that make her quiver. They sit like that, the two of them together, not saying anything, not even one word.

9

Opening Day

1979

MARNIE'S MOTHER IS WIPING away the blobs of spilled pancake batter from the stove when it comes to her. 'We have to dye your hair for the game,' she says to her daughter and her niece, Teresa.

The girls are by the sink. Teresa rinses off the dirty plates and silverware before handing them to Marnie, who then carefully places each item in the dishwasher. Breakfast had been blueberry pancakes and bacon, and the smell of maple syrup and cooked meat still lingers in the kitchen at Teresa's house.

In a few hours, they are going to Fenway Park to see the first baseball game of the season there, and everyone is rushing around, getting ready. Teresa's older brothers, Sean and Pat, are looking through boxes of Red Sox paraphernalia in their closets. Aunt Cath has gone to buy red plastic necklaces, foam fingers and banners from the women who set up tables in the Star Market parking lot on major game days, like this one. And Uncle Mike, who is always fixing something, is out in the garage getting his toolbox, so he can try to sort out the washing machine that's been leaking for almost a week.

At breakfast, Uncle Mike said he felt hopeful, that this could be the year. 'You always say that before the first game,' Aunt Cath said. 'It's the Red Sox, remember.'

He shook his head, as if she just didn't understand. 'It's the start of a new season,' he said, 'so anything is possible.'

Now, Denise holds the sponge in the air with her right hand. 'You think you got any red Kool-Aid mix, hon?' Denise asks Teresa. 'We can make our own hair dye. It's really easy.'

Teresa turns off the sink and drags a stool over to the top cupboard by the refrigerator. There are boxes of Kool-Aid mix, including red Tropical Punch, and she takes it out to show her aunt. 'Oh, this is perfect,' Denise says. 'You guys want red hair for the game?' She smiles wide.

'Yes, yes,' Marnie and Teresa say in unison. They hold hands and skip together in a circle. 'Yes, yes, yes,' they sing.

Marnie's mother sends Teresa up to the bathroom to fetch Aunt Cath's hair conditioner. Then the girls squeeze out most of the bottle into a tin mixing bowl, stirring in water and the Kool-Aid powder.

'This is what we used to do when we were kids, remember, Mikey?' Denise says to her older brother when he comes into the kitchen with his metal toolbox. 'You never went to Opening Day without red hair, right?'

He mumbles something, distracted, as he walks past them. 'Cath know you're doing that?' he says, looking back at Denise and the girls, still in their pyjamas, stirring something red in Cath's mixing bowl. Even though Aunt Cath and Uncle Mike are both the parents, both the adults in the house, Marnie's aunt is the one who says yes or no to things, makes the decisions and seems generally more in charge.

'It's just Kool-Aid and water, basically,' Denise says. 'It washes right out of everything. I'm sure she won't mind.'

He crinkles up his face and it looks like he is about to say something, but instead he heads to the basement to fix the washing machine.

When the hair dye is ready, Teresa carries the bowl upstairs to the bathroom with Marnie trailing behind, clutching the soup ladle and some large spoons. Once there, Denise instructs them to take off their pyjama tops, kneel on the tiled floor and lean over the edge of the bathtub. She gives each girl a washcloth to cover their eyes. Then she spoons the home-made dye onto Marnie's hair. The mixture is cold, but it feels soothing to have her mother's fingers massaging her scalp. When it's Teresa's turn, she squeals when Marnie's mother puts the dye into her hair.

'Don't move, Risa, baby, OK?' Denise says.

'It's so slimy.' Teresa opens her mouth wide and makes a face at Marnie. Both girls shriek and laugh.

Marnie and her mother have been excited about this trip for weeks, as soon as Uncle Mike called to say he got tickets for Opening Day. The night before they drove up here, Marnie had trouble getting to sleep because the anticipation was almost too much. She loves coming to her cousins' house, loves her aunt and uncle, her two older cousins, Sean and Pat, and most especially Teresa. Even though she is a whole year older, Teresa says they can still be best friends, they are best friends, that she has a school best friend and also Marnie. And yesterday, after Marnie and her mother arrived, they made it official when they become blood sisters, pricking their right index fingers with a safety pin and then pressing them together.

'It feels oogley,' Teresa says now, and the girls laugh even harder.

The red mixture drips onto the white porcelain of the bathtub. Her mother drapes towels over their shoulders and covers their hair in plastic bags because they don't have any shower caps. Her mother tells them to sit still while the mixture soaks in. They sit cross-legged on the floor while Marnie's mother calls for the boys.

When they pound into the bathroom, Teresa moves to the toilet and Marnie sits on the step stool that they all used when they were so little, they couldn't even reach the sink. The boys bend over the edge of the tub and wiggle around. Denise tells them to hold still while she applies the dye. But Sean shouts as Denise ladles it over his head and shakes his head. The dye splatters all over the tub and onto the shower curtain.

'Oh my God.' Denise covers her mouth. 'Seanie, look what you did. Oh my God.'

'Sorry,' he says, and smiles a fake smile. Then it's Pat's turn and he doesn't move at all during the entire procedure.

'See,' Denise says to Sean. 'That's what I call holding still.'

By now, the bathtub has red stains all over it and the dye is on the tiles and all over the bathmat and the shower curtain. There is more on the floor. The boys switch seats with Marnie and Teresa. Denise rinses their hair and then blow-dries it. She repeats the same steps with the boys.

Marnie and her cousins stand in front of the mirror, admiring themselves. Her dark blonde hair now has streaks of red in it, bright red streaks. Teresa's hair is darker, same as her brothers, yet still the red dye is clearly visible. 'Wow, it really worked,' says Teresa.

'I love it, Mommy.' Marnie hugs her mother.

'This is excellent.' Sean looks at himself in the mirror. 'Thanks, Aunt Dee.'

They hear a door slam downstairs. 'I'm back,' Cath calls out. 'Hey, where is everyone?'

'We're up here. Come see the kids, come see,' Denise shouts.

'Mommy, we made you a surprise,' Teresa yells.

The bathroom is right at the top of the stairs and Cath is smiling at first when she sees all four kids crowded in the bathroom with their shirts off, their hair streaked red. Then her face changes.

'What's all this, then?' Her eyes dart from Marnie and her cousins to the piles of towels and the red stains on the floor. 'What'd you do, Dee?'

'Aunt Denise dyed our hair,' Pat explains. 'For the game.'

'It was so fun, Mommy,' Teresa adds. 'Don't you like it?'

'Well, I can see that,' Cath says. 'I can certainly see that. Not sure I like the mess.'

Denise starts laughing. 'It's just Kool-Aid. Don't worry, Cath. It cleans up so easy. Honestly, it's so not a big deal. We used to do this all the time when we were kids. It'll come right out, it really will.'

Cath lets out a long exhale and suggests that the kids go get dressed. They slip past their mothers, who seem to be transitioning from a mild disagreement into an out-an-out fight.

Marnie follows Teresa up to her bedroom, which is in the attic and can only be reached by climbing a vertical ladder. She's got bunk beds and a swing and a big dollhouse that the girls play with all the time. They change into Red Sox shirts that Uncle Mike had given them the night before and head downstairs.

Cath and Denise are still in the bathroom. 'You had to use the white ones?' Cath has all the towels gathered up in her arms. 'You couldn't have at least used the ratty old towels?'

Marnie's mother is on her knees, scrubbing at the bathtub. 'I didn't know you had like towel categories, did I? And I can wash them right now. Honestly, it will come right out. I promise.'

'The washing machine is broken, Denise!'

'Come on.' Teresa grabs Marnie's hand. 'Let's go play until we have to go.'

They head out to the backyard and then they are running, Marnie and her cousins, and even though it is spring and already April, the air still has a crisp sting to it. Yet, everything has come back to life after looking dead all winter long. It seems like there must be thousands and thousands of birds singing and singing, the crocuses are starting to shoot up, blossom forming on the trees. In a few weeks, when Marnie and her mother return for Marnie's April break from school, everything will be bursting.

They start in on a game of tag, and Marnie is It. She runs and runs, but her seven-year-old legs are no match for ten-year old Pat, or Sean, who is almost thirteen. They keep coming near her, almost within reach, but duck away just as she is about to touch them. Teresa is calling out to her from the top of the slide on the swing set. Then Sean and Pat race up the ladder on one side of it, climb across, over the swings, then hustle down the other side. They run towards the large tree in the middle of the yard and clamber up the rungs nailed into the trunk and hide in the tree house. Marnie runs over to the tree, but before she can even get one foot up, Sean climbs out onto a limb and grabs hold of the rope with the tyre swing and slides down, yelling that his hands are burning. Then he lies on his back in the grass until Marnie comes running over to him. 'You got me, you got me.' He gets to his feet, picks up Marnie and swings her around.

That's when Marnie's mother comes out the back door. 'Marnie, we're going,' she yells.

Uncle Mike follows closely behind Marnie's mother. 'Come on, Dee, don't be like that.' He wipes his forehead. 'You guys don't need to leave. You're overreacting.'

She turns to him. 'I'm not the one who is overreacting, Mikey. She is. She's the one. It's fine. We can just go to a game another time. I don't even like baseball, it's really boring.'

Sean has stopped spinning Marnie around. He's got his arm draped over her. Pat climbs down from the tree house and Teresa skips over from the swing set.

'I said we're going,' Denise shouts across the yard. 'Didn't you hear me?'

'What?' Marnie asks.

'Dee, would you stop?' Uncle Mike says to her. 'Cath's just a little upset about the towels. They're brand new, that's all. But they're just towels. It doesn't matter now, does it? They're just towels.'

Marnie's uncle is waving his hands around while he talks. He is so much bigger than her mother. Sometimes, Marnie and Teresa play a game that involves climbing Uncle Mike, pretending he's a mountain. Expeditioning, they call it, and he'll stand with his arms and legs outstretched while they clamber up him. Then he'll scoop Marnie and Teresa into his arms and pretend to be a monster and run around with them. It's the most fun to play the game in the water, so they always hassle him when they go to the beach or the town pool. He'll float with the girls on his stomach, saying, *I'm going to eat you, I'm going to eat you.*

'Marnie,' she says, her voice wavering, the way it does right before she cries. 'Let's go, come on.'

Uncle Mike offers Denise a cigarette, steers her to the plastic lawn chairs and they both take a seat and light up.

Teresa grabs Marnie's hands and spins her, claps her hands to Marnie's and starts chanting the words to a hand game. *Miss Mary Mack, Mack Mack, All Dressed in Black, Black Black, With Silver Buttons, Buttons, Buttons, All Down Her Back, Back, Back.*

Marnie goes along with it, but keeps an eye on her mother. She can't understand why they would be leaving now. This would be Marnie's first baseball game ever. Her mother has been saying for weeks how she hasn't seen the Red Sox since she was a kid, how much fun it's going to be, that Fenway is the best ballpark.

Her uncle says something to her mother, who smiles slightly, and then she is laughing. Marnie loves her mother's laugh, which starts slowly and builds and builds. She runs over to them. 'Are we still going to the game?' Marnie looks from her mother to Uncle Mike.

''Course you are,' Uncle Mike says, as if she just imagined the whole thing.

'I was just being silly.' Her mom exhales a large cloud of smoke. 'You know me.'

Then they are in her uncle's orange VW bus, Marnie in the back, in between Teresa and her mom. They are kneeling, facing backwards, looking out the rear window, pointing at people who they think look funny and making up names for them: Lord Long Nose for the man waiting at a bus stop. Lady Poodle Head for the woman with tight curly hair putting coins into a parking meter. Queen Blondie Blonde for the tall woman with super-long blonde hair that is blowing all over her face as she walks. Marnie laughs along with her mother and her cousin, squished in close together.

Uncle Mike parks near a commuter rail station, so they don't have to drive all the way into Boston and deal with finding a space and all the expense, her aunt explains to no one in particular. While they wait for the train, the platform fills with people who look like they are heading into downtown for Opening Day. Many of them are wearing Red Sox hats or players' shirts, or dressed in the entire uniform. Kids are waving around banners and foam fingers. Some even have red streaks in their hair, just like Marnie and her cousins.

A train rattles in and everyone piles on, jostling for a place. It gets more and more crowded at each stop, until they are all pressed up against one another. A group of young men are already drinking beer, singing, chanting when they switch at Park Street. By the time they reach Kenmore and everyone gets off, the station is crammed full. One person is so drunk, he throws up into a trash can.

Uncle Mike leads them through the station, and they follow him up the stairs and out along Commonwealth, before taking a left on Brookline Ave and another left on Lansdowne. Marnie feels like she is being swept along in this tidal wave of people, grabbing hold of Teresa's hand and her mother's so she doesn't get lost. Finally, they take their seats just before the two teams come out onto the field. Once the game starts, it's hard to see exactly what is happening on the field, the players are so far away, the baseball so small.

The game lasts for hours and hours, and by the time it's over, Marnie is tired and not sure she'll be able to walk all the way back to the station. Her hands are sticky with the remnants of cotton candy and Cracker Jacks and ketchup. She is sitting on her mother's lap and she curls up to rest, just for a minute, before they start the long trek back. Below the seat, Marnie can see lots of empty plastic cups from all the beer her mother drank throughout the game. Her mother is shouting, *let's go Red Sox, let's go Red Sox*, even though it's over. Aunt Cath is whispering something to Uncle Mike, pointing at Marnie's mother with her head. 'You OK there, Dee?' Uncle Mike asks her.

'I'm great, man, I'm totally great,' Denise says.

People are starting to make their way out of the stands. Denise gathers her daughter in her arms, stumbling for a second when she stands up and almost drops her, before regaining her balance. 'I got you, Marn, I got you.'

Marnie nestles her face into her mother's neck and closes her eyes. 'You're my girl, Marnie Marn,' her mother says. 'You're my girl.'

10

Waiting

1979

ALICE IS WAITING FOR Marnie at the school bus stop, just around the corner from home. The air is thick with the smell of the sea. An early December snow fell on Sunday night, and a thick white cottony coating remained on the trees, roofs, stoops, porches and front lawns for several days. But a freezing rain that lasted all morning has turned it all into a grey, icy slush. Now everything has a dull, metallic sheen to it. Occasional cars trundle through puddles, sliding along the road.

It has been seven long hours since Alice last saw her granddaughter when she headed off to New Jordan Elementary earlier this morning. She has been waiting for this moment ever since. The moment when the yellow school bus approaches.

The day began the way it always does, with Alice waking up an hour before Marnie so she has time for a cup of tea and some breakfast before readying her grandchild for school. Denise works late most nights, and so she is always asleep in her bedroom this early in the morning. If she's made it home, that is. But her absence in the mornings is just as well. She can't really cope with the basics of looking after Marnie – can't really cope with much of anything. But Alice was no better herself when she was raising Sonny all on her own.

When it's gone seven, Alice gently coaxes Marnie out of bed. She fixes her a thick piece of toast slathered with butter and honey, along with a small cup of hot chocolate, which is mostly warmed milk mixed with a sprinkling of cocoa. She has the radio on, tuned to a station that plays jazz in the mornings, the volume low. Alice has noticed that Marnie needs quiet when she has first woken up so she leaves her granddaughter alone, doesn't pester her with questions and conversation as she eats her breakfast, often in a daze, staring off into space. What could she be thinking about, Alice wonders as she makes up her packed lunch: a cheese sandwich, an apple and a packet of crisps. By the time she has finished her breakfast, Marnie will have finally woken up. She'll go off to get herself dressed in the clothes that she and Alice laid out the night before. Then she makes her bed, because that's what people do when they respect themselves. Besides, she wants Marnie to learn how to take care of herself, how to take care of a home. By the time she was seven – Marnie's age now – Alice was helping her mother with all the household chores, the laundry and cooking and cleaning, and she wants to pass on those skills to her granddaughter.

Once she's brushed her teeth, Alice will fix her hair, and that's when they go over the plans for the afternoon.

If the weather forecast looks bad, they'll plan to go to the library. Otherwise, they'll head to Crane's Beach. It feels important to Alice to remind her granddaughter that it will only be a few hours and then they will be together again. Mostly, though, she is reassuring herself.

When Marnie is ready, they'll walk to the end of their street, take a right and wait on the corner at the bus stop, standing slightly apart from everyone else. Marnie stays right beside Alice, holding her hand, and doesn't ever talk to the two boys who always tussle with each other, or the three older girls who stand in a tight circle, whispering and giggling. After the bus pulls up and Marnie climbs the stairs and takes a seat, they'll wave to each other. Alice always waits there until the bus is out of sight, a pinched feeling spreading in her chest.

The rest of the morning is spent tidying up the apartment. If Denise is home, she usually stays in her room, waiting until Alice heads out to do the errands. Instead of going to the supermarket, Alice tries to get most of the groceries from the smaller stores along South Street. She prefers the Butcher Block, Wilson's Fruits and Vegetables, Olsen's Bakery, which are more like the shops of her childhood in Spithandle. Once home, she'll knit and read while listening to the radio until it's finally time to go and meet Marnie's bus.

Just before Thanksgiving, she received a letter from Sonny, saying he thought it would be for the best if he no longer had any contact with Marnie or Alice. 'I don't want my daughter to be anything like me,' he wrote in blocky capital letters. 'I am full of poison and the only thing I can offer is to stay far away from her.' She thought about burning the letter, but instead, she folded it up and put in a shoebox that she keeps under her bed. She never told Denise or anyone else about the letter.

She knows that time is running out on these afternoons with Marnie. Next fall, she'll probably want to be with her friends after school, and when she's a little older, she might even play a sport or be in a school play. So Alice wants to make the most of these afternoons while she still can. Then she sees it – the yellow school bus rounding the corner. When it comes to a stop, the door swings open and Marnie runs towards her grandmother.

It has been a long day. When Marnie and her grandmother walked to the bus in the morning, it was pouring, and she was wearing sneakers instead of waterproof boots. The rain had soaked through to her socks and her feet had been wet and cold for the entire day. Her friend, Sarah, was out sick, and although she was friendly with some of the other girls in her class, enough to be invited over to their homes and to birthday parties, none of them were as easy to talk to, to be around, as Sarah. She always felt out of place whenever her friend wasn't at school. By the afternoon, Marnie was having trouble concentrating when Ms Stuart read to the class. All she could think about was being with her grandmother.

Finally, the school day is over and she's back home. The first thing she always does is go into the bedroom she shares with her grandmother and change out of her school clothes. Mid-afternoon December light filters into the room, and the branches of the maple tree outside brush up against the window by Marnie's bed.

Her mother's bedroom is directly across the narrow hallway, the bathroom in between. Denise's door is always closed, no matter if she's home or not. When they are running low on cups and glasses, her grandmother sends Marnie in there to 'do a sweep'. She'll gather up mugs half-filled with congealed coffee, beer cans, lipstick-smudged glasses with cigarette butts floating in wine, every inch of the floor covered in clothes, shoes, pantyhose, so the rug isn't even visible. The bed is usually unmade and the air stale with cigarette smoke. Denise had taken down the gauzy white curtains Alice had hung in the windows when Marnie was a baby and often slept in this room. Instead, dark blue shades are always pulled down. Gone as well are the pictures of butterflies, kittens and puppies and Peter Rabbit.

On the afternoons when the weather is particularly bad and they aren't going anywhere, Marnie will change right into her pyjamas and slippers after school. But today, they decided on the walk back from the school bus that since it wasn't raining that hard anymore, they would go to Crane's Beach after Marnie has her snack. She pads out into the kitchen, where her grandmother has set out cookies and milk and grapes. Her mother has already left for work, so it is just the two of them in the apartment, like usual.

JUNCTION OF EARTH AND SKY

Noise is the first thing Marnie notices when she goes to other people's homes. She finds it overwhelming and she'll keep checking the clock, counting down the minutes until she can leave. Marnie doesn't understand her classmates' desire to spend so much time with one another. She would always rather be home with her grandmother. Every once in a while, she'll get invited to someone's house and she'll agree to go, although reluctantly, because it's the polite thing to do, her grandmother always says. Aside from Sarah's home, which is as calm and quiet as her own, she never enjoys the experience. She's been to Margaret Winston's house, but she has three sisters, three dogs, and the television in the kitchen blaring afternoon game shows. Still, her mother's voice is even louder than all of that combined. Tracey Newberry has an annoying little brother, and the one time Marnie went to her house, he chased them around, screaming, while he tried to wipe his snot on the girls. And when she went to Liza Smith's house, her mother yelled so much that Marnie asked to go home almost as soon as she'd arrived.

After Marnie has finished her snack, they make the short drive to Crane's Beach, which is less than a mile away. Marnie's grandmother always says she can't imagine living further away from the sea. She hates it when she has to go more than even one day without looking at it. She says the hardest time in her life was when she was evacuated and had to go live up north, so far away that she didn't see the ocean even once for eighteen long months.

They park and walk along the sand, looking for sea glass and shells and rocks to add to their collection. The storm has caused unusually big waves and there are a couple of surfers in wetsuits out in the swells. A thin grey line separates the water from the sky. The wind whips as they walk along the shore and Marnie clutches her grandmother, her small, warm hand inside Alice's. Then they pretend to look for pirates out on the sea before heading back towards the parking lot. But before they get there, Alice spreads her arms wide, leans back and sticks out her tongue.

'You look silly, Nanny.' Marnie laughs. 'What are you doing?'

'I'm drinking rain, love.' Alice closes her eyes. 'Oh, you must try it. It's absolutely delicious.'

Since they are the only ones on the beach and no one can see them, not even the surfers, Marnie sticks out her own tongue. As the rain pelts her upturned face, she listens to the rhythm of the waves pounding the shore, the build, the retreat, over and over again.

11

What Remains

1940

ALICE WATCHES THE TWO Simms sisters arguing in the Flights' front room, wishing more than anything that their mother didn't leave them here when she went with Auntie to see what was what.

'We're going to miss everything, we are,' Renie, Mrs Simms' younger daughter, says. 'The fire brigade will have been and gone by the time we're allowed out and it will all be sorted.'

'I don't want to see, I don't.' Pearl starts crying. She is in between Lou and Alice on the settee. The older Simms girl, Mary, is on the footstool, and she punches her little sister, who is sat on the floor beside her, tells her to shut her mouth. 'You heard our mums, same as us. They'll murder us if we go outside.'

'Ow. What'd you do that for?' Renie scrunches up her face. 'Miss *Mary*. *Lady Mary*. Miss Perfect.'

'Oh, why can't you ever keep quiet?' Mary scowls.

'But couldn't we just go outside for a minute, like?' Renie looks to Alice and Lou, as if they might be willing accomplices. 'There might still be things on fire. If we ran, we could make it back before them, surely.'

'Absolutely not. What is wrong with you?' Mary exchanges a look with Alice and Lou to indicate her disapproval.

'I saw that, Mary, you know?' Renie whines. 'I hate you, Mary. You're the worst sister ever.' She gets to her feet and starts pacing the small front room. But she can only take about five or six steps before she reaches the end of the room and has to turn around. This gets Mary more aggravated, and she moans at her sister to stop.

Before she left, Auntie insisted the girls stay inside with the windows shut and the heavy blackout curtains drawn. It's barely daylight, yet already the room is sweltering, but they aren't allowed out in the back garden.

Last night, Alice had been woken by the air-raid sirens. They went off all the time, and the girls thought nothing of it as they made their way down the stairs with Auntie, clutching their gas masks. But just as they reached the bottom of the staircase, there was a loud blast; the house shook. The girls screamed. It was so loud they knew somewhere close by must have been hit by a bomb. They didn't have enough of a warning to make it to the next-door neighbours', who had an Anderson shelter in their back garden. Instead they huddled under the table with their gas masks on and waited for the all-clear. Pearl was crying so hard that she got the hiccups. Then they heard another explosion, and another, but they sounded a little farther away. Alice wasn't certain that she took even one breath until she heard the all-clear an hour later.

The girls had been preparing for this moment since the war started, almost one year ago. Air-raid drills at school were performed in three stages: first they were told to stand, then to move their chairs to the right, and finally to sit under their desks with their backs to the teacher. The whole thing made Alice giggle.

Now, though, Alice couldn't believe she used to find anything funny at all about air-raid sirens. Dogfights between Spitfires and German bombers have been increasing over the last month, and there have been heavy bombings all along the south coast. Just last week, the Tangmere airfield, less than fifteen miles away, was hit by dive-bombers and all the hangars were either badly damaged or completely destroyed. On several occasions, Alice and the girls have been out when the air-raid sirens have gone off and they've had to take shelter in strangers' homes.

After the all-clear, Lou and Alice rushed to the windows to try to see what had happened, but Auntie shouted at them to keep away. She was still under the table, holding on to Pearl, with her hand over her mouth, and for a brief moment it looked like she would begin weeping herself. Alice had never seen her look so scared. But she quickly regained her composure and said in a softer tone that it might be wise to stay away from the windows for the time being.

They could hear sirens from the fire brigade and Lou thought they sounded close by, maybe even on the next road. Then Mrs Simms was knocking on the door with her daughters, and the two women went to try to find out what had happened, leaving the girls behind.

Finally, the women return. Auntie asks Lou and Alice to come upstairs with her and help sort out her bedroom. Once there, she explains that Mrs Little, who lives on the next road, is going to be staying with them because it was her house that was hit.

'Oh, that's awful,' says Lou. 'Poor Mrs Little. Was anyone killed?'

Auntie takes a deep breath and swallows before replying. 'Yes. Her son.'

'Funny Teddy?' Lou asks, and her mother nods and closes her eyes.

Everyone called him that. Alice had just seen him last week when she and Lou took Pearl to the park. He was sitting on the swings, pumping his legs back and forth. The swings were much too small for his adult legs, and he had to bend them so his feet wouldn't scrape the ground. While he glided back and forth, he sang a song to himself that Alice had never heard before. Something about a bird and a sunny day, and the way he sang it, out of tune and with no rhymes, made her think he was making it up as he went along. His voice always sounded funny when he said hello, like the words were getting stuck somewhere inside him and he had to think extra hard to get them out. Alice couldn't believe he had been killed.

'Mrs Little will be here soon. She had to go to the hospital with . . . with the . . . you know, and fill out some forms and that. You girls go on out, all right? Take Mary and Renie and Pearl with you, will you, please? We need a few hours to get her settled in. You can imagine she's in a bit of a state.'

It's the stillness on the road that Alice notices first when they leave the house. No one is riding bikes or skipping or running up and down or screaming or laughing. Across the road, two of the Christie sisters are sat outside quietly playing marbles, looking glum. Even Renie no longer seems excited as they head towards Half Moon Lane, where Mrs Little lives.

Her road is lined with people silently watching the fire brigade dousing the charred house. No one says anything; they just nod to one another while they watch the men work, as if they are all thinking the same thing: *That could have been us, that was almost us, a few hundred yards, here or there.* The house looks as if it's been cut in half. The entire front has been demolished, crumbled into a pile of bricks. The narrow staircase is still there but the second floor is gone. Downstairs, the front room has been reduced to rubble and the kitchen behind it is singed black. Alice cannot understand how Mrs Little survived.

Pearl is clutching tight to Alice and Lou's hands. The girls don't say anything, but Renie and Mary start their bickering all over again.

'There, now you've seen it,' Mary says to her little sister. 'Are you happy?'

But instead of a sharp retort, Renie just stares at what remains of Mrs Little's house. 'It's so awful,' she whispers.

'Well, what did you expect?' Mary says.

Renie starts to cry. 'You're being horrible to me, you are.' She sniffs. Mary puts her arms around her little sister, and tries to soothe her.

No one feels like doing much of anything after that. They wander over to the park and lie on the grass in the shade. Alice wishes they could go home. All she wants to do is lie in bed under the covers. After a while, Renie and Pearl go off together to climb one of the trees.

When they get back home, the front room is filled with women bustling around with tea and toast. Upstairs, Mrs Little is crying out *Teddy, Teddy, Teddy*, in between letting out guttural moans, a sound Alice has never heard a human make before. The girls don't need to be told to get out of the way. They hurry out to the back garden and sit and wait. Alice hopes that someone can do something to make Mrs Little feel better and settle her, stop her anguished cries.

Later on in the afternoon, Alice meets Danny outside the Turners' farm when he's finished work. They walk together holding hands along the dirt path that leads back to their neighbourhood, like they have done most afternoons since they first met. Usually, they talk the whole way, but today they don't say anything. It's been a long, slow, hot afternoon, and Alice has hardly eaten or drunk much of anything; she feels light-headed. They take a seat under a large elm tree and lie together in the heat, with their eyes closed, not exactly sleeping, but not quite fully awake either. Next week, he will be gone.

After a while, Alice lifts her head. It must be getting on and she should go home, she tells him. When they get to their feet, he explains that his mother decided this morning, after the bombing, to go back to Ireland for a while; she says she won't feel safe here now, especially once Danny is gone. Alice fears her throat will close when they say their goodbyes. She won't feel safe here without him either.

One evening, a few days later, Auntie tells the girls it's simply too dangerous here in Spithandle, and that the local authorities are offering to evacuate children to somewhere safer, somewhere that isn't being bombed. The way children from London came down here at the start of the war. The girls will leave on Friday, in two days' time.

Pearl begins to cry, and her mother picks her up and cradles the little girl in her arms.

'Where will we go?' Lou asks. But her mother says that no one yet knows.

'Mummy, are you coming with us?' Pearl asks.

'Just children are going,' Auntie says. 'But you three will be together. And you'll get to go on a train journey. Won't that be exciting?'

'Without mummies?' Pearl looks even more worried. 'A train journey without any mummies at all?'

Her mother explains that their teachers will travel with them, and if they end up being away for longer than a few months, she'll join them, no matter where they are. Pearl tucks her head under her mother's chin, as if she is trying to burrow inside. Her mother holds her tight, her eyes shiny and wet.

Alice excuses herself, saying she needs the loo. But really, it's so she can be alone in the back garden. Her chest feels like it might explode, and she wants more than anything to be with Danny right now, to hear his soothing voice. It's quiet out there, with only the muted sounds of the radio drifting from open windows, a mixture of music and news reports.

Finally the smell of Mrs Little's burned house has gone away. She left to stay with a sister in Hastings. Before she went, Mrs Little gave each of the girls one of Teddy's handkerchiefs. They were silk, she explained, and had been in the family for a long time. She wanted the girls to have one each, so whenever they felt sad, they'd have something soft to wipe away their tears. Teddy was such a gentle soul, she'd said, and, more than anything, he hated seeing people upset.

Lou and Pearl had both put theirs at the very bottom of the chest of drawers, under their knickers. But Alice has kept hers tucked in a pocket, and she pulls it out now. The light blue square is almost big enough to tie around her neck and make a scarf, and Alice presses it to her forehead, her eyelids, her cheeks. The fine, soft silk is soothing as she gently caresses it on her skin. Even though it's gone seven, there is still plenty of daylight. In just a few weeks, at this time of day, it will be dusk. Alice looks at the sky, waiting for the darkness that is coming.

12

Still Life

1990

THE VORTEX IS WEDGED in between Cash King and Beverage Mart, that has bars on the windows and plenty of forty-ounce bottles of malt liquor and shot-sized ones of cheap booze favoured by the homeless men who hang out on the sidewalk in front. There is nothing else on the block besides the two stores and the club, just boarded-up storefronts on one side and a burned-out building and an empty lot surrounded by a chain-link fence on the other.

Even though it's not even five and the Vortex won't be officially open yet, Marnie always heads there straight after work on Fridays. It takes two buses plus a long walk to get home, a good hour in total. It's not worth it when all she is going to do is turn right around and head back out again. Because Friday nights are for partying at the Vortex. Besides, Carl bartends on Fridays, and he'll let Marnie come in early to hang out and draw. She likes the way the afternoon light hits the bottles along the backbar, the shadows that fall on the empty tables and chairs.

Except for coffee and some dinner rolls she snagged at the senior centre where she works, Marnie hasn't eaten all day. She threads her way through the huddles of men along the block, ignoring their catcalls. *Hey, baby, check you out, girl, why such a rush?* and *where's my smile, where's my smile?* A few are nodding off, slumped against a pile of milk crates. Four of them stand in a tight circle, laughing hard at something. Two other men are screaming at each other. 'I got the money, I got the money,' one of them insists. Another man lies flat on his back in the middle of the sidewalk.

Once inside Beverage Mart, she heads straight for the soda section on the far wall, grabs a Coke and a bag of Doritos. She crouches down, rips open the bag and eats quickly, in between gulping down the soda. There are yet more men hanging out with the cashier, as usual, and so long as you're not trying to steal liquor, he doesn't pay much attention to what's going on in the aisles. Marnie survives on candy bars and Doritos, boxes of macaroni and cheese, instant ramen noodles eaten straight out of the Styrofoam cups. She hasn't had a real meal or felt full since she left New Jordan over six months ago, and there has been a constant gnawing sensation in her stomach ever since.

Once she's finished 'dinner', she stuffs the empty soda bottle and Doritos bag behind a box of Oreos. Then she buys a forty-ouncer of Olde English, and brings it with her into the Vortex. Carl will pretend not to notice her sipping from the brown bag by her side while she draws.

His face brightens like it does every week when Marnie walks in. 'Well, look what the cat dragged in.' He comes around from behind the bar to give her a hug. 'My favourite artist.'

Marnie takes her usual stool in the far corner where the bar curves around. She pulls out her sketchbook to work on a drawing of the bottles that she started last week. Carl concentrates on readying for the approaching evening. There won't be anyone else in there for at least another hour, when customers will begin to trickle in, along with musicians lugging their equipment to the band room, followed by the sound engineer. For the next half hour, Carl is back and forth from the kitchen to the bar, in between answering the phone. Marnie draws, sips at her drink and blows her nose. She has had a cold since moving here – the outskirts of Worcester – with her friend Tim in January. He left several months ago, but she's still living with his friends who are in a band – the Texas Chainsaw Massacres – and Gracie, their manager. They're crashing in a loft in a former paint factory, and the abandoned building is inhabited by artists and musicians. Although they have managed to install plumbing and electricity, the walls are more or less held together with posters from shows. Marnie sleeps on a mattress she found on the sidewalk, and even in summer, the rug in her bedroom is so damp, if she leaves her clothes on the floor overnight, they are wet by morning. The Buildings Department keeps threatening to condemn the place and evict them all.

Carl sets up his cutting board and a bowl of lemons and limes and starts to slice them up. He and Marnie talk about the bands playing there later on, how weirdly cool it's been for late June, and how much they wish they were closer to the coast so they could go to the beach, instead of being a good couple of hours away.

'Hey, you were going pretty hard last weekend.' Carl looks at her.

Marnie blushes. She had hardly eaten anything last Friday night and got very drunk, very quickly. One minute, it seemed, she was dancing with Gracie, and the next, Carl was waking her up after she'd passed out on the floor. He ended up giving her a ride home. 'Sorry about that. I'm so embarrassed.' Marnie covers her face in shame at the memory.

'Please, I'm a bartender. I've seen everything. But maybe just take it a bit more slowly tonight, OK?'

'OK, *Dad*.' The regulars started calling him that after his thirtieth birthday last month.

'And since we're having a little father/daughter talk, if you guys are going to do coke here, at least be a little bit cooler about it. OK, dear?' He puts the lemons and limes in the metal containers by the sink behind the bar and heads back into the kitchen.

Marnie thinks back to the previous Friday. It comes to her in flashes, and she remembers vaguely that Gracie was flirting with some guys in business suits, trying to get them to share their drugs. An image comes to her of snorting coke in the bathroom, and then again out in the bar. She'd forgotten all about that part of the night, until just now.

'Oh God, Carl, sorry about that, too,' she tells him when he returns with trays of clean pint glasses and starts to arrange them underneath the bar.

The wait staff are beginning to trickle in. Gracie and the Massacres will be arriving in a little while to do their sound check, along with the rest of the evening's lineup, mostly local bands playing short sets, which some nights can be up to eight bands in total.

Carl says it's cool about the coke and asks about the road trip. Gracie just got the Massacres their first out-of-town gig in Troy. The show wasn't that well attended, but still, it was a start. They didn't have anywhere to stay so they'd all slept in the van in a parking lot. 'They got a mention in the paper,' Marnie tells Carl. 'Things might be about to happen for them.'

'Look, dear, I hate to break it to you, but nothing is going to happen to them.' Carl goes on to say that if he's being honest, and he likes to be honest, the Massacres are barely tolerable, and they're lucky to have this gig.

Marnie laughs. 'Wow. You're a good actor, you know that? This whole time I totally thought you liked them, Dad.'

'I just wouldn't pin all my hopes on the Massacres.'

'They're just fun to hang out with. That's all. I don't have any hopes pinned on them.'

'Oh, yeah? So what do you have all your hopes pinned on?' Carl stops putting away the glasses and settles in front of Marnie, and it occurs to her that this is no longer the fun banter they usually have with each other on Friday afternoons. That he is, in fact, lecturing her. He looks around to see if anyone can hear him and then back at Marnie. 'How old are you, anyway?'

'Twenty-one, Dad.'

'Cut it out. I'm serious. I don't care about the ID thing. Just for real. How old are you?'

'Eighteen.' Marnie looks away.

'Let me ask you something. You're not from around here, are you?'

She shakes her head.

'Do your parents know you're here? Are you like a runaway or something?'

Marnie blinks, willing herself not to cry.

'Sorry, OK, I'm sorry. It's none of my business, I shouldn't have asked. It's just . . . Look . . . You're obviously really interested in drawing – I see you working at it every week. And you seem really bright, and I mean, look at your friend Tim, man. That could have been you, I bet. I don't mean to sound like a douche bag, it's just I wish like anything I had gone to college when I had the chance.'

'So why don't you, if it's so great? And what makes you think I have a chance?' Marnie starts to tear up.

'Hey, come on, don't get upset. I don't know what I'm saying. The only thing I know is that shitty clubs and lame-ass bands, we're not going anywhere.' He spreads his arms out. Then he leans in closer to talk to her. 'You like maybe got something here.' He points at her sketchbook. 'And those guys, Gracie and them?' He lowers his voice. 'Those guys are such . . . losers.'

Marnie is so angry, she can't even look at him.

'Whatever, don't listen to me. Nobody ever does.' He grabs a piece of paper and a pen and writes something on it. 'Here's my number, OK? And my mother's number. You ever need anything, that's how you find me.' He puts it in front of her and turns his attention back to prepping for the evening.

Marnie considers the scrap of paper for a minute before putting it in her wallet. Behind the picture of her grandmother, in the compartment where she keeps everything important. The liquor bottles shine in the late afternoon light.

13

Moms' Night Out

1980

It's Moms' Night Out, and Denise and her two best girlfriends are gathered around the kitchen table getting themselves ready, giddy in anticipation of what the night could bring. The possibility that Two-For-One Tuesdays at the Mamma Mia Lounge, Thirsty Thursdays at the Aloha, or TGIF at Lady Pearl's Bar and Grill will be the on-ramp access to all their dreams coming true.

For Denise, the dream includes not only a man who treats her right, but a man who will take her away from this cramped two-bedroom apartment that isn't even her own home. It's been six years since she and Sonny divorced, yet still, here she is, sleeping in her ex's childhood bedroom. Which is humiliating enough, plus there is her mother-in-law to contend with. Uptight Alice, who tries to control everything Marnie does. *Her* daughter, by the way. Alice has so many rules about Marnie's bedtime and what she eats, and how much television she's allowed to watch and what shows are appropriate, and on and on and on. If only Denise could afford her own place. If only.

She has the hair dryer going, feathering back her hair, and she's wearing tight jeans and a green midriff top with long billowing sleeves and swirly patterns on it. Her friend Linda is applying black eyeliner, putting on blue eyeshadow and shellacking red on her lips. She's dressed in a miniskirt and cowboy boots. They are gathered around the large mirror Val has brought, along with her huge makeup bag, which they all help themselves to. Val sells Avon products and works at Ames, where she gets an employee discount, first dibs on the new line of beauty products, and free samples.

The women complain about their creepy bosses while they smoke and drink from a large jug of Paul Masson white wine, which is in the middle of the kitchen table. The radio is tuned to the station that plays Top 40 hits and turned up loud.

Tonight, Marnie is in her footsie pyjamas on the couch, pretending to read. But really, she is watching the familiar routine of her mother getting ready with her friends. Her grandmother has a sour look on her face like she always does when Denise has her friends round. There isn't a door between the kitchen and the living room, and they are separated only by a large oval passageway, so there is no escaping the sounds of the three women enjoying themselves.

Denise notices her daughter staring at them. 'You want to come to Mommy's party?' Denise waves her over. 'Come here, sweetie.'

Marnie scoots off the couch and slides on her pyjama-covered feet like she's ice-skating into the kitchen. Linda pats the chair next to her and Marnie takes a seat.

'Don't you think Marn would look so cute with a little makeup?' Val asks. She has a large puff of red hair and the biggest breasts Marnie has ever seen.

'You want me to put some eyeshadow on you?' Linda uses a baby voice when she speaks to Marnie, even though she just turned eight.

'OK, sure,' Marnie says and closes her eyes while Linda rubs a tiny brush over her eyelids as she tells her friends about her latest weight loss plan. Even though she is already very thin, Linda obsesses about her weight and only drinks vodka because she says it has less calories than wine.

When Linda finishes with Marnie, it's Val's turn. She strokes blush on her cheeks, but it feels tickly and Marnie keeps giggling, which makes all three women laugh.

Her mother says she is going to do her hair, and Marnie leans back so she can brush it first. Val suggests a French braid, but Linda says to put it up in a bun: 'You know, like a ballerina or something.'

After her mother is finished with Marnie's hair, she tells her to pout her lips out so she can apply lipstick.

'Look at you! Look at my beautiful baby!' her mother shrieks when the women are all done fixing and fussing with Marnie. 'You look like a movie star. Here, dance with Mommy.'

She pulls Marnie out of her chair and holds on to her hands as they start to sway. Val and Linda join them. Then Stevie Wonder's 'For Once in My Life' comes on the radio, and all three women squeal and turn it up even louder.

Marnie's mother swings her around and dips her backwards. It's Val's turn to dance with Marnie next, and then Linda's. Her mother takes her hands, pulls her in close and slow dances with her. Marnie closes her eyes and holds on to her mother.

The music stops suddenly. 'That's enough.' Alice has switched off the portable radio on the counter. 'It's late. Denise, time to make a move. All right?' She takes Marnie's hand. 'She needs to get to bed now.'

Alice turns to go into the living room, and when she does, Marnie notices her mother making a face behind her grandmother's back. Val and Linda laugh at Alice.

'Come on, ladies,' Denise says to her friends. 'Let's go paartay!'

'Woo-hoo!' says Val.

'Let's rock and roll!' says Linda.

Marnie's mother kisses her on the cheek and gives her a hug and says goodnight, and Val and Linda do the same. Then the three women are clicking in their high heels and boots through the living room, and Marnie can hear them laughing and laughing as they make their way down the stairs.

'Phew,' her grandmother says. She collects the dirty wineglasses and brings them to the sink, empties the ashtray into the garbage. 'We can have a bit of peace and quiet now. Go and wash that nonsense off your face, love.'

'OK, sure.' Marnie never disobeys her grandmother. Yet once she's in the bathroom, she stares at herself for a while in the mirror above the sink, as if she looked hard enough, she might be able to see a grown-up version of herself somewhere deep inside the reflection. Then she takes a washcloth and wipes it all away.

Later, Marnie is woken up by the sounds of her mother stumbling around in the bathroom. Some nights, her mother comes home crying. But now, Marnie only hears the toilet flushing, followed by the light being clicked off and her mother's bedroom door closing. Marnie rolls over and squeezes her stuffed dog. Her mother is back home, safe, not upset, and alone.

Sometimes, after Moms' Night Out, Marnie hears a man's voice in her mother's bedroom. Or there's a man leaving her room, the morning after. Once, Marnie saw a guy in the kitchen wearing only his underwear, searching for aspirin. Other times, the phone will ring over and over in the middle of the night, and it will be a bartender explaining to Alice that Marnie's mother is so drunk, no cab will take her home, or it will be an ER nurse, or the police. Sometimes, after Moms' Night Out, her mother doesn't come home at all until the next day, or even the one after that.

But this morning, her mother gets up earlier than usual. She takes a shower and washes her hair, wraps it up in a towel and makes coffee in her bathrobe. She has several hours before her shift starts at Massey's Seafood Saloon, the restaurant by the Point Judith ferry terminal where she waits tables. Instead of taking Marnie along with her to do the Saturday morning shopping, Alice asks if she would rather stay home. She'll be certain to get back before Denise has to leave for work.

JUNCTION OF EARTH AND SKY

Once Alice is gone, Denise puts on cartoons for her daughter. She says that Val left a bottle of nail polish that's a really pretty shade of red. 'How about I do your nails while you watch TV?' her mother asks.

'Yes, yes, yes, yes, yes!' Marnie says.

After washing her hands and feet, Marnie's mother trims her nails and files them. Denise lays down a paper towel on the sofa cushion and paints the nails on her daughter's right hand, then her left. Marnie's feet are ticklish, and she laughs when her mother winds toilet paper in between her toes to separate them. After her mother is finished painting her toenails, Marnie leans back in her mother's arms while her nails dry.

Then the phone rings in the kitchen and her mother gets up to answer it. 'Hey, Val,' she says, and lights up a cigarette, pulls the cord out into the living room so she can cuddle up with Marnie and talk to her friend at the same time. Her mother laughs while they go over the details from last night, recounting every moment they can remember.

Their phone call is interrupted by the doorbell and the sudden buzzing startles Marnie and her mother. Denise drags the phone cord over to the window to see who it is. 'Shit,' she says extra slow, drawing out the word so that it sounds like it has three syllables instead of just the one, *Shiiit*. 'I can't believe it, I can't fucking believe it. Don't answer it, baby,' she tells Marnie.

The doorbell goes again, and then a third time. Denise holds her head in her hand, rubbing her temples. 'You're not going to believe who's at my door right now,' she says to Val. 'Yup. Donnie. Was he there last night?' Pause. 'God, I was so wasted, I didn't even notice him. That guy is fuckin' nuts. Like one night together and he's acting like we're getting married or something.' Pause. 'You don't need to come over. I can handle him.' Her mother's hands shake when she lights up yet another cigarette, like they always do when she's stayed out late with her friends. 'Alice is going to freak if this is still going on when she gets back. I better go deal with this asshole. I'll call you later.'

The man downstairs presses the buzzer for a whole entire minute. Marnie covers her ears. 'Denise! I know you're up there,' he shouts. 'Come on, Denise! I need to talk to you!'

The Finnegan sisters, the two older women who live below them, are thumping a broom on their ceiling, shouting to *keep it down up there.*

'I don't know why he's acting so crazy,' Denise says to herself. She crosses the room to let him in. 'Baby, go to your room and stay there until I get rid of this bozo, OK?'

Marnie rushes to her room, slams the door behind her and dives onto her bed, burying her face in her pillow. She wishes her grandmother would hurry up and get back, and make the man go away. The front door groans open.

'Are you trying to humiliate me, Denise?' the man shouts. 'Is that what you're doing? Acting all like you don't know me? You think you're too good for me, is that it?'

The Finnegan sisters downstairs thump their broomstick again. For once, Marnie is grateful that they are so nosy, and only one floor away, listening in on everything that's happening up here.

Then there is a loud crashing sound and her mother screams. 'Help me. Please, somebody help! Marnie? Marnie? Help me, baby. Call 911!'

Marnie runs from her room into the living room. Her mother is on her side, shielding her face with her arms, and the man has the empty Paul Masson bottle, holding it above her mother's head. He's enormous, with an oversized head and no hair, and he looks like one of the ogres in Marnie's story books.

'Mommy!' Marnie stops in the entranceway to the living room. The telephone is in the kitchen, and she has to go right by the scary man to reach it.

'Who the fuck is this?' He turns away from Denise, and she crawls on her hands and knees towards her daughter and they cower together. Her nose is bleeding and a few droplets fall onto Marnie's pyjamas.

'You have a fucking kid? What the fuck, Denise?' He throws the wine bottle against the wall and it smashes, the glass fragments spraying everywhere. More broom thumping from the Finnegan sisters. 'What's going on up there?' one of them shouts.

'Please just leave us alone. Please,' her mother cries.

'You're crazy, you know that, Denise?' He starts for the door. 'You're crazy.'

He slams it behind him and Denise gets up and double bolts it. She turns and rushes towards Marnie, and picks her up. She carries her to the sofa and holds her daughter on her lap and they both cry. 'It's OK now, everything is OK.' She strokes Marnie's hair. 'Don't tell Alice about him, OK, baby? Please don't tell Alice. Whatever you do. Promise me?'

Marnie worries for the rest of the morning, long after her mother washes the blood out of her pyjamas and cleans up the broken glass. By the time Alice returns with the shopping, everything is all taken care of and you can't even tell that any of it happened. Still, Marnie worries. She worries while she helps her grandmother put away the groceries, placing the butter, milk, eggs, a chunk of Cheddar cheese, and a pound of hamburger meat in the fridge, the new box of Cheerios next to the almost-empty one, the tea in the drawer by the stove, the bread in the wooden box by the toaster. She worries while she is getting together the library books that need to be returned. She worries collecting newspapers and old mail to take to the dump to be recycled, along with the glass jars and her mother's empty bottles of wine. She worries after her grandmother makes herself a cup of tea and heats up some milk for Marnie's hot chocolate, and they are sitting together at the kitchen table, sipping their drinks.

'You're awfully quiet this morning, love. You all right? Cat got your tongue? Is that it?' her grandmother asks.

The way her grandmother looks at her, her hazel eyes filled with concern, makes Marnie well up. She thinks of the expression on her mother's face when the man held the wine bottle up above her. What would have happened if he had smashed it on her head instead of against the wall? She knows she is not supposed to tell and tries to hold it all in, but the tears start leaking out anyway.

Alice reaches across the table and squeezes her granddaughter's hand. 'Oh, love, it's just a silly expression. Nothing's happened to your tongue, now, has it?'

Marnie sniffs hard, sucking back the tears.

'Why don't we check just to make sure, then? Let's have a look, then, shall we?'

Marnie wipes at her face and sticks out her tongue. 'Looks perfectly fine to me,' her grandmother smiles at her. 'Quite a long tongue, now, isn't it? But a healthy tongue in my opinion, and clearly no cat has got anywhere near that.' She pats Marnie's hand and they finish their drinks. 'Come on, then, let's stop all this, why don't we? And look, it's such a lovely day.'

14

Summer is Money

1981

HER MOTHER-IN-LAW'S HOME IS haunted. That's what Denise tells her girlfriends, her co-workers, the regulars at Massey's Seaside Saloon, anyone who will listen to her. How else to explain the bumps and groans in the middle of the night. Once, she put a glass down in the living room, went to the toilet, and it wasn't in the same place when she returned.

'Swear to God,' she says now at the bar in Massey's. The kitchen has been closed for an hour, but the manager has the bartender stay on if there's enough wait staff sticking around, taking advantage of their employee drink discount to make it worthwhile. Like tonight with the hostess, three other waitresses besides Denise, and a couple of the food runners and dishwashers, as well as the manager, all having after-work drinks at the bar.

'How come she's your mother-in-law if you and Sonny are divorced?' asks the bartender, the only one still listening to Denise.

'She'll always be my mother-in-law, no matter what. That will never change. I'll never be rid of Alice. But you're missing my point. The place has fucked-up vibes. It's no wonder Sonny turned out the way he did.'

'You heard from him?'

'Nope. *Nada*. Nothing. Not even a phone call in I don't know how long. I have no idea where he is. He never sends any money for Marnie. If he did, I could afford my own place. Seven years I been there. Seven fucking years.'

Alice is having the same thought. It's like living with a teenager, instead of a grown woman. Her bedroom is always in a state. When Denise isn't home, Alice ventures in to collect the damp towels, glasses, mugs, plates of rotting food that are strewn all around the room. The woman doesn't seem to know how to hang up a coat or her purse, and her shoes, balled-up socks and pantyhose are always in a heap by the door. She spends ages in the bathroom, using every last drop of hot water, leaves blobs of toothpaste around the sink and damp towels on the floor, and never puts away her makeup or the hair dryer. Every time she gets something to eat, she'll stand in front of the refrigerator with the door wide open while she decides, wasting all that electricity before settling on a bowl of Cheerios, managing to spill some on the floor when she's tipping them out of the box, slops milk on top, leaving a puddle on the counter. And always, it seems, right after Alice has finished a big clear-up.

The woman never stops talking, her voice grating, like being scrubbed with shards of glass. Always on the phone, complaining about everything to one friend, then hanging up and calling another one and telling her the exact same story all over again, all morning long before she leaves for work.

Then there is the constant stream of different men. Men in Alice's shower, the living room, helping themselves to the contents of the refrigerator, drinking beers with Denise at six in the morning. And once, when Alice had got up in the middle of the night for a glass of water, she'd been so startled to cross paths with one of them that she'd actually screamed before realising he was with Denise. They had both laughed at her. Some mornings there were sounds coming from Denise's bedroom, sounds that were inappropriate for someone Marnie's age to be hearing, and Alice didn't care to hear them either, thank you very much.

'Oh, I think I've just about had it,' Alice says to her friend, Dolly. They're sitting in their favourite booth at Mabel's Coffee Shop, the one by the front window with a view of the harbour. 'It's time she got her own place.'

'What about Marnie? I mean, it's none of my business, but you do everything for her. How would that work if they weren't living with you?'

'Oh no, she's not taking Marnie. Absolutely not. Can you imagine? Denise could never cope with her on her own. She's more like a big sister to Marnie. Not a mum, if you know what I mean.'

'What a shame.' Dolly grimaces. She retired from New Jordan Elementary only a few years after Alice, to run the Seaview Motel and Efficiencies, and the two women have met for lunch on Mondays ever since. It's the only time that Dolly takes off until Memorial Day weekend, when the motel becomes too busy for such a luxury.

Even though it's almost noon, a grey fog remains on the wharf and there's a heaviness in the air, and the smell of damp and salt holds on tight. The sky has been the colour of dirty dishwater for almost a whole week now.

'Do you remember Celia Robbins who used to teach kindergarten?' Alice asks.

'Oh, yes. She was a nice girl, wasn't she?'

'Yes, she was. Is. Well, we've kept in touch all these years. Turns out her husband manages those new rental units on the other side of the harbour. Harborview Homes.'

'Does he? Those look very smart. At least from the outside.'

'Well, I've been talking with Celia and there's still plenty of availability. They're really quite reasonable, and she said that her husband would be certain to give Denise a good deal. And they're very close to Massey's. It would make so much sense. And I think it would be good for her, to be honest, to finally live on her own.'

'It would be good for you too, wouldn't it? What does Denise think? She must want her own place at this point, surely?'

Before Alice can explain that she hasn't yet mentioned the idea to Denise, but is planning to do so this very afternoon, as soon as she gets home from lunch, Vicki, the waitress, comes over to take their order.

'Well, if it isn't my favourite customers,' she says.

'You say that to everybody.' Dolly smiles.

'Oh, but I don't.' Vicki cackles a deep, cigarette-smoke-basted throaty laugh. 'So what'll it be this week? Same, same?'

'You know us. We like what we like,' Dolly says. She goes on to enquire if business is picking up now that it's getting warmer, and they share weather predictions for the upcoming holiday weekend. After she shouts their order through the window to the cook in the back, Vicki returns with a cup of chicken noodle soup for Alice. She crumbles a packet of saltines into it and stirs the pieces around before taking a spoonful. 'These noodles.' Every week, Alice praises their thickness.

The rest of the food arrives shortly after. Dolly always has a poached egg on toast because she loves someone else making her breakfast. Alice gets a BLT because she finds its American-sounding name amusing, and Mabel's uses just the right amount of mayonnaise, not too much, which can make the toast soggy, and the bacon is cooked so that it's nice and crispy but not hard and brittle, the iceberg lettuce cold and crunchy, the tomato juicy.

It's still quiet, but after Memorial Day weekend the docks will start getting busy and there will be long lines for the restaurants, the salt-water taffy place, the ice cream parlour, and the nineteenth-century merry-go-round. The two municipal parking lots will be constantly filled, and the entire area around the harbour will remain busy for the rest of the summer weekends. Alice sighs at the thought of what's coming.

'What is it?' Dolly asks.

'This is bloody paradise when it's like this. I absolutely dread the summers here. Don't know how you can stand dealing with all those tourists. It's awful really, isn't it?'

'Summer is money,' Dolly says. 'That's what summer is. I mean, we couldn't survive without it. But I prefer when it's busy here. Makes the time go faster.'

The women finish up their food. Vicki clears their plates, refills their coffee mugs, asks if they need anything else, which they decline, so she brings the check. Dolly insists that it's her week to pay and then they head outside.

The fog has lifted off the harbour and now the water is visible as the two women walk alongside it. 'I hope you don't mind me asking, but will you be able to manage without Denise – financially, that is?' Dolly asks. 'She must help with rent and that.'

'She does,' Alice says. 'She pays rent plus a bit for groceries. I do have some money saved up, but I'm hoping to keep it that way. It's for Marnie, for college. So I'll have to go back to work. All things being well, Denise can move out this summer, and I'll find something part-time in the fall. I'm considering going back to New Jordan Elementary once the term begins.'

'If you're looking for something sooner, I need someone to help me supervise the summer cleaning staff. Like I said, summer is money. This is when we make most of our profits, so if the rooms aren't clean, we're sunk.'

'You're always saving me, aren't you? That's a lovely offer, but I don't know what I'd do with Marnie all day.'

'There's a kiddie programme right here on the beach that starts when the school year ends,' Dolly says. 'Perhaps Marnie could do that?'

When Alice gets home from lunch, Denise is on the couch with the phone cord pulled all the way from the kitchen wall. The television is on. She nods a greeting to Alice, and continues to drone on about last night's shift, how she hates working Sunday nights, how bad the tips were, how that creepy guy came in again and wouldn't leave her alone.

Finally, she gets off the phone just before she's about to leave for work. Alice says that they need to talk.

Denise crosses her arms. 'What is it?'

Alice swallows a few times before beginning to speak. Denise can be foul-tempered and Alice isn't in the mood to be yelled at. She asks in her most gentle voice if Denise has ever considered getting her own place, tells her about the apartments near Point Judith and her connection, that she could help Denise get a good deal. And what with her schedule and all, wouldn't it be less of a disruption for Marnie if she stayed here, with Alice? Denise could have a place all to herself. Surely she deserves that, after everything she's been through.

Denise doesn't say anything while she searches for her cigarettes, lights one up, exhales a large cloud of smoke that hovers for a moment before dissipating throughout the room. Another thing Alice dislikes about living with her is the constant reek of cigarette smoke that has permeated everything, no matter how often Alice cleans. 'Let me get this straight. You're kicking me out? Because I don't like living with you either. And this place gives me the creeps, if I'm being honest.'

'No, Denise, that's not what I meant. Don't be silly. 'Course I'm not. You're welcome to stay here as long as you want. I just think you shouldn't be stuck here with me. It's not fair on you now, is it? Sonny's gone off and left you here. And it's time. It's time you had some independence, don't you think? Get on with your life.'

Alice waits for her to say something nasty in return, but instead, Denise begins to cry.

'Oh, love, what is it?'

Denise closes her eyes and tries to collect herself. 'I've never lived on my own before. I went from Aunt Shirley's to Aunt Lucy, to my cousins, to living with Sonny, and now here. It's just a lot of financial responsibility. What if I can't do it?'

''Course you can. And we'll help you.'

'We who?'

'Everyone. All of us.'

A few weeks later, Denise signs a lease on an apartment with a view of the harbour and plenty of light. There is even a second, small bedroom for Marnie, whenever she wants to stay over, she tells her daughter. Before she moves in, Uncle Mike paints the whole apartment white and yellow. He brings some things from his basement that Cath approved for Denise, things they no longer needed:

a small sofa from the early days of their marriage; a few lamps; a fan; and some dishes and silverware. He takes Denise to yard sales and they find a table and chairs, pots and pans, more dishes and glasses. They pick up an easy chair at a used furniture store.

The day of the move, Mike drives down in his work van with Sean and two of his friends. By early afternoon, all of Denise's things are in her new apartment. Alice and Marnie bring her flowers and home-made chocolate chip cookies and some drawings that Marnie made for her. Alice sewed white curtains which they hang in the bedrooms. They help her unpack and settle in and then the three of them go to the IGA and Alice buys Denise her first round of groceries.

On the way home from Denise's, Alice and Marnie stop at Crane's Beach. Usually, the beach is busy on a Sunday afternoon in June, but the foul weather has kept most people away. Still, it's warm and they can walk barefoot in the sand by the edge of the water, the gentle waves washing over their toes. Marnie holds her grandmother's hand and splashes in the sea.

Alice wondered if the girl would ever say anything about her mother moving out, but Marnie took the whole thing in her stride, as if she'd been expecting it to happen all along.

'Do you think, if we looked really hard, we might be able to see across the Atlantic?' Marnie asks after a while. 'I think I can just about see England.'

Alice kisses her granddaughter on the top of her head. 'You keep looking, my love.'

'Nanny, the water looks spooky, don't you think?'

'Why's that, then?'

'It looks like something is going to leap out of it. How many things are in that water?'

'So many. I can't even imagine. A whole world under there and we only see the surface. Don't we?'

'Someday I want to see all of it. I want to see everything under there. Every single thing. Do you think I could? If I looked really carefully?'

Marnie looks up at her grandmother for an answer, but Alice is staring at the sea and doesn't say anything. Gazing hard out over the calm, grey water. Maybe her granddaughter is right, and it's merely a matter of looking in just the right way. Maybe it is possible to see everything, even across to England. Home.

15

Early Bird Singers

1982

Tom Anderson taps Alice's shoulder and asks if the chair next to her is available in the crowded New Jordan Elementary auditorium. She'd been saving the seat for Denise, keeping an eye on the back doors, hoping that, somehow, she might actually show up to see her daughter's solo performance in the Early Bird Singers' spring concert, the final one of the year. But the concert is about to begin and at this point, she'll have to stand in the back with the rest of the latecomers, so she says he is welcome to it. Besides, now that Alice is this close to him, she finally understands all the fuss about Tom Anderson. His eyes really do look like Paul Newman's and you *can* see his biceps bulging under his blue button-down shirt, just like she'd heard the mothers whisper and giggle about to one another. As if they were schoolgirls themselves. He settles in next to her and she is thankful that she has just eaten a breath mint.

Since his wife died last year, Tom Anderson has become school-wide famous among the mothers. In addition to the tragedy, he is widely admired for his ability to get his son and two young daughters to school on time every morning, dressed in season-appropriate clothing, the girls' hair brushed and in tight braids. On top of that, he is on the PTA, volunteers at school events and chaperones school trips. The only father in the whole school with such an exemplary record.

Alice and Tom both start to speak at the same time.

'You must be . . .'

'Isn't this . . .'

Tom puts out his hand. 'I'm Tom Anderson.' As if she doesn't know.

'Alice Butler.' Alice flushes at the touch of his skin when they shake hands. 'You're Neal's father, aren't you?'

'I am indeed, and you're Marnie's mother?'

He must be having her on. 'Excuse me?'

'Sorry, did I say something wrong?'

'I'm Marnie's grandmother.'

'God, I'm always saying the wrong thing.' He shakes his head. 'I just thought . . . Well, you look very young to be a grandmother, if you don't mind me saying. I guess I've only seen Marnie with you, so I just assumed . . . I didn't mean to offend.'

'Not at all.' Alice is so nervous, she begins to perspire.

The students walk onto the stage, signalling that the concert is about to start. Alice and Tom join in the polite applause that spreads throughout the audience.

Marnie takes her place in the centre of the front row. She is wearing a white blouse and black trousers that Alice ironed for her last night. Her hair is pinned back in a bun, just like all the other girls on the stage. She looks bright and hopeful, focused on some point in the way back, and Alice feels a tightness spreading in her chest at the sight of her. She has one last glance around, but, of course, Denise isn't there.

Marnie has been in the Early Bird Singers club for three years now. It meets before school on Tuesday and Thursday mornings, with four performances throughout the year, and in all this time, Denise has only made it to one. When Marnie came home from school one day with the exciting news that she'd been offered the coveted solo for the end-of-year concert, she immediately called her mother to tell her. Denise said she would definitely be there.

'You know how her schedule can change at the last minute, right, love? She might have to work,' Alice told Marnie this morning when she was getting ready. They had got up earlier than usual to make time for all the extra preparations.

'I know,' Marnie said, but Alice could tell she was holding on to the hope that this time would be different.

Marnie's song, 'May Day Carol', is the second to last, and Alice's eyes are wet the whole time. Whenever she practised the song at home, it made Alice feel a deep longing for England – for Danny and Lou and Auntie, and even for her mother – and she suggested Marnie practise in the bathroom because the acoustics would be better. But really it was because she didn't want Marnie to see her crying.

Marnie had been worrying her voice would crack or she'd forget the words, but she gets through the song perfectly, and by the end, Alice notices that she isn't the only one dabbing at her eyes with a tissue.

'Marnie has such an amazing voice,' Tom whispers, gently gripping her forearm.

'She was smashing, wasn't she?'

'Completely smashing.' He smiles at Alice.

The last song is 'Blowin' in the Wind', and by the time the students are taking their third and final bow, both Alice and Tom are wiping away tears.

'Here.' Tom hands her a Kleenex. 'I've learned the hard way to never leave home without these.'

'Ta, thanks.' Alice blows her nose.

'We're a sight for sore eyes, aren't we?'

'Yes, a right pair we are.'

They get to their feet and join in the standing ovation. When the applause has died down, the aisle is so busy they have to wait a minute before they can move.

'Your Marnie is so talented, isn't she? What a voice!' Tom says.

'So is your Neal.'

'Marnie seems like such a nice girl. Neal talks an awful lot about her. I think he might have a crush on her.'

'Oh.' This makes Alice blush, and she can't think of what to say.

'I really love this club. Ms Addleson does a great job with them, doesn't she?'

'Marnie loves it so much.'

The crowd has thinned out and they shuffle down the row. When they reach the aisle, Tom stops and turns to Alice. 'Listen, I'm not sure if Marnie mentioned this to you, but we're having a barbecue on Saturday. I know Neal would want Marnie to be there. And it would be lovely if you both came.'

Alice's face flushes again. Marnie hadn't said anything about the barbecue, which must mean she didn't know about it. Maybe Tom is wrong about his son's feelings for Marnie. Her granddaughter is shy, and although she's good friends with Sarah and a couple of other girls, Marnie rarely went round to their homes after school, like other children seemed to do on a regular basis. 'Well, that's awfully kind of you, but we don't want to impose.'

'Oh, please do come. I should have mailed out invitations. That's the kind of thing my wife did. But I'm not that organised. We always have a barbecue over Memorial Day weekend, and the kids wanted to keep up the tradition, even now that ... Anyway, it's at four, on Saturday. Our house isn't far from here, actually. How about I give you directions from school?' He searches in his backpack for a pen, rips off some of his newspaper and, after writing down the information, passes it to Alice. 'I look forward to seeing you there.'

'Thank you. This is lovely. What can we bring?'

'Oh no, don't worry. We always have too much food, more than we can possibly eat. I'm so pleased you can come, and sorry we didn't get you the invitation sooner.'

*

Saturday turns out to be sunny and clear, and it's still warm by the time Alice and Marnie arrive at the Andersons' in the late afternoon. A sign on the front door says to go to the back of the house. Marnie holds Alice's hand as they walk around the side of the large, blue Colonial. When they reach the backyard, a group of girls call out to Marnie. They are gathered around a rope swing hanging from an ash tree in the middle of the yard. Marnie rushes off, leaving Alice by herself. Some of Marnie's classmates are playing on the swing set and others are running around on the wide, lush lawn with their siblings. A few little ones toddle on the purple and grey slate terrace where the grown-ups have congregated. A wooden picnic table is covered with potato salad, corn on the cob, watermelon, barbecued hot dogs and hamburgers, buns, ketchup, paper plates and napkins weighted down by a brick. Nearby, there's a garbage can filled with beers, soda cans and white wine. Alice puts the bottle of red wine that she brought on a side table among the stacks of plastic cups and pitchers of water, iced tea and lemonade. She makes her way through the groups of parents clustered together, balancing plates of food and drinks, nodding to the few mothers that she knows, searching for somewhere to sit.

'Oh, Alice.' Mary Ronson grabs her arm. 'You're here.'

She's with four other mothers from Marnie's class, and they spread out so Alice can join their circle, greeting her with small nods and slight smiles, looking her up and down. After many outfit changes, Alice finally settled on a low-cut sundress which she bought last month with Dolly.

'Well, you can definitely see your boobs in that one,' Dolly chided her when she came out of the dressing room at Ames. They always waited at least a month into the season to do their shopping in order to take advantage of the sales.

'Is it too much?' Alice looked at herself sideways in the mirror.

'Depends on what you're doing. Maybe I wouldn't wear it to fetch Marnie from the school bus. But you look gorgeous in it. Go on, get it. Live a little.'

Now, she can sense the mothers' surprise at the revealing dress and immediately regrets her choice. Mary Ronson resumes talking about the diet she has her daughter on, and the exercise video they are trying. 'Have you seen that Jane Fonda workout video? It's just amazing! I'm just trying to nip this in the bud before it gets any worse.'

The women nod and smile. Then the group is broken up by the arrival of more families, and Alice slips away to snag a chair in the shade. Marnie is running around with some of her classmates, and Alice watches them venture to the picnic table and help themselves to the burgers. Once they've eaten, they grab slices of watermelon and have a seed-spitting contest until a few of the mothers notice and tell them to cut it out.

Then she sees Tom heading towards her with two plastic cups in his hands. 'There you are. You made it. I didn't realise you were here. Would you like a glass of wine?'

'Oh, ta, thanks.' Alice takes a cup, and he pulls up a chair. 'What a beautiful afternoon,' she says.

'Yes. Somehow, it always manages to be nice when we've had this barbecue. Did you get anything to eat yet?'

'Yes, thank you,' Alice lies. She has yet to touch any of the food. Even after all these years in America, she still can't get used to their idea of a barbecue, with grilled hot dogs and hamburgers, which she can't stand. 'Thank you for having us. This is really lovely and Marnie is having a smashing time.'

'Of course. So I know this is a stupid question, but you are from England, right? Like England, England?'

'I am.'

'How long have you lived here?'

'Let's see ... Well, I came here in 1942.'

'Wow! In the middle of World War Two! Blimey,' he says and smiles. 'Sorry, that was my bad attempt at a joke. Did you come with your family?'

'Just by myself.' Alice swallows a large mouthful of wine.

'That's very brave of you. Have you been back much?'

'Never.'

Nick Swander shouts from the grill that they need *a re-up on the dogs*. 'To be continued, mysterious lady from England.' He winks at her and then adds quietly, 'Listen, I'm really glad to be talking to you. I've always wanted to get to know you better.' He squeezes her knee before standing up.

This makes her hands tremble so much that she almost drops her cup of wine, which has made her feel lightheaded. It's time to eat. She heads over to the picnic table and helps herself to a dollop of potato salad, an ear of corn, a watermelon slice, before returning to the lawn chair.

Tom loads up a platter with a fresh round of burgers and hot dogs, and brings it over to the picnic table. A group of boys are waiting and as soon as he sets down the meat, they pounce, filling buns, squirting ketchup and grabbing at the bowl of chips. He comes back to check if Alice wants more wine, which she declines. They talk about the Early Bird Singers, how quickly the school year has gone by, how much they like the new principal. Tom asks where Alice and Marnie live, what part of England she is from and how she likes living in America.

Then his youngest daughter appears on the terrace, in tears after falling off a swing. Tom goes to her and holds her tight, wiping away the grass and dirt on her knees. Margaret Lewis is suddenly there, too, with a damp paper towel, and Tom takes it and gently pats it on his daughter's broken skin. Mary Ronson comes over to make sure everything is OK. Three other mothers follow closely behind, until he is surrounded.

Alice feels foolish in her low-cut dress, sitting by herself. She looks around for Marnie. Maybe she could persuade her that it's time to go home. When she stands up, the lawn chair sticks to the backs of her legs. 'Bugger,' she says to herself, and peels it off. Marnie is with the same group of girls, sitting together on top of the swing set, laughing. She looks very far away from wanting to leave.

Tom is coming back towards her, but Beth Seaver trails along with him. Tom tries to include Alice in the conversation, but all Beth wants to talk about is the PTA proposal to upgrade the girls' bathroom sinks. Does Tom think that's a proper use of funding expenditure, wouldn't the money be better spent on refurbishing the library? Alice has no opinion on this matter, plus Beth is quite pretty, has just got divorced and is much younger than she is. It's starting to get buggy and people are beginning to leave. She excuses herself and crosses the yard to tell Marnie that they should get going. 'OK, sure,' she agrees. Her knees are covered in dirt, her hair matted down with sweat. She looks tired and happy from all the running around and playing.

'I'm just going to the loo first and then we'll go,' Alice tells her.

She trudges across the lawn feeling old and defeated, collecting a few paper plates and cups in a feeble attempt to help with the clean-up. Already the kitchen is buzzing with a cadre of mothers busily straightening things up, so she tosses the plates in the trash and goes in search of the bathroom instead.

The ground-floor bathroom is occupied, so she heads up the carpeted staircase, hoping she isn't violating some sort of privacy rule, but she's too desperate for the toilet to wait. She finds it easily and there are paper hand towels by the sink, as if he was anticipating its use at the party.

When she comes out, Tom is right there. 'Here you are.' He takes her hand. 'I just had a question.' He leads her into his bedroom, shuts the door behind them: 'May I have permission to kiss you?'

'Permission granted.'

Alice leans into him and Tom kisses her, long and deep; the last time she was kissed like this was with Danny. It goes on for a few wonderful minutes, their tongues wrapping around each other, his large soft hands finding their way inside the front of her dress.

The sounds of the mothers cleaning the kitchen echo up the stairs. A loud screech from Beth Seaver makes them break away from each other.

'Would you like to come over for lunch on Friday?' Tom strokes the side of her face. 'It's my day off and the kids will be in school and I won't have a house full of guests. We can have a little more privacy. How does that sound?'

Alice tries to control her breathing. 'Sounds lovely.'

On the drive home, Alice thinks about Friday. After walking Marnie to the bus, she'll skip going to the bank like she usually does. That will have to happen Thursday this week. Instead, on Friday morning, she'll go straight home and have a bath with one of those oils that Denise left behind, and some lavender from the window boxes filled with herbs in the kitchen. She'll give her legs a thorough shave, working her way carefully around her knees, making sure not to miss any spots on her shins or the three wiry hairs sprouting out from her big toes. Neaten up her bikini line. Another item on this week's to-do list will be to buy some new knickers for the occasion, and a decent bra. Her giant, white underwired one just won't do. She does have a new blouse, and finally a chance to use the expensive red lipstick Dolly gave her two birthdays ago.

She's so busy planning her outfit that she misses the turning for their street and has to make a right at the next one. She looks over at Marnie, expecting her to say something, but the girl is fast asleep, her head lobbed over to one side. Alice makes a careful U-turn before putting her foot on the brake. There is no other traffic, so Alice stops the car and shifts to park.

The sun is just starting to set, and the street is bathed in orange light and it streams in through the car. Alice rearranges her sleeping granddaughter, gently moving her head so it's upright. She stirs for a moment, a slight smile crossing her face. The way she sometimes looked when she was a baby, napping in her cot. Alice leaves her hand resting on the side of Marnie's face, like she used to all those many years ago, leaning over her while she slept. Her smooth infant skin a warm comfort in Alice's hands.

16

The Arrival

1940

Alice feels like she has been travelling all day. Moving from one location to another. Carrying a satchel containing all the things she selected to take with her after finding out she was being evacuated. Now, there is only one last place she has to get to, and the walk to Silverdale Road from the village hall in North Winstead isn't far, Mrs Newsom tells Alice when they set off. She is almost there; she has almost arrived.

But this is the part she has been dreading most of all. The end of the journey. Reaching the final destination. No longer will she merely be anticipating this moment, preparing for it, thinking about it. When she reaches the Newsoms' home on Silverdale Road, all of it will be over. With each step she takes, the reality sinks in just how incredibly far away she is from Spithandle and Auntie and home.

And worst of all, so incredibly far away from Danny.

It's dark and raining, and Mrs Newsom and her husband, the older couple who Alice is billeted with, walk briskly ahead of her and don't offer to help with her bag. She must walk fast not to lose sight of them on these unlit, unfamiliar streets. At one point, Mr Newsom looks back and says something to Alice, but she struggles to comprehend his northern accent.

'Sorry?' She skips to catch up to them. He doesn't repeat himself, just turns to his wife and asks why they'd been burdened with a 'simple one'. That, Alice can understand.

'Well, we didn't have much choice in the matter, did we?' Mrs Newsom says. 'She was practically the last one left. At least we didn't have to take that little one who was crying for her mammy.' She glances back at Alice, whose face flushes hot with shame, even though the rain has soaked into her hair, her coat and her shoes. 'Anyway, she doesn't look simple to me. She's too pretty to be simple.'

They don't say anything else. Their footsteps echoing along the pavement are the only sounds apart from the rain. By the time they reach their home – a small terraced house – Alice feels like she's been walking for hours and hours, instead of less than ten minutes.

She was among the last of the children from Spithandle to be selected by the families who were waiting for them when their train finally arrived. They had been badly delayed – they had to get off the train and shelter in a station on the outskirts of London because of heavy bombing. The jogging of the train had made Alice nauseous, along with the smell of sick that permeated their carriage. She was already worn out when the train stopped and the children were all told they had to leave and take their bags with them. Pearl couldn't manage her things by herself, so Lou and Alice took turns helping her. They walked down a steep set of stairs to the very bottom of the station and waited there, it seemed like forever, huddled together on the tracks underground, and Alice worried the whole time about mice and rats climbing over them. Finally, they were told it was safe and they had to walk all the way back up the stairs. In addition to carrying their bags, they wore their overcoats because there was nowhere else to put them, and Alice felt she'd never been so hot in her whole life, and that she might pass out.

It was dark by the time they finally reached North Winstead, about twenty miles north of Nottingham, and were taken to the village hall next to the train station. Although they hadn't eaten or drunk anything for hours, Alice felt so sick after the long day of travelling, she barely touched her buttered roll and managed only a few sips of the tea the children were given when they arrived. Pearl curled up in Lou's lap and they waited while the teachers who had travelled with them conferred with the local authorities as people from the area arrived to take in the children. The older, bigger boys were the first to be chosen since they would be the most useful, as many people in North Winstead had farmland. Although older girls, like Alice and Lou, were also deemed worthy because they could be more helpful with household chores than the little ones, Mrs Flight had instructed the girls to stay together. A few families had wanted to take in Lou or Alice, but not all three girls, and so they had waited in the hope that someone would come along who had room for them all. Finally, they had given up, and Lou and Pearl had gone off with a young couple who had a baby. Meanwhile, Alice was left waiting with some of the very small children. She was among the last when the Newsoms arrived.

Once they are inside the house, Mr Newsom takes off his coat and heads straight up to bed without saying anything to Alice. Mrs Newsom shows her where to hang her overcoat, which is soaked through, and to put her shoes by the coal fire. Although the house is similar to the Flights' – a two-up, two-down, with a small front room and a loo out the back – instead of a cosy settee and two comfortable armchairs and a thick rug in front of the coal fire, it's sparsely decorated, with one wooden straight-backed chair, a rocker and a small armchair pulled around the coal fire and the wireless.

'Mr Newsom hasn't been well,' Mrs Newsom tells Alice. 'We're expecting help.'

'Of course.' Alice nods and waits for her to say more.

'Right then, off to bed with you.' Mrs Newsom shows Alice upstairs, where there are two small bedrooms and a washroom. Her room is the one right at the top of the stairs, with a narrow bed, a bureau and a washbasin.

Once she is alone, Alice places her bags on the floor and sits on her bed. She thinks back to the very beginning of the day. She had sneaked out of the house early in the morning before daybreak, like she had done so many times over the summer. She knew how to ease herself out of the bed without waking Lou, asleep beside her, or Pearl. She had dressed and crept out of the room and down the stairs, avoiding the steps that creaked. The girls still didn't know where they were going and wouldn't find out until they got to the train station in a few hours' time. Danny would be leaving the following day.

It was still so early the sun had yet to rise. Once she made it out of the house without Auntie noticing, she didn't care if she was stopped by soldiers for violating the curfew. She'd tell them to sod off. She needed to see Danny, one last time.

Even though it was already September, the air in the early morning was thick and close, as if it was still the middle of summer. Alice tried to keep from perspiring as she made her way along the dark streets until she reached the narrow dirt lane that led to the Turners' farm, kicking bits of flint and chalk as she went. She took deep breaths, wanting always to remember the smell of late summer on this lane, and the way the brush looked when it was just beginning to brown, the sound of the doves, the magpies and the seagulls.

Danny was waiting for her by the elm tree where they always met. It was just beginning to get light. He didn't say anything at first, just pulled her into a tight embrace.

'Oh, Alice,' he said. 'Oh, my Alice.'

He could still make her feel light-headed, still made her swoon, and a trembling feeling had come over her, just like on that very first day when his mere presence had caused her to drop a teacup.

JUNCTION OF EARTH AND SKY

He had brought a woollen blanket and laid it out beneath the tree. He took her hands and they began to kiss, slowly at first, and then more urgently, until they were practically inhaling each other. His right hand caressed her hip, his left around her back. Gently, he guided her towards the blanket. First, they were on their knees, and then they lay down and began kissing once more.

'Alice.' He pulled away from her. 'I'm trying to control myself here.' He put his hands over his face. 'What are you doing to me?' He closed his eyes and took some deep breaths to steady himself.

Finally, he turned to her. 'Think I've got myself better sorted now.'

The sun was starting to rise. He stroked her hair and told her that she was the most beautiful girl in the whole entire world, and she burrowed her face into his chest. She knew the minutes were ticking down much too quickly, speeding towards their final farewell.

'Alice, there's something I have to say. But you have to stand up.'

'What are you on about?' Alice smiled. 'I want to stay lying down with you as long as possible.'

'We can lie down again in a minute, I promise.'

'Promise?'

'Yes, now come on.' Danny helped her to her feet, and then he got down on one knee and took out a piece of wire twisted into a circle with a blue bead in the middle. He held her hands. 'I know this isn't a real ring or anything. But, even so, Alice, will you marry me?'

At first, she thought he must be joking, but his face was so serious, she finally realised he meant it. She put her hand over her open mouth. 'Danny,' she said. She sat down once more and he took her in his arms.

'Actually, don't say anything, Alice. This mustn't be it. I'm going to get you a proper ring, and we're going to do this again. When I come back. When the war is over. After we've won. We'll do this with an actual ring. But hold on to this for now.' He placed the ring in her hand and clasped his hand around hers. 'Not to wear on your finger. But if you keep hold of it, it will bring me good luck.'

'What if . . .?' She began to cry.

'No! You mustn't say it. You mustn't ever think it. Promise me, you won't think that. I'm going to get a real ring, Alice, a posh one, and we're going to do this again. Promise?'

'Promise.'

'Do you remember when I said I'd save myself for you? That morning up at the Miller's Tomb?'

''Course I do.'

'Well, I meant it. I want you to be my first. I love you, Alice. I'm coming home, for you. And we're going to have a family. We are.' They embraced again as he sketched out their future. How someday, they would be married and have a family, a boy who they would name Sonny, after his father, and a girl that they'd name for Alice's mother, Betty. And in that moment, everything Danny said seemed possible. When they kissed for the last time, Danny told her not to turn around when she started for home because that would bring them both bad luck.

The rest of the day was awful. She didn't want any of the special breakfast Auntie fixed for the girls: real eggs instead of powdered, bacon and beans on toast with actual butter, not just lard. She had gone to a lot of trouble, bartered to get the eggs and the butter and the extra rashers of bacon yesterday, so she could fix the girls this one last meal, so Alice had to somehow finish everything on her plate. But it was tasteless and she struggled to get it down.

At the railway station, Pearl was so upset she had been sick to her stomach, right there on the platform. Once the train approached, it wasn't just Pearl crying, though, and the other children and most of their mothers were also in tears as they started their goodbyes. The teachers gathered everyone up in their usual cheerful manner, as if the morning bell at school had just rung. Pearl howled and clung to her mother's leg so she couldn't move at all. Alice had managed to collect herself enough to comfort Pearl, telling her that she had a special story for her once they got on the train.

After they settled into their compartment, they waved goodbye out of the window. Alice could tell that Lou's mother was trying not to cry when the train pulled out of the station. At first, Lou and Alice distracted the little girl by pretending to be famous actresses heading off to London. They had brought a packed lunch of butter and jam sandwiches and apples, which was supposed to last all day, but they ended up eating most of it within the first hour, just to keep Pearl occupied. The journey quickly became tedious. When they got back on the train after the long delay on the outskirts of London, it seemed to go on for hours and hours more and felt as if it would never end.

Now that the long day is finally over, she wishes more than anything that it wasn't. She pulls out Danny's ring and kisses it, places it under her pillow. It has stopped raining and a sliver of moon is visible, and she wonders if Danny is looking at it, as well. But even if he isn't, they are still under the same night sky, in the same country. At least for now.

17

Blue Mornings by Cold Storage Beach

1991

ON HER LAST MORNING in Provincetown, Marnie wakes early. Even at dawn, during the busy summer months, the last of the late-night revellers would be careening down Commercial Street, making their loud, tumbling way home, weaving around the early-morning deliveries. But it's a week after Labor Day and summer is over, which means Marnie can pedal her bike the whole way from the West End to Route 6A without once having to pull over to make room for an oncoming car or truck, or a large group of partiers teetering along, singing, arms wrapped around each other, yelling, throwing things, like she might have encountered just a few days ago.

As she bikes along Commercial Street, she passes the landmarks of her summer hook-ups. The beach by the Coast Guard pier, with a cashier from the A&P in July for moonlit sex in the sand. The punk rocker from New Haven who worked in the custom T-shirt store. A cleaner from one of the whale-watching boats. The dishwasher from the Lobster Pot. The lifeguard she met on the pier when she was doing mushrooms on 4 July, who took her out to Race Point Beach.

But then she met Vincent at the beginning of August. He had a motorcycle, and took her on late-night rides along Route 6 and saved his best cocaine for her. She has been sleeping with him exclusively ever since. Later today, they are going back to Weymouth, where he lives the rest of the year.

It's muggy, and Marnie is sweating when she reaches 6A; the chain on her bike is rusty and creaks as she pedals along Cape Cod Bay. She continues up the hill towards the motels and holiday cottages. When she reaches the white clapboard cabins named for flowers, she stops at the one called Marigold, the one Uncle Mike and Cath always rented for a week or two, many summers ago. She locks up her bike and walks out onto the sand. The light is just spreading across Cold Storage Beach off in the distance, the tide coming back in. She takes off her clothes and wades into the bay until the water is up to her waist, dives under, and then lies flat on her back with her toes pointed out towards the deeper part of the ocean.

Those summer vacations with her cousins every August from the time she was seven until she was in middle school were a highlight of Marnie's childhood. Six summers of leaving at dawn in Uncle Mike's orange VW bus, which was packed and ready to go since the night before. When they drove over the Sagamore Bridge, Marnie and her cousins would stop the pillow fights and playing Guess

Whose Head under the blankets, roll down the windows, stick their heads out and start screaming.

Uncle Mike and Cath were different people out here. Moving slowly, not wearing shoes. There was no talk of mortgage payments or medical bills or the small business loan that Mike had been struggling to pay off, or Cath's mother, and which nursing home they were going to have to put her in and how much longer they could wait. No worried whisperings about Denise.

Every morning, Marnie and Uncle Mike were the first ones up, and they sat together on the back porch that looked out over the water. It was so early, even before dawn, and the light on the bay by Cold Storage Beach was a washed-out blue, which Uncle Mike always pointed out. Marnie was hunched over her drawing pad with her hot cocoa and Mike had his first cup of coffee, taking big sips, exhaling loudly after each one, his binoculars around his neck, thumbing through his guidebook of sea birds. No one else was awake for at least another hour, so it was just the two of them watching the tide going out, leaving behind motor boats in a slick debris of seaweed clumps, shells, barnacles, buoys, anchors and chains. The sky slowly became streaked with pinks and purples, then a slight yellowing before the sun made its entrance, reflecting off the water.

'This is it, Marn, this is it,' Uncle Mike said from time to time.

When it became full-on daylight, they went across Shore Road to Millie's Bait and Tackle and picked up a dozen doughnuts and Portuguese rolls still warm from the oven and the *Boston Globe*, before a stop at the farm stand out front for vegetables and fruit. Uncle Mike made sure that Cath could sleep in, bringing her a cup of coffee when they returned. By that time, everyone else was awake and hassling to get to the beach. He fried up bacon and egg sandwiches for himself, Cath and Sean, and everyone else helped themselves to the doughnuts while running around getting ready. Teresa and Marnie assembled sandwiches, Cath stirred frozen lemonade concentrate into the thermos, cut up slices of watermelon, threw bags of potato chips into the beach bag. Sean and Pat helped load up the car with beach chairs, the umbrella, blankets, towels, boogie boards, gathered the buckets and shovels.

They spent the whole day at the beach with Cath's two sisters and their families, racing to find the perfect spot and dump all the stuff on the sand. There was always a contest to see who could get in the water first, Uncle Mike walking as fast as possible, almost running, laden down with the cooler, bags of towels, chairs, yet somehow always managing to beat everyone into the waves.

Cath and her two sisters sat semi-circled in low-to-the-ground beach chairs, slathered in Bain de Soleil, shrieking gossip to one another while their husbands and children rode waves in the frigid Atlantic water on the outer reaches of the Cape, made sand forts, ate damp sandwiches, potato chips, cookies, grapes, drank lemonade from the large thermos, the sisters occasionally moving altogether as a group to float on pink and orange noodles when the water was calm, the sun high in the sky.

They went to the beaches on the bay side and out by the lighthouse, and the one with the seal colony at the far end. The water was always bracing, even on the hottest days. The best body surfing was at the beach with the sandbar, but the lifeguards wouldn't allow anyone out there until later in the afternoon. In the minutes leading up to that moment, Marnie and Teresa lined up in the water with everyone else, waiting for the signal. After the sharp bleating of the lifeguard whistles, they were off, swimming across the narrow stretch of deeper water between the coastline and the sandbar, along with hordes of other children, screeching, tugging boogie boards, inflatable tyres and wave boards behind them. The waves hit the sandbar in a way that made them perfect for catching the crest. Then they were carried along towards the shore, before crash-landing. Over and over they did it, limbs thrashing in the seawater froth, sand in every crevice of their bodies. They stayed in the water as long as they could stand it, until they were purple, their fingertips shrivelled, their lips cracked with salt water.

Back at the cottage, Marnie and her cousins rode their bikes barefoot up and down the road out front, played in the sand when the tide was out in the bay while the grown-ups started in on cocktails and beer before grilling hot dogs and burgers, boiling corn on the cob, making potato salad, cutting up more watermelon. Sometimes they packed a picnic dinner to take to the beach and watch the sun set, or got seafood out on the commercial fishing pier, which Marnie and her cousins would leap off afterwards, she and Teresa scrambling up the ladder, trying to beat the boys. There were family bike rides through the National Seashore, whale-watching trips, car rides to the area lighthouses and the drive-in movie theatre.

But when Sean and Patrick went off to college, they no longer wanted to go and Teresa began spending her summers working as a counsellor at a sleepaway camp, so the vacations came to an end. Marnie hasn't been back since she was thirteen.

It was Patrick who suggested going to Provincetown and living with him when she saw him last Christmas. They were holed up in her cousins' basement rec room getting stoned on Christmas Eve, the only ones home. Everyone else in the family – Teresa, Sean, Uncle Mike and Aunt Cath – were out at parties, catching up with old friends.

'We are officially the family outcasts.' Patrick lit the bong and handed it to her. Marnie inhaled and the water bubbled.

They sat on the fold-out couch, a large bag of Doritos between them, their fingertips basted orange, cans of Diet Pepsi on the side table, while Patrick tried to convince Marnie to join him.

Marnie and Teresa weren't close anymore; their days of being inseparable during Marnie's visits were over. She wasn't even there when Marnie first arrived, had already gone out with her friends from high school. Cath asked if Marnie wouldn't mind staying in the basement rec room, instead of in Teresa's room. She'd been sharing a room with two other girls all semester at Penn, which had been insanely busy, what with juggling being on the swim team and pre-med. She just needed some space, Cath explained to Marnie. Most evenings during the rest of Christmas week, Teresa went to parties or to friends' houses, and never once asked Marnie to come along.

So she hung out with Patrick instead. He dropped out of UMass Amherst and moved to Provincetown last summer and Uncle Mike and Cath were furious. He hadn't yet told them he was gay, but everyone else knew it without him even needing to say anything.

Provincetown is paradise, he told Marnie. 'You remember how great it is out there, don't you? Imagine what it's like being there every day. *Every* day.'

One April morning, several months later, Marnie decided to go. She took a bus from Worcester to Boston, changed to another in South Station headed for Provincetown – seven hours in total. When she stepped off at the last stop on the wharf, Patrick and his boyfriend, Devin, were waiting for her. Commercial Street was crowded with beautiful men spilling out from the bars and clubs, the air thick with the scent of the sea. Marnie was certain she would never leave.

She loved everything about Provincetown. She loved living with Patrick and Devin in their two-room cottage on a quiet back street up on a hill with a view of the bay. She loved their landlord, a mom with six kids who lived next door and dealt pot and speed out of her kitchen, stray cats and dogs running around the house. She loved biking to Herring Cove in the early morning and swimming off her hangover before going to work, cleaning rooms at the large hotel by the breakers. She loved her co-workers – hippies and punks from all over the country, who came here every summer to make some money and have a good time.

But mostly Marnie loved the partying. It started as soon as her 8 a.m. to 4 p.m. shift was over. There was a group of cleaners who met in the hotel parking lot and walked across the dunes to smoke joints and do shots on the beach, swim wasted in the waves until the sun set. She'd go home to clean up before joining Patrick and Devin as they did their nightly circuit of bars and clubs. She loved snorting coke and angel dust in the bathrooms, dancing and laughing and drinking and not ever remembering how she got home. She loved the casual hook-ups until she met Vincent, part of Patrick and Devin's crowd who kept them supplied with drugs all summer long.

It all came to an end Labor Day weekend. The hotel laid off the summer staff, including Marnie. Patrick and Devin moved to New York City, where Devin would be starting art school. Just before they left, Patrick finally came out to his parents, telling them about Devin, but Uncle Mike and Cath were upset he had kept such a huge part of his life from them. They all said things they regretted, but in the end, Patrick said he wouldn't be coming home for the holidays, and wouldn't relent, even after Cath pleaded with him to change his mind.

Marnie dunks under the water and lies flat on her back. During those long-ago summer vacations, the boys would tease Marnie and Teresa about the dangers of the ocean. She remembers a wild, rainy day walking along one of the beaches with the wind whipping them, the surf pounding so hard that Sean and Patrick told the girls that if their feet touched the water even for the briefest moment, the sea would suck them so far out, they'd be lost forever. The boys always hassled to go swimming at night. There'd be an argument with the grown-ups first, about who was old enough to go along with them, a strong enough swimmer. Teresa always insisted that she and Marnie be included. But as soon as they were in the water, the boys would start describing the opening scene in *Jaws*, start chanting the shark attack music, tease the girls that they could see dorsal fins off in the distance. The girls would scream and start back to shore. Towards Uncle Mike and Aunt Cath around a bonfire on the beach in front of the cottage. Towards safety.

Now, floating in the water, the memories are so vivid of those summers, when she turns back to look at the shore, she almost expects to see her aunt and uncle keeping an eye on her. Waiting for her to come out of the water with towels and open arms.

18

It's Too Late

1983

IT IS A DREARY March day, and the rain arrives just as Marnie's bus departs. This school year, there are a couple of new children, young ones, waiting at the bus stop with Marnie. Alice watches their mothers, the three of them, head off together to have coffee, like they do most mornings, never inviting Alice to join them.

But today is Friday, and Alice smiles to herself as the trio trudge off to spend a miserable morning together, complaining about how hopeless their husbands are, how they can't seem to do anything useful, how they almost don't even dare to leave them alone with their children. Things she hears them say to one another when they are all waiting at the school bus stop. Some days, it stings when they leave together, barely even acknowledging Alice's existence. But not on Fridays.

On Fridays, Alice is certain that she is the only one hurrying home to run a bath filled with fragrant oils and lavender. The only one giving her legs a thorough shave. Putting on special black lace knickers and red lipstick, spraying perfume on her neck and her breasts. Only Alice is hoping not to attract the attention of the neighbourhood snoops, feeling like a teenager sneaking out of the house as she gets in her car, checking herself in the rear-view mirror before driving over to Tom Anderson's house for their Friday morning rendezvous.

Although Alice has been going to Tom's house almost every week since his barbecue last May, still there are many things she can't do without feeling an overwhelming amount of anxiety rise up inside her. She can't be alone anywhere, except the bathroom. She can't wait for him in his bedroom if he's in the kitchen because she panics at the sound of his footsteps on the stairs. She can only manage to take off her clothes once she is actually in bed and under the sheets, and only after having a drink. So they always begin the visit in the kitchen. Tom fixes her a white wine spritzer, and he has a whiskey. They sip their drinks and catch up on the week sitting, fully dressed, at his kitchen table. Tom always has fresh flowers, which he buys especially for her.

The first time they were together, Alice was terrified, and explained in a tumble of words that it had been a long time – a very long time indeed – since she had been with a man. She hoped that would be enough of an excuse as to why she panicked at his touch. Tom had trouble himself with guilt, felt like he was betraying his wife, Claire, who had died the previous year. So Tom and Alice had just kissed and held each other, and she avoided having to do the thing that she dreaded. But as their relationship progressed, Alice has found that if they kiss for a long time first, then the rest of it goes quickly enough, and the alcohol loosens Alice up so that she can do the things that make Tom happy. The kind of things she had hoped to do with Danny one day. The kind of things she did on occasion with a few men in those first years in America, when she was so lonely that she would do anything for a night or two of companionship. Even that. And although men often flirted with her, which could be enjoyable, it's only Tom she's been able to trust enough to let things develop into something more than just a brief fling.

This morning, after the drink downstairs, they head up to the bedroom and sprawl out on top of the covers, facing each other, propping themselves up on their elbows. Alice leans in towards Tom for a kiss.

'Is it OK if we just lie here for a moment, you know, before . . .?' he asks.

''Course it is.'

He studies her face and strokes her arm. 'Oh, you are lovely, aren't you?' He smiles at her. 'Did I tell you how beautiful you look today?'

'You did. When I first arrived. Like you always do.'

He lies back on his pillow and closes his eyes. 'Oh, good. At least there is that. I'm not myself today, I have to admit. I've slept so terribly all week.'

'Oh, I am sorry to hear that. I hate it when that happens.'

He opens his eyes and looks up at the ceiling. 'I've been so looking forward to this all week. I kept telling myself, it will be Friday and then you will see Alice. Just get through each day. That's what I said to myself every morning when I woke up, and it still wasn't yet Friday. And now, here it is. And you are here, at last.' He looks over at her and begins to cry.

'What is it? What's all this?' Alice reaches for his hand.

'God, Alice. I'm such a mess. I just ... It's still ... I'm sorry. It's been a really bad week.' He reaches for a Kleenex and blows his nose. 'It was Claire's birthday on Tuesday.'

'Oh, Tom.' She reaches for him and lies in the crook of his arm, stroking the tuft of hair in the middle of his chest as he weeps.

'I'm sorry, this isn't very romantic, is it?' Tom says after a few minutes.

'Don't be stupid,' Alice says. 'Why don't you tell me about her, if you like?'

'Oh, she was wonderful.' He cries harder. 'I miss her. I miss her so much. I miss my wife. I'm so sorry.'

Tom sits up in bed, his head in his folded arms, and sobs. Alice cradles him. 'I still love her. You are so lovely, but I still love her. I still love my wife.'

'Of course you still love her. It's OK. It's really all right.'

They hold each other and Tom continues to cry. 'I think it's too late,' he says. 'I think Claire was it, and it's too late for me to fall in love, ever again.'

Later, when she goes to collect Marnie from the school bus, Alice can hear the trio of mothers who never invite her for coffee, before she even rounds the corner. Alice has overheard them debating her connection to Marnie. Clearly, she is too old to be Marnie's mother, she heard one of them say. Another wondered if she's the babysitter or live-in help. Once they finally figured out that she was the grandmother, the trio moved on to gossiping about Denise.

Alice has tried to make her presence known as soon as she rounds the corner, saying an abrupt 'Afternoon,' and pursing her lips to indicate she can hear them. The trio say hello back, just a little too quickly, before readjusting themselves, like pigeons interrupted by a speeding bicycle. Finally, the school bus arrives and there she is, Marnie, coming through the door as it swivels open.

They get soaked on the way home, and thump up the stairs, prompting a shout from the Finnegan sisters to *keep it down, will you please?* By the time they have tumbled into the apartment, they are both laughing.

'Better get yourself out of those clothes, then,' Alice says. 'Just go ahead and put on your pyjamas, why don't you? It's that kind of afternoon. I'll put the kettle on.'

In her bedroom, Marnie peels off her wet trousers and sweater and changes into the green and blue plaid flannel pyjamas, her favourites, that she's left neatly folded on top of her quilt. Marnie pats her hair dry with a towel and goes into the kitchen while Alice fixes the tea.

After boiling the water and pouring it over the tea bags, Alice lets it brew in the pot for a good five minutes while she arranges home-made sugar cookies on a plate, still warm from the oven. Marnie fetches the milk and the sugar bowl and they sit together at the kitchen table. Rain pelts the windows and the radiators hiss on.

After her snack, Marnie will do her homework while Alice fixes a shepherd's pie. They are warm and dry, and they are together. And for now, this is more than enough.

19

Conditional Probability Equations

1984

IT'S FRIDAY NIGHT, AND Marnie and her mother are on their way to her cousins' house. Her mother drives fast, like she always does, despite the snow pummelling the windscreen, causing low visibility on the highway, her right hand on the steering wheel, the left one for her endless cigarettes. They are both excited. Not only is it the start of Marnie's February break from school *and* snowing, but also her mother got the whole, entire holiday weekend off from work, which hardly ever happens. Usually, she can stay only one night when she brings Marnie to her cousins' house. Sometimes, her mother has to turn right around when they arrive, and head straight back home. But this time, she'll be there until Monday. Three whole days.

'Hey, I was thinking we could go skating together this weekend, just the two of us?' her mother says at one point during the drive.

'I didn't know you could skate,' Marnie says.

'Totally can. Might have even played a little ice hockey in high school.'

'For real?' Sometimes Marnie forgets that her mother was once a kid.

'Totally for real. We could go to Spy Pond. Used to go there all the time. So much more fun than a rink. Especially at night. How does that sound?'

'Fun,' Marnie says. And it does. Skating outside with her mother at night.

But everything is about probability, says Ms Stubenski, Marnie's sixth-grade accelerated maths teacher, and everything can be turned into an equation. And Marnie worries about the probability of going skating with her mother when they drive past the exit for her cousins' house and take the next one instead. The exit for Discount Liquors.

When they get to her cousins' house, Teresa comes bursting out to greet them the moment they pull into the driveway, like she always does. Marnie is barely out of the car when Teresa picks her up and twirls her around.

'You're here, you're here, you're here,' Teresa shouts.

Uncle Mike has followed behind his daughter and he envelops Marnie in his arms. 'So happy to see you, Marn,' he says. 'And Dee! You guys made it. Let's get you inside.' It's snowing even harder now, and they get covered during the brief moments it takes to bring the bags from the car into the warm kitchen.

Cath hugs and kisses Marnie and gives Denise a quick peck before turning her attention back to the stove, where she's fussing over a large pot of marinara sauce. Meatballs simmer in another pan.

JUNCTION OF EARTH AND SKY

'Oh God, that smells incredible.' Denise is still in her coat, taking out the large bottle of Paul Masson white wine, which she bought at the liquor store, and placing it on the table in the breakfast nook.

'Dee, can we take your coat?' Cath looks at the trail of snow that Denise has left on the floor.

'Oh, sorry, yeah.' Denise shrugs off her coat and drapes it over the bench, before helping herself to a coffee mug from the dish drain. She twists off the wine cap and fills her mug. 'Man, that was some crazy-ass drive. You guys want some wine?'

Uncle Mike and Cath both decline, saying they are going to wait until dinner, and besides, they're going to drink red. 'Since it's spaghetti with meatballs,' Cath explains – Marnie's favourite dish, that she always makes for her first night here. 'You want a wine glass, Dee?'

'Nah, this is good,' Denise says.

After watching Denise fill the coffee mug with wine all the way to the top, Cath suggests Teresa help Marnie bring her things up to her room, and says that dinner should be ready in about half an hour.

How many glasses of wine per thirty minutes equals her mother being drunk by dinner, Marnie wonders as she picks up her duffel bag, noticing a wordless exchange between her aunt and uncle. It only lasts a brief moment, but she's certain they're doing the same probability equation.

Teresa has dismantled her bunk beds; she says she's too old for them. Now, there are two twins, side by side. She flops down on the one against the wall and clicks on her clock radio, which is tuned into a heavy metal station. She starts pumping her fists when they play 'Cum on Feel the Noize'. Marnie sits on the other bed. The glossy photos of kittens and puppies and Pippi Longstocking have been replaced with posters of U2, Van Halen, Led Zeppelin and Madonna, and there's a pile of music magazines by the side of Teresa's bed.

Teresa turns down the music once the song finishes. 'So I have news. Big news.' She moves her eyebrows up and down. 'I think I have a boyfriend.'

'Really?' Marnie blushes. She can't imagine it.

There's a new boy in her class, Teresa explains, who arrived right after the Christmas break. All the girls have crushes on him. 'But he picked me.' Teresa looks up at the slanted attic ceiling. They hung out one day after school a couple of weeks ago, she tells Marnie. And then last weekend, they kissed. 'Have you ever kissed a boy?' she asks.

'No.' Marnie blushes even harder.

'It's the only thing I want to do now. The only thing.'

Marnie struggles for the right thing to say. 'That sounds . . . cool.'

'Kissing is so cool.' Teresa sighs and studies her fingernails. Marnie's cousin seems much older than at Christmas. 'I wish I had blonde hair.'

Marnie can't think of a reply.

'Do you ever, like, want to just, like, run?' Teresa says. 'Like, just run forever and ever, until you get to some place where there is no one else around and, like, nothing. And you could, like, yell your head off. Or, like, swim way out, like, so far out into the ocean, like, past where the boats even are and just, like, float out there alone in the waves? I really want to do that.'

'Yeah?' It sounds scary to Marnie, swimming so far away from the shore.

Then Cath yells up the stairs that it's time to eat. Dinner and weekend breakfasts are always taken together in the dining room. They settle around the table, with Sean and Pat on one side, Marnie in between her mother and Teresa on the other side, and Mike and Cath at each end. Her mother already has that cloudy unfocused look she gets when she drinks a lot. Everyone begins to eat, passing around the Parmesan cheese, a plate of garlic bread, and salad. There isn't much in the way of conversation, just the sounds of silverware clinking against china. Marnie tries to just enjoy the delicious food and ignore her mother's cup and the ever-decreasing level in the Paul Masson bottle by her side. Outside, it's still snowing.

Denise is the one to break the silence. 'You guys got any skates?' she blurts, a little too loudly. Sean and Pat stifle a laugh. 'Thinking to take Marnie skating at Spy Pond.' She smiles, as if expecting praise.

'Oh, they don't allow skating there anymore,' Cath says. 'There was an accident a few years ago, and a kid broke through the ice and drowned or something, right, Mikey?'

'Yup.' He nods his head. 'But we might go skating when we're in Vermont.'

'Vermont? When are we going to Vermont?' Denise looks confused.

Mike reminds her that they talked about the possibility of going to Vermont for a few days the following week. They have some friends with a cabin. But Denise says she doesn't remember being told about that.

'Well, is that OK with you? If we did that? Took Marnie to Vermont next week with us?' Cath asks her, exchanging a look with Uncle Mike.

Denise refills her mug. 'Oh, so you're going without me. I don't get to go to Vermont, is that it?'

'No, Dee.' Mike closes his eyes and scrunches up his face. 'Like I told you, we can't go this weekend. It's our friends' cabin, and they're going there this weekend. But they offered it to us for a couple of nights in the middle of next week, when they won't be there.'

'Still sounds like I'm not invited to Vermont.'

A long minute passes where no one says anything. Marnie twirls spaghetti around her fork, then takes a bite of a meatball. 'This is so good, Aunt Cath,' she says.

Aunt Cath reaches over and squeezes her hand. 'I'm glad you're enjoying it, sweetheart.'

Denise crumples up her napkin. 'Yeah, that really was good, Cath.' She pulls out her cigarettes. 'You don't mind if I smoke, do you?'

'No, it's fine.' Cath's face tightens.

'Still snowing.' Mike says. He always talks about the weather when he's uncomfortable. 'Some people are saying it could be a nor'easter. We might get over a foot.'

'How'd they come up with the name nor'easter anyway?' Denise ashes in the remains of her food. 'I mean, nor.

That's not even a word. And what the fuck does Easter have to do with anything?'

'I think it's short for north-east, like north-east wind.' Mike sounds tired. They never let their children swear at the dinner table, or anywhere else.

'Sounds like a fart or something, doesn't it?' Denise exhales.

Teresa and her brothers start to giggle, but Marnie's face flushes hot. She notices Cath give Uncle Mike yet another look, and indicate towards Denise with a slight nod of her head. Uncle Mike makes a small gesture with his mouth and hands, like there's nothing he can do about it.

Denise helps herself to more wine, but she overfills her cup and it spills onto the table. 'Oopsie.'

Cath stares hard at Uncle Mike. 'Think maybe you've had enough there, Dee,' he says finally.

'I'm an adult, OK?' Denise says. 'I'm allowed to have a little wine on a Friday night. What are you, the Fun Police?'

'Mom, please don't,' Marnie says quietly. When her mother drinks too much, she can get mean.

'Please don't what?' Denise says to her daughter. 'Look at you, so sullen, with your sullen, grouchy face. Such a grouch face.'

'Denise,' Uncle Mike says, extra quiet and slow.

Marnie concentrates on her plate.

'Don't "Denise" me. You have no idea what she's really like. So rude to her mother, such a fresh mouth.'

'Denise.' Cath shakes her head.

'She thinks she's better than me.' Marnie's mother stares straight ahead at nothing in particular. 'Alice is always telling her she's special. So she thinks she's better than her mother. She's not better than me, and she's not special either.'

'Denise! That's enough now!' Mike slams his hand on the table.

'Are you guys finished?' Cath means her children and Marnie. 'You guys are excused, OK?'

Marnie folds her napkin and thanks Cath for the meal, the way her grandmother tells her to when she's in other people's homes. Even here at her cousins' house, her grandmother says. She pushes in her chair and, without looking at her mother, carries her plate to the sink in the kitchen, rinses it off and puts it in the dishwasher. Her cousins do the same thing.

'Oh, I get it.' Denise's voice is getting louder. 'You embarrassed of me? Is that what you guys are, Mikey? You and your snotty little wife? Well, fuck the both of yous.'

Sean asks if they want to go watch the Olympics. Teresa grabs Marnie's hand and they head down to the basement rec room. Downstairs, no one says anything about her mother, which makes it even worse. Sean turns on the TV and takes the La-Z-Boy chair, where he always sits. Teresa and Marnie spread out on the orange couch, and Pat sits on one of the beanbag chairs. But even with the television on, they can still hear Denise shouting upstairs.

Marnie lies with her head on the arm of the sofa. Her mother always drank, for as long as she can remember.

But it seemed like Denise used to enjoy it and have a good time. Now she just gets angry. Marnie tries to think back to when her mother's drinking started to make her behave badly. From the way Uncle Mike and Cath are acting, it has probably been going on for a long time, way before Marnie noticed.

After a while Marnie drifts off to sleep. The next thing she knows, Uncle Mike is rousing her. The room is dark and she's alone.

Her uncle stands over her. 'Hey,' he whispers. 'You don't want to sleep down here all night. It gets really cold.'

'Where'd everyone go?' Marnie stretches and yawns.

'Bed. It's really late. You need anything, Marn?'

'No, I'm good.'

'Goodnight, then.' He turns to leave.

'Night.'

'Hey, Marnie? You're a good kid. And you are special, OK? You really are.' Her uncle makes a thumbs-up sign and gives her a weak smile before heading upstairs. Marnie sits up, rubs at her face, and gets off the couch. When she reaches the top of the basement stairs, she hears her mother crying in the kitchen.

'I'm such a fuck-up,' her mother weeps. 'I'm such an asshole. I hate myself, I fuckin' hate myself.'

Then there's the sound of crashing and something shattering on the floor.

'Oh, for the love of Pete,' Cath says. 'Give me a hand, would you, Mikey? Help me get her up. Jesus Christ!'

Marnie hurries up to the bathroom on the second floor. The wind whips against the house while she brushes her teeth. She presses her face up against the window. Snow pelts the screens and swirls around the backyard.

The next morning, when Marnie and Teresa go down to the kitchen, the house is quiet and it seems everyone else is still asleep. The entire backyard – the tree in the middle of it, the swing set, the tree house, the trees on the side, the grass – all of it is buried in deep snow.

Teresa takes out the black cast-iron pan and Marnie opens a package of bacon. They lay out the meat in vertical strips and turn on the heat, flipping them over with a fork as they cook. Cath comes shuffling in, mumbles good morning, and pours coffee into the large mug with *I'm the Boss, Goddamn It* written on it. She carries it over to the breakfast nook and sits down on the bench. She has crevices under her eyes, and her hair spills out of a drooping bun.

They can hear Uncle Mike shovelling the driveway. It's then that Marnie looks out the kitchen window and sees tyre marks where her mother's car was parked the night before. 'Where's my mom?' Marnie asks, even though she already knows the answer.

Cath swallows. 'Oh, honey.' She gets up, comes over to Marnie and gives her a long hug.

By late morning, Marnie is at the top of the sledding hill in Elm Park, which is covered in eighteen inches of fresh snow, thinking again about probability. If she hits the two bumps halfway down the hill at just the right angle, she might even lift off and be airborne. Marnie's cousins are already going down it – the steepest and longest hill in their neighbourhood. Every child who lives near Elm Park seems to be here, sledding, building snowmen and snow forts, having snowball fights, making snow angels. Although the streets have been ploughed, hardly anyone is venturing out in their cars, so the only sounds are the scraping of shovels and children playing in the deep snow.

'Wait up, I'll go with you,' says Kev, Pat and Sean's friend who lives just down the street from her cousins' house. 'You'll go faster with me.'

Marnie concentrates on not falling off the sled as Kev manoeuvres them down the hill, steering around two small children up ahead who have fallen off their plastic disc, and a girl lying flat on her back after being thrown off a toboggan. The wind rips at Marnie's face as the sled propels her and Kev faster and faster down the hill. He grips her tight.

They hit the first bump and bounce, then the second one, and that's when it happens. They are in the air, rising above the snowy hill for a full ten seconds before landing with a thud. Kev holds on to her and they manage to remain in the sled.

Marnie would need to know the exact distance from the top of the hill to the bottom in order to figure out their speed. Their combined weight would be a component in calculating how fast plastic can travel along packed snow.

Sometimes equations are simpler, like how a bottle of Paul Masson white wine equals her mother leaving early in the morning, embarrassed and hung-over. Without saying goodbye to her daughter. Without staying for the whole weekend and taking Marnie skating. Without calling. Without.

20

Smouldering

1985

SEVENTH GRADE SLUMBER PARTIES verge towards danger. And Marnie wants some of that, all for herself. The thrill that was giggling on Nikki Fantana's swing set last Saturday night with the girls from 704 and a stolen pack of Virginia Slims. When the patio lights flooded the grass, they quickly crushed out the burning embers and ran, shrieking, back inside the house. A long session of Truth or Dare followed and Marnie discovered which girls had gone to second base, drank rum, loved Mr Donnegan, the science teacher who was in possession of both a ponytail and a motorcycle.

Now, it's Tuesday afternoon and Marnie rests her head against the cool scratched glass of the window in the third row of the school bus, pretending to listen as Margaret Winston complains about the maths homework. But really, she's plotting.

'I think I finally figured out what I want to do for my birthday,' Marnie tells her grandmother after she gets off the school bus. Marnie is much too old for an escort, but when she sees her grandmother waiting for her in front of the Liptons' house, all the things that have or haven't happened in her life don't matter anymore.

'About time,' her grandmother says. 'We've only been talking about it for a month.'

'Two months actually.' Marnie threads her arm through her grandmother's. 'And I think it's *you* who's done most of the talking.'

'Well, thirteen is a big birthday,' Alice says. 'You're becoming a big scary teenager. I left home when I was fourteen, you know?'

'Oh, I know. But you had to, you were evacuated. There was a war. Things were different then, as you would say.'

'Still, thirteen deserves a proper celebration. Not just you and me and a slice of cake at Chadwick's. So, what are you thinking, then?'

Marnie takes a deep breath and tries to muster up the courage for her request. 'Could I have a party? Like a slumber party? Like Nikki Fantana's slumber party? If it's not too much trouble. I can help pay for it, I've got money saved up.'

''Course you can have a slumber party. And don't talk daft. You're not paying for a thing!'

Their feet slap against the wet sidewalk, which is uneven and crumbled in places with dirty snow caked at the edges, the remnants from last week's storm. The trees are still barren, with green nubs dotting the branches. In a month, they'll be covered with leaves and white blossom.

'Could we decorate the living room?' Marnie pictures Nikki's party, and what would be possible to replicate in her apartment. Even though she doesn't live in a spacious four-bedroomed house with a manicured backyard tended by a weekly landscaper, or a basketball net in the driveway, a wood block kitchen island where parents can gather round drinking wine, a golden retriever, or siblings, she can provide the girls in her class with an amazing meal. 'Do you think Dolly would make her spaghetti and meatballs?'

''Course she would. What else would you like?' Alice squeezes Marnie's hand.

'Would you make cupcakes?'

'Absolutely not.'

Marnie stops walking and turns to face her grandmother, who smiles back at her. 'This is a special birthday and we're going to get a cake, a seven-layer or something like that, from Olsen's.'

'Nanny! But those are so expensive!' Marnie says.

'Listen to me. You just tell me what you want, all right? No more fretting about costs.'

'OK, fine. But just so you know, I did really like a slice of cake at Chadwick's with just you and me.'

'Me too, my love, me too.'

The morning of the party, Marnie's mother comes over before work so she can help with the preparations. While Alice is out buying groceries for the special dinner and picking up the cake, Marnie and her mother work on the decorations at the kitchen table. Marnie cuts pieces off the rolls of purple and yellow streamers and puts masking tape on the back so she can hang them from the ceiling.

Denise writes out *Happy Birthday Marnie* in pencil before highlighting the bubble letters in purple and yellow markers on a large piece of white paper. It's her fourth attempt to make a sign.

'Oh my God, this one looks terrible, too.' She holds it up to show her daughter. 'Looks like a three-year-old made it, doesn't it?' She laughs at herself. 'We should have just bought a sign.'

'I like it, Mom,' Marnie says. 'Home-made is better anyway.'

'Well, that's good, 'cause home-made is what you're getting.'

After she's cut several dozen pieces, Marnie crosses through the oval passageway into the living room. She arranges the pieces on the top step of the wooden ladder and climbs up before attaching the streamers in neat rows along the ceiling. When Denise is finished with the sign, she cuts up more streamers and hands them to Marnie, who moves the ladder around the living room. Once all the streamers are up, they take a seat on the couch to admire their work.

'Hey, this looks pretty good, doesn't it? We did it!' Denise puts her hand up to high-five her daughter. 'So how many girls you got coming over?'

'Ten.'

'That's amazing, baby.' She looks at her daughter, plays with her hair. 'I can't believe you're thirteen, I can't believe it.'

'Well, almost. I'm still twelve for a few more hours. Wasn't I born in the afternoon?'

'You were born at 2.17, if you want to be exact.' Denise pulls her into an embrace and Marnie lies back with her head in her mother's lap. Denise fiddles with her daughter's hair. 'You want your present now, baby?'

Marnie sits up and looks back at her mother, nodding. 'Yeees!'

Denise squeals and springs off the couch for her bag, reaching in it for a small box with a purple ribbon. She hands it to Marnie and bites her lip as she watches her daughter open the present. 'I hope you like.' She grits her teeth. 'I'm so nervous.'

It's a pair of silver dangle earrings with glass circles at the end that twinkle in the light. 'Mom! These are beautiful. Oh my God.' Marnie hugs her mother and puts them on. 'Where did you get them?'

Denise wells up. 'You like them, baby? Really?'

'I love them, Mom. Look, what do you think? How do I look?' Marnie cups her hands under her ears to show them.

'You look beautiful, baby.' Her mother wipes away her tears with her fingers. 'They were my mother's.'

'Oh, Mom.' Marnie hugs her again. 'Thank you!'

When it's time for her mother to leave for work, she says that she should be able to be back by 9.30 – 9.20, even – so she won't miss the whole party. Marnie says they'll wait to have the cake when she gets there.

A little while before the girls are supposed to arrive, Dolly comes over to help Alice prepare the food. She has already made her marinara sauce with meatballs, and she heats it up on the stove. Alice runs hot water over two cans of frozen lemonade concentrate. Then she empties the contents into a plastic pitcher and smashes up the pink goo with a wooden spoon before adding cold water and ice. Dolly stirs the sauce, and begins to make the garlic bread.

Right before the girls are due, Marnie goes into her bedroom and lies down, wishing she could go back in time and erase the moment she thought having a party and inviting Nikki and the girls from 704, especially Lucy D. *and* Lucy M. – the Lucys – was a good idea.

Nikki Fantana and the girls from 704 have never been to Marnie's home before. She might be the only one who doesn't live in a house with a yard, or with at least one parent. And now the girls from 704 will know everything. Plus, somehow, she has to entertain them, here in this small apartment, for a whole night and into the next morning, with her grandmother and Dolly. *They're going to be so bored*, she thinks. *And they hate being bored. More than anything.* But then the buzzer is going. The party is happening, and now there's nothing Marnie can do to stop it.

Lipstick, deodorant and dampened paper towels. Denise's weapons of choice to transform herself into a smouldering beauty. She applies makeup in the restaurant bathroom mirror, after finishing her shift. Charlie waits for her at the bar.

Denise can't remember the last time a man made her feel like this. Her legs are shaking, as if he's Mick fucking

Jagger or some shit. She noticed Charlie noticing her all evening. Now that he's back in town, most nights he comes into Massey's alone, has a few drinks at the bar and makes small talk with the manager and the bartender. Tonight, he requested a table in Denise's section; the manager told her, the bartender confirmed it.

When Denise cleared away his seafood combo platter, he asked if she wanted to grab a drink when she finished work. And it's something when a man without a wedding ring who owns a boat – possibly even a yacht, if you believe what some people say – pays some attention to Denise.

The kitchen closes at nine during the offseason, but the manager keeps the place open for as long as it's worthwhile. When the weather starts warming up, most Saturday nights there are a good number of waitresses, and the male customers they have attracted drinking until midnight. Sometimes they move as a whole unit on to JJ's Bar & Grill, which doesn't keep regular hours, or maybe even to someone's house. On those nights, Denise can be found fending off the fishermen who've been out on the water for weeks, blowing their earnings in one fell swoop.

But Charlie is a seasonal regular, part of the cadre of customers who frequent Massey's once April arrives and then disappear after Columbus Day weekend, heading down to the Carolinas, Florida, or maybe even the Caribbean. But seasonal regulars are trying to be part of the community and might actually be looking for something more meaningful. A second wife, even.

Everyone at Massey's claims to know a little something about Charlie. Divorced, with a winter home in Sanibel, beach house on Block Island. And that boat. He has four daughters, the youngest at college, the oldest working on Wall Street. The other two in law school or medical school. Something along those lines. Those type of people, the waitresses gossip with one another, in between balancing trays loaded up with baskets of lobster rolls, clam strips, fried calamari. The restaurant is by the entrance to the wharf, filled with commercial and game fishing boats, the ferries running back and forth to Block Island, sailboats, motorboats. And somewhere, Charlie's yacht.

In the bathroom, Denise blots at her armpits with wet paper towels and pink liquid soap from the dispenser by the sink. She puts on deodorant, changes into a clean blouse and high heels and a thong, which she always has in her bag along with makeup and a toothbrush. Just in case.

It's the beginning of the season so there aren't many after-hours customers. Most of the waitresses have gone home except Jean Anne, polishing off a margarita with the manager. Two newly hired waitresses are huddled in a corner with some college students. The bartender dries off glasses with a white dishtowel and preps for the following morning's brunch rush. Behind the small window where the waitresses shout orders, the cook scrapes off the grill. The two busboys, brothers who just moved down here from Providence, drag leaking bags of garbage out back.

'Well, hello there,' Charlie says when Denise emerges, her brown curls let loose out of her hairnet, blouse unbuttoned just slightly too low.

'Hey.' She gets comfortable in one of the high-backed stools that line the bar. The bartender makes sure there is a vodka tonic waiting for her. Denise's lipstick remains on the glass after a large swallow. 'Whoa, that was a long day. And boy, was it jumping. The whole freakin' time. Nonstop.'

'I really don't know how you do it.' Charlie has white flecks scattered throughout the remains of his hair and the stubble framing his mouth. 'Must be tough dealing with us assholes all day long.'

'Not *everyone* is an asshole.' Denise tries to lift her drink without him noticing that her hand is shaking. 'Haven't seen you in here for a while. You just get back?'

'Yeah, a couple of weeks ago. I'm putting my house on the market, so I've been busy getting it fixed up. Winter was brutal.'

'Tell me about it,' she says. 'This winter sucked big time. Your place get messed up?'

'Roof almost caved in. We . . . I have a house on Block Island.' He indicates with his thumb, but of course Denise already knows about his beachfront property through the waitresses. 'I was lucky. Some homes really took a beating.'

'I heard a few might need to be torn down?'

'Yup. The ones on the hills. Couple of them are beyond repair.'

'That's terrible.'

They catalogue the storms and cold weather, comparing it to other years. They talk about the damage on Block Island and Cuttyhunk. Charlie signals the bartender for more rounds each time their glasses are empty.

After their fourth drink, Charlie asks if she wants to go for a walk. 'It's really such a beautiful evening,' he says. 'The sky is unbelievably clear tonight. I'm somewhat of a constellation freak.' He sounds almost apologetic. 'Unless you're too tired.'

'No, that's sounds awesome,' Denise says, though she has been on her feet for close to ten hours.

Charlie pays the tab and leaves two crisp twenty-dollar bills folded under his empty glass as a tip, Denise notices. Then they walk out to the wharf. Charlie explains the different types of boats that are moored, and tells her stories about some of the owners. Like the guy who is rumoured to be a fugitive. People say he kidnapped a little girl, escaped from prison and lived in Alaska for years before coming here. Things Denise has already heard, but pretends to be finding out for the first time.

There's a slight breeze and a bright half-moon in the sky. He points out the Big Dipper, Orion, and how it's possible to see Mars. Denise isn't quite sure which shiny thing he means, but she nods anyway, as if she can tell one from the other.

At one point, Charlie takes hold of Denise's hand, as if it's the most natural thing in the world, then he puts his left arm around her, and it feels so good to be drunk and walking by the water in the moonlight with a nice man. A man who is a real adult. A man with means.

Charlie tells her about his divorce, how it crushed him to live apart from his daughters, missing the everydayness of their presence. He rented an apartment near his old house, so he could be close by. But the new place was too quiet without his children and he couldn't bring himself to buy anything permanent, just ate off Styrofoam plates and paper towels. It took two years before he felt anything aside from total despair. Then he got his boat and everything changed. *So where is it*, Denise wonders. *Where's the boat?*

'I'm being a real motormouth. Think I maybe drank too much in there. I don't mean to be talking so much about myself. Are you free tomorrow night, by any chance? Could I take you to dinner, and over a bottle of wine, maybe I could hear the Denise Life Story, now that you've heard mine?'

She quickly agrees to the date and he offers to come pick her up. As he walks Denise to her car, she is already worrying about what she could tell him about herself that wouldn't scare him away. At least they have some things in common. Both divorced and both of them are parents.

After she gets in and rolls down the window, Charlie leans in and kisses her. She gives him her address and begins the short drive to her apartment, smiling to herself along the way. She has a real date – dinner with a man who, for once, isn't a total loser. And he actually seems interested in *her*. She really wants another drink, but there's nothing at home, so she heads over to Lighthouse Liquors and picks up a quart of vodka. She takes small swallows on the way home, a wondrous smooth feeling spreading throughout her body.

It's at the stop light at the intersection of Market and Green, only a few minutes from her place, that she remembers about Marnie's sleepover. She makes a U-turn to get on Route 1 and heads in the opposite direction.

She'll say she got out later than she expected. That there was a large party celebrating a fiftieth wedding anniversary. How they got slammed last minute. She'll take Marnie shopping or to the movies this week to make up for it. Besides, what thirteen-year-old wants their mother around their friends?

She pulls up in front of her daughter's home and gulps down a few mouthfuls of vodka. Then she gets out of the car, drops her keys and her purse, and trips over as she's bending down to retrieve them. When she stands up, all the drinks hit her at once. 'I'm fine,' she says to herself. 'I'm totally fine.'

Upstairs, Marnie is snuggled into her sleeping bag while Lucy M. holds the flashlight against her chin and tells the scary story about the babysitter getting phone calls, asking if she's checked the children. A few girls have already drifted off, but Marnie is wide awake. She heard Nikki tell Lucy D. that this was the best slumber party ever. 'Except mine,' she added quickly.

The girls loved Dolly's spaghetti and meatballs. Alice let them play Manhunt out in the street, then they watched *Grease* and sang along to all the songs, and Alice kept bringing in bowls of hot, salted popcorn smothered in butter.

They waited almost an hour for her mother to arrive, and then Alice decided they should just go ahead with the cake, that her mother must have been delayed. It was OK that she wasn't there, in the end. Everything had gone so well.

Lucy M. passes the flashlight to Nikki, who starts in on the story about the hitchhiker and the bloody hand on the car window. Then the front door of the apartment explodes open, startling the girls.

It's Denise, in a low-cut blouse revealing her pink bra. She dances into the room singing 'Happy Birthday', closing the door too hard behind her. 'Whoops.' She giggles after it slams. 'That was loud. Hey, girls. Wow, this is a real party, huh?'

'Who is that?' Lucy D. whispers to Lucy M.

'I have no idea,' Lucy M. whispers back.

Alice comes out of her bedroom in her bathrobe. 'Denise, it's almost midnight. What are you doing here?'

'I know, I'm so late, but I just thought I'd stop by anyway. I didn't want to miss all the fun.' She stumbles through the tangle of girls in sleeping bags on the floor and trips. She sits down very suddenly in Alice's armchair and flops over. 'Oh, shit,' she says. 'Sorry, did I just step on a body? Oh, shit.'

The girls laugh nervously.

'What's so funny?' Denise sits up straight. 'Who's laughing at me?'

Everyone goes quiet, and Alice offers to call Denise a cab, but she says she wants a piece of cake first, to hang out with her daughter a little while.

'The cake is all gone, Denise.' Alice's voice sounds rough, the way it does when she first wakes up. 'I'm calling you a cab.'

Denise goes into the kitchen, saying she wants cake. The girls are trying to stifle their laughter. Denise shouts again. Marnie gets out of her sleeping bag and tries to talk to her mother quietly in the kitchen, hoping the girls won't hear. 'Mom?' she whispers. 'Please, Mom, you're embarrassing me.'

'Don't talk to me like that. I'm not embarrassing, I'm not. And I met a man, Marnie. A nice man, a really nice man. Aren't you happy for me? Why isn't anyone ever happy for me?'

Her mother's voice seems to be getting louder and louder. 'Please, Mom.'

Her mother slaps her hard across the face. 'Please, Mom, what? I gave you a nice present, didn't I?'

Alice says again that she's going to call a cab, or maybe Denise just wants to lie down in Marnie's room for a bit. But Marnie's mother shouts that she just wants to have a piece of birthday cake with her daughter, and is that really too much to ask? It was a long night, it's not her fault she's so late. They got slammed at the last minute because of a fiftieth anniversary party, or maybe it was a work do, or something. Anyway, it just happened and she should have called, but she thought it would be better to just get here and she didn't realise how late it was, and please, Alice, please can't I stay and just have a piece of cake with my baby? My baby is thirteen, my baby is a woman now, look at her, Alice. Look at my baby.

While Alice calls a cab, it feels like Marnie is stuck in a movie in slow motion that will never end. Finally, Alice manages to get Denise out the front door and onto the landing. *Fuck you, Alice*, she yells. *Fuck you, you don't get to decide everything, she's my daughter, she's mine.* The Finnegan sisters yell up the stairwell and Denise tells them to fuck off, and Mr Conner on the third floor comes out and asks if everyone could please be quiet, and the Finnegan sisters threaten to call the police, and Denise says, just go ahead then, fucking call the police, and Alice says, come on, Denise, let's just go downstairs, the cab will be here soon for you and you can come back in the morning and have breakfast with us, how does that sound, and Denise is asking if Alice promises that she can have pancakes with Marnie and her friends, and Alice says yes, of course, and so finally, Denise agrees to leave and take the cab and the police don't have to be called, so at least there is that.

Once Denise is safely on her way, Alice trudges back up the stairs.

'Sorry about that, girls,' she says to the eleven shapes on her living room floor. It is too dark even to make out which one is Marnie.

The girls don't say anything after that. Not one word. They lie just there, pretending to be asleep. Even Marnie. As if it's just like anyone else's slumber party. As if none of it happened at all.

21

That Kind of Gone

1941

THUMP, THEN PAUSE, THUMP, then pause. Thump. Pause.

The sound means only one thing. Mr Newsom's crippled brother has got out of the armchair where he sits all day long, and is slowly heading towards the staircase with the help of his crutches.

Upstairs, Alice is on the edge of the narrow bed in her room, which is not much bigger than a closet. Her heart pounds, a fist pummelling inside her ribcage. It is Tuesday evening, when Mr and Mrs Newsom go to their church to pack boxes for the war relief effort. They also go on Thursdays, so Alice is left alone with the crippled brother twice a week.

Thump. Pause. Thump. Pause.

Mr Newsom's crippled brother has been living here in the Newsoms' house for the past month. Alice doesn't know why. All she knows is that one morning she came down for breakfast, and there he was. He hardly ever speaks, just sits in a chair in the front room. Sometimes, he is gone for days at a time, and Alice will hope maybe that's it, maybe he has left permanently. But he always returns.

Thump. Pause. Thump. Pause.

Alice weeps as she sits on the bed, even though she'll be sixteen next month and much too old for tears. She tells herself bad jokes, trying to calm herself.

What's orange and sounds like a parrot?

A carrot.

But the joke only reminds her of when they first arrived in North Winstead last year, and Pearl would cry for her mother, and somehow this stupid joke made her laugh. It got to the point where all Alice or Lou had to say was *what's orange?*, and a smile would appear on the little girl's face, before she started laughing. 'See,' Alice used to say. 'It's all right then, isn't it? Everything is going to be just fine.'

Alice had no idea what was coming.

Thump. Pause. Thump. Pause. The sound of his slow, laboured movement has reached the bottom of the stairs. Alice has already pushed the bureau up against the door. She touches the satchel of letters from Danny that she keeps under her pillow. *My Alice*, the letters begin. She reads them out loud to herself in an Irish accent, making sure that Mr and Mrs Newsom are far enough away so they can't hear her. Danny has so many plans for the two of them, his most recent letter said. He heard from his cousin who lives in Boston. When the war is over, his cousin told Danny, he must come there. That's where all the opportunity will be, Danny wrote. There'll be plenty of work. They can raise their children there. Sonny and Betty.

Mr Newsom's brother coughs, clears his throat. Then he starts to climb the stairs. Thump, creak, pause. Thump, creak, pause.

Mrs Newsom often complains about her crippled brother-in-law to her neighbour, an unpleasant woman who manages to find something *negative* to say about anything, even the rare sunny days. His war injuries are too much for her, Mrs Newson says, in between drags on her rollie, and it isn't just the crippling. There's something in the way he just sits in that chair in their front room, staring and staring at nothing for hours at a time. Well, it gives Mrs Newsom the chills, quite frankly, she says. She can't be expected to look after him forever. It isn't right that the government puts the burden on families for the convalescence without proper compensation. Always been trouble, he has. Could never look after himself. Useless, really. Can't imagine how he managed to survive at all, fighting over there. The neighbour replied, but Alice had no idea what she said.

Even after living in North Winstead all this time, Alice still struggles with the northern accents and often has to ask Mr and Mrs Newsom to repeat themselves. This makes Mr Newsom especially cross, and Alice avoids him as much as possible.

It rains most days here and Alice never feels warm. Her toes constantly ache with cold, and most nights she shivers under a thin blanket, wrapping it tightly around herself, longing for the warm bed she shared with Lou.

Thump. Creak of the wooden staircase. Pause. Thump.

Alice puts on the sweater that Mrs Newsom made for her. She had given it to her out of the blue, just presented it to Alice one morning. Until then, her communications had been mostly gruff instructions about the chores, the shopping, to do this or that around the house. Alice couldn't understand how two elderly people generated so much work. She was constantly darning socks, repairing tears, helping Mrs Newsom sew new clothing, washing the clothes, ironing them once they had dried on the line, scrubbing the floors, doing the washing-up, sweeping and dusting, going to the parade of shops in the town centre first thing every Saturday morning with the ration book to get in all the food shopping, and then carrying it all back home by herself. So when Mrs Newsom gave the sweater to Alice, she had started to tear up. Mrs Newsom was so startled, she even gave Alice a one-armed hug.

Thump. Creak. Pause. Thump.

The first time Mr Newsom's crippled brother ended up in Alice's bed, she'd been asleep, and had woken up to him lying next to her, playing with himself. It was a Tuesday night and Mr and Mrs Newsom were out at the church. It happened again two nights later, when they were out, and then again, the following week, but only on the nights she was left alone in the house with him. Alice dreaded Tuesday and Thursday nights, and as soon as Mr and Mrs Newsom left, she'd go up to her room and pray that somehow, it wouldn't happen. But it did anyway. He would rub himself up against her, the rusty bedsprings squeaking, squeaking with his movements, and then there'd been dampness in the sheets. But it didn't count. Danny could still be her first and they could still have a proper wedding. Danny would never have to know. She wouldn't tell anyone.

But it kept happening and happening and happening. And then there was last Thursday. There was last Thursday, and Alice could never do that again. Not ever. Not even with Danny.

Thump. Creak. Pause.

In the evenings, Alice is always the last one waiting outside on the large grassy square in the middle of the neighbourhood, long after Lou, Pearl, and the rest of the children have been called in for their tea. Mrs Newsom told her not to come back inside the house until seven. It didn't seem there were exceptions for bitterly cold days or when it was heaving it down. Lou and Pearl would wait with her for as long as they could stand the cold.

'Mum's coming for us,' Lou told her yesterday, her face bright with the news. 'It's all sorted out now. Two weeks' time and then we're leaving.'

Auntie had been up a few times to visit, but she would not be able to bring them back to Spithandle, like she had wanted to. Instead, they were going to stay with relatives on a farm in Yorkshire for the remainder of the war. Alice hoped she was going with them, but she was too scared to ask in case the answer was no. She couldn't imagine being left here on her own. When Lou and Pearl offered to stay outside with her as usual, even though it was dark and had started to rain, she insisted they go home. She wanted to be alone when she cried, worrying about what would happen when Auntie arrived. She stood by herself under a tree while the rain pelted her, everyone else inside their warm homes, until finally, it was time to go in.

Thump. Pause. Thump. Pause.

When Mr Newsom's crippled brother has reached the top of the stairs, Alice goes to the window and opens it as wide as it can go. The roof flattens slightly under the window frames and if she can manage to make her way along it, there is a tree at the edge of the house and she could climb down it. She hoists herself up on the edge of the window, crawls out onto the ledge as the doorknob to her bedroom starts to turn. The bureau wobbles with the force of the heavy door being pushed against it. Alice slithers along the edge of the roof, towards the tree. When she reaches it, she grips the trunk tightly with her arms, wraps her legs around it and begins to shimmy to the ground. That's when she hears it: the sound of the bureau crashing to the floor.

When her bare feet touch the damp soil and grass in the back garden, she pads in the quiet darkness along the narrow passageway on the side of the house until she reaches the street. Then she starts to run.

The rain has finally ended and the clouds have given way to a clear sky, and a quarter moon is visible. No one is out at this time of night and the road is empty. There are no seagulls in North Winstead, and it seems so long since Alice has heard them. Her mother used to say that the sound seagulls made were the cries from sailors lost at sea.

Lou and Pearl are billeted with the Moltons just over on the next road, and Alice runs the whole way there. When she arrives at their front door, she is out of breath.

She knocks a few times and waits, hopping from one bare foot to the other, shivering, hugging herself. She hears footsteps inside and then Mr Molton opens the door.

'What's this, then?' he says. 'It's gone nine o'clock. Why are you out and about, young lady, dressed like that? Now go on home. Off with you, then.'

He tries to shut the door, but Alice steps onto the threshold, blocking him. 'Please.' Her teeth chatter with the cold. 'Please can I come in?'

Mrs Molton is making her way down the stairs. 'Who's that at the door, lovey, at this time of night?'

'Well, it's Alice.' He moves aside as if he is presenting her.

'Look at you out in your nightdress,' Mrs Molton says. 'And no shoes on? You'll catch your death. Come on, then, let's get you home, silly girl. You can see Lou and Pearl in the morning, now, can't you?'

'Please can I stay here tonight? Oh, please?' She doesn't care how mad it sounds. She can't go back to the Newsons' house.

'What you on about?' Mrs Molton asks. 'Does Mrs Newsom know that you are out in the dark after curfew? Dressed like this? Surely not?'

Alice explains that they are out, at Saint Edmund's, that they go Tuesdays and Thursdays.

'Were you scared, then? In that house on your own. Suppose there's no harm in you staying here for one night. Come on, then.' She turns to her husband. 'Lovey, can you pop round and leave Mrs Newsom a note, slip it through the letterbox. We don't want them worried, now, do we?'

They bicker for a moment about whether or not to let Alice stay, but in the end, Mr Molton agrees to the arrangement. Once he has set off to leave the note for the Newsoms, Alice begins to cry.

'There, there, now, you're a big girl to be carrying on like this, now, aren't you?' Mrs Molton looks her over. 'Let's get you settled down, then. Would you like a cup of Ovaltine to help you sleep?'

Alice nods and wipes at her face, and Mrs Molton wraps her up in a blanket on their settee in the front room by the coal-burning stove. Alice reaches for the woman and pulls her into an awkward embrace and sobs. The woman pats her back, and says Alice will feel all better after the hot drink.

The Newsoms return home later that evening to find the note from Mr Molton and the tipped-over bureau in Alice's room. Mr Newsom's crippled brother isn't there. The following day, Mrs Newsom brings over all of Alice's belongings to the Molton home, where she stays until Mrs Flight comes to collect the girls. When Alice becomes sick in the mornings and misses several periods, she tells Lou that something 'funny' happened with Mr Newsom's brother. Mrs Flight takes her to a doctor, helps arrange her emigration to America and a place for her to live with relatives in Providence, where Sonny is born on a hot July night in 1942.

Alice writes to Danny, telling him that he doesn't need to 'save himself' for her anymore. She won't be returning to Spithandle, and she can't do any of the things they talked about. But he will be much better off without her. He'll find someone else who will make him happier than Alice ever could. She is only thinking of him, and is so very sorry, but she knows that in the end, he will be the better for it.

But all that is yet to happen. For now, Alice falls asleep before Mrs Molton even begins to heat up the milk. She is so exhausted that she sleeps all through the night, not moving at all, waking up in the exact same position, unaware of the new life forming inside her, thinking she is safe and that, finally, everything bad is behind her.

22

Force of Your Suck

1992

MARNIE IS BEHIND THE cash register at Sister Midnight Records, her chin resting on top of her fists, waiting for customers that will never come. It's Monday, already past two, and they haven't had a single person come in. They only stock vinyl, mostly used, so this store is for those with integrity, says Carl, the manager. He is clinging to a firm belief that there are still enough people who want to spend their afternoons looking through records in dusty milk crates to keep the store afloat.

Sister Midnight does have a cult-like following with the deejays at the local college radio and alternative stations, music journalists and music heads, and collectors. It's also a mandatory destination for local bands who linger here on the weekends, trying to garner Carl's interest in their self-produced, self-pressed LPs, hoping to convince him to play their single, maybe even arrange an in-store gig. He claims to have 'zero interest' in attracting the kind of customers who prefer brand-new CDs and shopping at Tower Records or the Coop, or even Strawberries Music.

Marnie is used to people being visibly disappointed when they do venture inside and find only unsigned bands and LPs dating back to the 1960s, with a decided deficit in classic rock and heavy metal.

This is what makes Sister Midnight unique, Carl likes to say, and the best record store in the area. Marnie managed to keep hold of his number after he gave it to her one afternoon at the Vortex. His bartending days are behind him, he told her when she'd finally tracked him down, and in fact he's quit drinking altogether. He left Worcester and came here when he was offered this job by a buddy, as well as booking bands at the Rat. Marnie called him crying after Vincent dumped her in the fall. She was broke and had nowhere to live, she explained. 'At least I got out of there, Dad,' she'd said. 'I haven't been in touch with Gracie or any of them. Aren't you proud?' Carl always said she was like the little sister he never had, and he gave her a job at the record store, even though he didn't really need anyone, and found her a place to crash with his friends in their illegal Combat Zone loft.

Marnie yawns and checks the time. Almost half an hour has gone by since Robert, her co-worker, left to do the Italian subs run. Marnie hopes he remembers drinks. Her mouth is dry, like it's stuffed with cotton balls soaking up the last traces of saliva.

Outside it is cold. News-item cold. Marnie woke up coughing and congested. The loft was perpetually freezing, so much so that she could see her breath in the air. Carl's friends taped plastic sheets and garbage bags over the windows. But they barely did anything to ameliorate the frigid outdoor temperatures.

Her cousin Patrick is the only person in Marnie's family who knows she's here, less than a fifteen-minute drive from Uncle Mike and Cath's house. She calls them from time to time so they won't worry, making sure to keep her whereabouts vague. A practice she adopted when she lived with Patrick in Provincetown. He was barely speaking to them by that point, and he didn't want them to know she was with him. She tells them she's staying with Nikki or Tim, her friends from back home, names her aunt and uncle recognise. And she has still made it to their house for Thanksgiving and Christmas these past few years, adding to the allusion that everything is OK.

Marnie is starving by the time Robert comes back. A blast of wind escapes into the store when he opens the door. 'Thinking Lou Reed would go well with these.' He holds up the brown paper bag filled with their lunch.

After putting on *Transformer*, they sit cross-legged in the middle of the rug on the floor. Fold-out tables are shoved up against the walls, with crates of records on top and below, and there are more in the storage room and the office in the back. Robert takes out the subs, bags of potato chips, Cokes, and a pack of Marlboro Lights. A square of sunshine filters in from Mass. Ave. Marnie bites into the soft bread roll filled with salami and cheese, diced pickles, onions, tomatoes, lettuce, hot peppers. 'Oh my God, this is so fucking good,' she says.

'Totally.' Robert shoves a handful of chips in his mouth. 'Did I tell you I'm considering vegetarianism.'

'Are you crazy? I could never do that. Could never not eat salami or bacon. They are like maybe my best friends.'

'Perfect Day' comes on. 'How great is this song?' Robert says. 'But doesn't the thought that you're eating something that used to be alive gross you out? Like, my sandwich used to be breathing and running around. My sandwich might have had hopes and dreams. My sandwich might have been in love the day it was slaughtered.'

'Stop!' Marnie says. 'Please don't ruin this moment. *My sandwich is the only good thing in my life right now.*'

'What are you talking about? You have this awesome job. And you get to hang out with me all afternoon.'

'You're right, my life *is* amazing!' She goes on to tell him about her freezing-cold apartment.

'I mean, if you're gonna live in a dump in the Combat Zone . . .' Robert says. 'I'm just saying.'

Marnie finishes eating and crumples up the wax paper wrapping drenched in olive oil and vinegar, and shoves it back inside the paper bag. 'Dude, I would so live somewhere else, if I could afford it.'

'You looking?' Robert rips apart the plastic seal around the cigarette box, taps one out and offers it to Marnie, then lights it for her. They remain on the floor while they smoke.

'I'm not looking or anything because it's totally cheap and it's all I can swing,' says Marnie. 'But fuck yeah, if something better came along, I would totally move.'

'You should check out my place.' Robert leans back on one arm as he smokes. 'It's really cheap. Some of my housemates are having this, like, gathering thing tonight. You should come.'

'You mean a party? And you didn't invite me?'

'First of all, it's not a party. Second, it's my housemates' thing. So I didn't exactly not invite you.' Their eyes meet and he looks away quickly. He stands up, shaking off the sandwich debris from his lap. 'Hey, guess we better look kind of like we are doing something. I know Carl is cool, but still, he won't like this. But, like, you should totally come check out my place tonight.'

The rest of the afternoon passes slowly, with a few lone customers trickling in from time to time, flipping through the milk crates. A group of teenagers wearing plastic vampire fangs come in after school, momentarily disrupting the quiet. No one buys anything.

Around five, Carl arrives with the manager of a punk band from Providence he's convinced is about to break. They are doing an in-store gig the following week to promote their new EP. After being introduced to Marnie and Robert and looking around for a while, the manager takes off and Carl retreats to his office. Usually, he spends most of his time talking with Marnie and Robert and the customers, but today he stays in his office with the door closed. The walls are thin though, and Marnie and Robert can hear everything while he makes phone calls to his sister, then his mother, dealing with some sort of family emergency. One of his cousins has been stealing money from their aunt to support his heroin habit. Carl suggests that his cousin come stay with him for a while, and give his aunt a break. 'I got this, Ma, don't worry,' he says before hanging up. 'What a fucking piece of shit.'

When Carl comes out of his office, he looks worried. 'Sorry to be so MIA this afternoon, guys,' he says to Marnie and Robert. 'I gotta hustle though. You can close up a little early today if you want.'

That night, Robert and Marnie start holding hands in the backyard at his place, a large house he's renting along with nine other people from an MIT professor who is on sabbatical with his family. Double the number of people that are supposed to be living there, but they keep it clean and take good care of the house, so, hopefully, the family will never know, Robert explains. They're using a home office, a den, the playroom and a large closet for bedrooms, so no one has to share.

It's even colder than earlier and Marnie is shivering, so they head inside and sit on the couch in the living room; tea light candles are dotted around the room. Spider plants hang off the window frames, and tapestries and art prints line the walls. The sofa is worn-in, but looks expensive, and matches the other couch and the two armchairs. The party is low-key, with people draped on the chairs or sitting on the floor, and even though there is music playing, no one is dancing, just bopping slightly in their seats.

Their fingers touch as they pass a joint back and forth to each other. Once they are good and stoned, Robert shows her the kitchen, explaining how they all share food and the cooking, and rotate the chores. Would that be a problem for her? Marnie has never lived anywhere with such a clean kitchen since she left home. The counters are uncluttered and not lined with dirty dishes, the refrigerator has food in it, and there are even ceramic canisters filled with flour, sugar, beans, coffee, tea leaves and a full spice rack. Marnie can picture mornings sitting in the living room, drinking freshly brewed coffee, sunlight pouring in, Robert making her eggs out in the kitchen. Walking to work together.

They go upstairs so she can see the bedrooms. Robert's has piles of philosophy and German history paperbacks by his futon. The walls are covered with posters of Lenin and flyers from political demonstrations. 'Feel free to look around,' Robert says.

There are two windows that face out onto the street and the room is sparsely furnished, with just a bureau, a desk and a small bookshelf. On top, there's a framed photograph of a boy with a bowl haircut in the front seat of a canoe, holding a paddle, with another boy in the middle and an older man in the stern.

'That's you, right?' Marnie picks up the picture. 'Eleven?'

'Twelve.'

'Nice haircut. With your dad and your brother?'

'That's my friend and our science teacher.'

Marnie turns around. 'Why are you in a canoe with your science teacher?'

'He used to do this thing where if you were a good student, as a reward, you and a friend could sleep over at his house and then canoe to school. He lived out in some suburb by the Charles.'

'That's really creepy. You slept at your teacher's house?'

'It wasn't like that. It was cool. His wife was there and everything. He was like the best teacher I ever had. He taught us how to blow things up, and we made model volcanoes. I feel like I learned everything important during seventh-grade science. Canoeing to school at dawn was one of my top-five middle school experiences.'

'Really? What were the others?' Marnie asks.

They are facing each other, and he takes hold of her hands and pulls her towards him.

'Maybe there weren't any,' he says.

They sit on his futon and start to kiss. He unbuttons her shirt and pulls his T-shirt over his head. They lie down and he undoes his jeans and takes them off, helps her wriggle out of hers. They get under the covers, their hands all up and down each other's bodies, and remove the rest of their clothing.

'I've been wanting to do that since I met you,' he whispers in her ear after they have sex. Marnie lies on his chest and he strokes her arm.

'Yeah?' She looks at him and they kiss for a while.

'Yes,' he says when they come up for air. 'Since that first day you walked into the store. But I thought you had something going on with Carl.'

'Carl's gay, dummy.'

'That's what I thought, but you guys seemed to have some sort of connection, so it was confusing.'

'I just know him from Worcester. It's just a Worcester thing.'

'If I'd known that, I would have made a move sooner.'

The sounds of the party filter up through the floorboards.

'So is the room that's available as nice as yours?' Marnie asks. 'Because I am definitely in.'

'This *is* the room that's available,' he says.

'Wait, what? This is *your* room. I don't get it.'

'I know. But I'm leaving. I got into graduate school at Berkeley. I thought you knew. Didn't I tell you?'

'No.' She tries not to sound hurt. 'I don't think you did.'

He thinks back. 'I think I found out before you started. Anyway, I'm going there this summer, taking a class before the programme starts in the fall. But you can totally have my room. It's totally yours if you want it.'

'When are you leaving?' Marnie asks.

'In a month. I'm gonna drive out there, visit people on the way.'

'That sounds so cool.'

'Yeah.' He turns to her. 'I really wish this had happened sooner, though.'

'Me, too.'

They kiss. 'Hey.' Robert pulls away. 'I know this sounds crazy, but maybe you could come with me? You know, like, drive across the country with me?'

Then they both start laughing and before she can say yes, that she'd love to do that, he tells her to forget it, that it was a stupid idea.

*

A week later, Carl brings his cousin into Sister Midnight for the punk band's in-store performance. The shop is hot and filled with the band's friends. Marnie notices Carl's cousin looking at her throughout the four-song set.

Afterwards, he makes his way towards her, threading through the crowd. He holds her gaze and she feels something as he stares at her. A jolt goes right through her when he shakes her hand and introduces himself and says, 'Hey, I'm Jimmy.'

23

Junior Life-Saving

1986

MARNIE IS TRANSFIXED BY her grandmother's mouth. The way her lips move around as she chews and swallows her dinner. She is telling a long story that Marnie is having trouble following because she is preoccupied. She can't stop thinking about Nikki Fantana and their plan – Nikki's plan, really, but Marnie has a crucial part to play in it. Nikki is going to call Marnie and invite her for a sleepover. Meanwhile, her mother thinks Nikki is going to Marnie's tonight. That way, the girls can stay out all night at the end-of-summer lifeguard party.

The only thing that Marnie has to do is lie to her grandmother, Nikki had told her. It's nothing, she promised. She lies to her parents all the time.

The clock directly behind her grandmother's head is counting down to the moment when Nikki is supposed to call with the fake sleepover invitation. Ten more minutes.

'And then Lou's granddaughter says, after all that, *but, Granny, I don't like lavender cake anymore. I think I might be allergic to it.*' Her grandmother laughs. 'Can you believe it? After she went to all this trouble, traipsing round practically all of West Sussex. And her daughter, Jean, says, *Mum, she hasn't liked that cake since she was three.* And this was supposed to be for her tenth birthday. Oh, I really laughed when I read that, I did. Typical Lou. I must write back to her tomorrow.'

Marnie hopes her grandmother doesn't realise that she isn't listening to anything she's been saying throughout this entire dinner. Active listening, Ms Stubenski, her maths teacher, calls it, where you use both ears – as opposed to passive listening, when you appear engaged but, in fact, you are not paying attention at all.

Alice is bent over her plate, cutting up the grey meat before dipping it into the gravy, which she eats slowly, followed by a string bean, then a piece of boiled potato. She dabs at her mouth with a napkin. Her grandmother favours meat-and-two-veg dinners which are too hard to get down in this kind of heat. Daytime temperatures have been reaching into the nineties this past week. Here, less than a mile inland from the coast, the air is thick and still, even with all the windows open.

After the phone call – after she lies to her grandmother – Marnie is supposed to meet Nikki in front of the Clam Shell Gift Shop before they head off to the lifeguard party. Sam Santiago is going to the party, Nikki keeps reminding her. Sam Santiago, who has this way of drifting down the long hill that leads to the beach access dirt road on his skateboard, banking left where the road curves round before hopping off and flipping it into his hands, all in one effortless motion. Nikki says he likes Marnie. She says tonight is the perfect opportunity to hook up with him because there is nothing more romantic than a beach party. They can tell their children about it someday. And Nikki will get off with Russ Weatherall, Sam's best friend. When they start high school in the fall, they can go on double dates together. She has it all figured out, Nikki does.

All Marnie has to do is tell her grandmother that she is sleeping over at Nikki's and go meet her. That's it. Simple.

'You've hardly eaten a thing.' Her grandmother pops in one last bite of potato. 'Are you all right, love?'

'Absolutely,' Marnie says. 'Totally.'

Her grandmother gives her a funny look, and Marnie feels panicked. What if she has already ruined the plan? What if Nikki doesn't want to be her friend anymore?

Every morning this summer, Marnie wakes up and she remembers. Nikki Fantana is her friend. She thinks about it when she showers, puts on her bathing suit and her Junior Lifeguard Summer Program T-shirt, which she got at the orientation after passing the open water swimming and calisthenics test. And then again as she wolfs down some toast with honey and tea with Alice. She bikes over to meet Nikki in front of the Clam Shell Gift Shop. They ride their bikes together along Route 1A, past Bigeye's Bait and Tackle, Salty's Landing, Breezy Acres Mini-Golf, the smell of the ocean getting stronger and stronger before turning on to the beach access road.

It's usually still cold enough on the beach in the early mornings for a sweatshirt. Marnie drinks too-hot cocoa, the Styrofoam cup woody against her teeth, and waits for the rest of the kids to arrive. The first hour is sit-ups, push-ups, and a run out to the lighthouse and back. They have relay races before learning CPR, mouth-to-mouth resuscitation, how to handle broken bones. After a snack, they get in the water and practise rescues, learn new strokes and how to surf, then more relay races.

They are finished by mid-afternoon, and the rest of the day is spent swimming with Nikki and the other kids, getting ice creams and sodas from the snack bar. When the lifeguards blow the final whistles, calling in the last of the swimmers, Marnie's lungs feel heavy with the sea air, the skin on her fingertips shrivelled up, her hair coated with salt water, feet rubbed clean by the sand. Then they slowly bike home, a whole group of them spread out across the beach access road, the boys popping wheelies. At home, Marnie inhales her dinner, barely makes it through an hour of television with her grandmother before crawling into bed. She is usually asleep within minutes.

Her friendship with Nikki started off slowly. First, she got invited to Nikki's seventh-grade sleepover and then Marnie invited her back. They remained friendly, but weren't real friends until this past fall, when Marnie caught her crying in the girls' bathroom. Everyone at school knew that Nikki's father had just left her mother and walked out on his family.

'Sorry.' Marnie hurried for the door.

'Don't tell anyone you saw me like this.'

'I won't,' she promised Nikki. 'I totally won't.'

Later that week, Marnie ran into her crying again in the school library. She ended up telling Marnie everything – the only person in the whole school Nikki confided in.

Nikki's parents had been arguing for a while, and her father started sleeping in their basement. Sometimes, he didn't come home at all. One Sunday morning, Nikki and her siblings were eating breakfast out of those individual cereal boxes, the kind that you can pour milk into, and her father was stumbling around drunk, shoving clothes in his suitcase, screaming at them if they said anything. A taxi arrived and he was gone. They hadn't seen or heard from him in weeks, and her mother said she didn't know where he was.

Marnie's heart was pounding. She'd never heard anyone talk like this. Nikki, of all people. With an older brother who worked at the gas station and could drive Nikki places, and an older sister who worked at Baskin-Robbins. And Nikki's mom, the cool mom, the one the dads were always checking out. The perfect family. It gave Marnie an ugly feeling in her stomach, thinking about how good things could vanish so quickly.

Nikki started coming over to Marnie's after school to do her homework while Alice fixed them tea, and she often stayed for dinner. Marnie's life at school changed completely. There were whole entire areas she had never even seen: behind the gym, where Nikki and her friends would sneak cigarettes during lunch, the outer reaches of the sports fields where they'd go to flirt with the boys during recess. Besides the classrooms, all Marnie had known before was the library, where she'd run to hide out during lunch and recess with her old friend Sarah, who was also shy and quiet. It was the only safe place to be when there was no adult supervision, and the same boy got beat up every day and no one told any of the teachers. Not even him.

Marnie knew they were truly friends when Nikki suggested they do the Junior Lifeguard Summer Program together.

The phone starts to ring.

'Who could that be?' Her grandmother pushes her chair back and gets up to answer it. Marnie scrapes her dinner into the trash with her fork. The slab of meat, the potatoes, the string beans slop on top of the tea bags, toast crusts, the remnants of their long-ago breakfast.

'Oh, hello, Nikki,' her grandmother says. 'Yes, Marnie is here. Let me just get her for you.' She hands the receiver to Marnie. 'It's Nikki.'

'Hey.' Marnie takes the phone and turns away. She can't bear to look at her grandmother while she lies to her.

'So, you ready to party?' Nikki says it so loud, Marnie is sure her grandmother can hear. 'Ask her, OK? Evelyn is right here, she's been practising sounding like my mom. Haven't you?' She can hear them both laughing now.

Marnie covers the phone and looks at the floor. 'Nanny, is it OK if I sleep over at Nikki's?'

''Course it is. How lovely.'

'You sure?'

''Course I'm sure.'

'I can come,' she says into the phone. Nikki and Evelyn cheer on the other end.

The whole ride over on her bike, she lags behind Nikki and Evelyn. She can't stop thinking about her grandmother at home by herself, and the lie between them. It can never be undone, not ever. Even if she confesses at some later point, she has deceived her. Like something her mother would do – let down the people she loves the most. Maybe she is more similar to her mother than she'd like to think.

Once they get to the beach, Marnie drinks two beers in quick succession with Nikki and Evelyn.

'Look at little girlfriend go,' Nikki says with admiration.

A calmness washes over her, and she feels powerful and fearless, like she can do anything. Even go sit next to Sam Santiago by the bonfire, which she does. And when a joint is passed around, she takes a long drag, her lungs feeling like they will explode with fire, but she doesn't choke it out, doesn't betray her inexperience. She is more relaxed than she has ever been in her entire life. Sam offers her a shot of tequila, shows her how to lick salt from her hand before downing it, suck on a lime afterwards, and wash it all down with a large swallow of beer.

After that, her limbs are liquid, and she is dancing with Sam Santiago to Run-D.M.C., the Beastie Boys, LL Cool J. It's dark, but the bonfire throws out enough light that Marnie can see her feet moving. Nikki and Russ are making out on a blanket and Evelyn is dancing with one of the lifeguards. Then people are taking off their clothes and heading into the water. The next thing she knows, she is bobbing on a wave, naked, her arms outstretched, her hair swirling around in the sea.

Marnie wakes up wrapped in a towel with her clothes on. There are clumps of bodies everywhere around her. Dawn is creeping up over the water.

Marnie knows she should wait, to make the sleepover story more believable, but she just wants to be home, with her grandmother.

Once she reaches her building, she pounds up the stairs. Her grandmother is at the kitchen table with a mug of tea, doing the crossword puzzle and listening to jazz on the radio. Like usual on Sunday mornings.

'You're home early,' her grandmother says. 'Wasn't expecting you for ages.'

Marnie rushes to her and gives her a hug.

'You all right, love?'

'Yeah. Just thought it'd be nice to spend the day with you. I've been so busy.'

'Well, that's lovely. And did they have weird things for breakfast at Nikki's?'

'That, too.'

'Eggs, then, it will be. Think I've got some sausages and bacon in the freezer. I can defrost them so we can have a real proper breakfast. How does that sound?'

'Sounds perfect.'

Marnie sits at the kitchen table while her grandmother rummages through the refrigerator, pulling out the eggs, butter and milk. Then she puts the bacon and some sausages in the oven. The smell of the cured meat begins to fill the kitchen. Marnie crosses her legs in her chair and watches her grandmother putting their breakfast together. It's only early morning and they've got the whole day stretched out before them, just the two of them.

24

Hidden Scars, Invisible Wounds

1988

THE TEARS BEGIN WHEN Alice first sees it – England, through the oval airplane window. When they dip below the clouds, the patchwork quilt pattern of fields and roads are suddenly visible below. Marnie is still asleep, curled into an L-shape, stretched across her grandmother's lap. Alice has only managed to doze every now and then throughout the entire flight. Marnie stirs when the landing gear groans into position before hoisting herself up to a sitting position. Alice wipes at her face, hoping her granddaughter doesn't notice she's been crying.

In the forty-six years she has lived in America, Alice has always dreamed of going back home. But it was hard to think it would actually happen, and she was beginning to accept that England might forever exist only in her memories.

That changed when a letter from Lou arrived after Christmas. Since her husband died in late November, she'd been struggling to cope, she confessed. Would Alice and Marnie consider coming to visit her, if Lou helped with the air fare? It would give her something to look forward to, she said, which she desperately needed. That cemented things into real, actual plans, with dates selected in the summer and flights booked.

'Oh, I'm so excited for you to meet Lou. You'll love her, she'll love you,' Alice kept saying to Marnie in the weeks leading up to the trip. 'I'm going to show you everything. Sea Place Beach, and where I lived with Lou's family and our school, and we'll have to go up the Downs and see the pier and . . . Oh, you'll love Brighton, you will. Lou says I'm going to be so surprised when I see Spithandle. You'd never know there'd ever been a war, she says. That it'd been bombed. You have to look really carefully to see the evidence. But it's definitely there.' Alice went on to explain that the remnants of the war were really obvious in the big cities like London, where there are new developments in places that had been badly bombed, right next to buildings dating back hundreds of years that hadn't been touched. 'But it's more hidden in places like Spithandle,' Alice said. 'You know – more like hidden scars, invisible wounds.'

The week before the trip, Marnie and Alice were so excited that they had trouble sleeping. Their bags were packed days in advance of the flight. Neither of them have ever flown before. Marnie kept asking about her grandmother's trip to America all those many years ago. What had it been like, she wondered? But the details aren't very clear to Alice, and she mostly remembers it as an awful experience. The boat seemed to take a year to cross the

Atlantic and she'd been nauseous most of the way, not only from seasickness and fear. She was also pregnant.

Now Marnie and Alice make their way to the lines for Passport Control, then collect their luggage and head through Customs. Alice tears up again at hearing so many English accents. They reach the arrivals area, and when she sees Lou standing there behind the barrier, she weeps harder as they embrace, even though she barely recognises her childhood best friend. They hug and shriek for a long time. Long enough to draw attention from other people.

Once they are settled in Lou's car and merge onto the motorway, Alice can't contain herself. 'I'm in bloody, sodding England!' she cries out.

'We're here!' Marnie chimes in from the back seat.

Lou laughs. 'Steady there, you lot. It's just the M25.'

Lou has told everyone about Alice and Marnie's visit, she explains on the drive down to Spithandle. She hopes they aren't too tired because none of them could wait to see Alice and meet Marnie, and a whole load of people are dropping by that very afternoon. 'You have a sleep as soon as we get home,' Lou says, 'and then you'll be right as rain by the time everyone comes round.'

The two women begin to tell Marnie all about their old gang, but each name gets the women sidetracked on a story that has them both laughing. Eventually, they give up and instead, Lou catches Alice up on everyone's marriages, children and general whereabouts. By the time they arrive at Lou's house over an hour and a half later, Marnie still has no idea who anyone is.

It's a clear, dry afternoon and after their naps, Marnie and Alice help Lou get ready for the guests. Lou has assembled 'nibbley bits': cheese and crackers, a bowl of cherry tomatoes, bread and dips, sliced celery and carrots and cucumber, and more dips. They bring it all into her extension, a glass-walled room that looks out to her back garden. People begin to arrive in the late afternoon and they sit outside on the patio, forming an ever-widening circle of chairs. Alice cries out every time a new person appears in Lou's back garden. There are two of the Christie sisters, who used to live across the road from Lou and Alice along with their husbands. Mary Simms on her own, divorced since the 1970s, and her sister Renie. Cindy Mason. The recently widowed Jack Brown, who has been coming round to keep Lou company. Tom Farley and his wife. The initial cups of tea quickly give way to wine, and then sausage rolls are passed around. Someone suggests a bonfire when the sun finally sets.

As the night wears on, the talk turns to the war.

'I'm right there, I tell you, right back in my shed.' Jack turns to Marnie. 'When I was a young lad, I had a shed in my back garden filled with bombs and swords and guns. It was a boys' paradise here.'

'You weren't evacuated, were you, Jack?' Lou asks.

'No, we had the run of the place, those of us still here. We'd blow up things in the fields behind the houses. It was great fun, it was. And when a plane came down, we'd wait until the soldiers had gone through it and then we'd strip the whole thing. But do you have this thing where decades ago is clearer to you than last week?'

'Yes, than two hours ago even,' one of the Christie sisters says.

'I couldn't for the life of me tell you what I had for breakfast, but I can tell you all about my shed.'

Marnie is so tired, she can barely keep her eyes open. She longs to go upstairs to bed. But her grandmother is wide awake, and no one seems close to wanting the evening to end. They talk and laugh until the last of the wood has been burned, and finally people begin their goodbyes and head home.

The following day is spent in and out of Lou's car, seeing the milestones of Alice and Lou's childhood. The first stop is Lou's house, where Alice lived after her mother died. They park in front and get out, pointing to the other houses. Alice and Lou can still remember the names of every person who used to live on their street.

'We knew everyone. Now I'd be lucky if I could name three of my neighbours, and we hardly ever speak to one another,' Lou explains to Marnie, who is taking photographs of everything: their old house, the road, the neighbours' homes. Alice asked Marnie to be in charge of taking all the pictures for the trip, because she says she's hopeless with the camera.

Next, they go to Alice's childhood home, Honeysuckle Lane, and the Downs where Alice and Lou played as children. They drive past their primary school, which has since been turned into a block of flats. Along the way, they point out Babs Bailey's house – Spithandle's one celebrity, who had a brief singing career in London. They walk around the town centre, which is almost unrecognisable to Alice, and aside from a barber shop and a frame store, everything is completely different, she says. Then it's on to the seafront.

When they first glimpse the English Channel and the pier, Alice gasps and screams.

'Nanny!' Marnie laughs. But then she realises her grandmother is crying. *Again.*

When they reach the Victorian-style pier, Alice breaks down completely. 'It's still here. I can't believe it. They blew up the middle during the war,' she tells Marnie.

Lou suggests they go all the way out to the end. They pass a restaurant and an amusement arcade and continue walking until they reach an empty pavilion, which used to be a disco club during the 1970s, at the very end of the pier.

'I haven't stood on this pier since I was fourteen,' Alice cries. 'I can't believe it's still here.'

'Oh, for God's sake.' Lou rustles around in her purse until she finds a tissue. 'Of course the pier is still here, silly woman. They repaired it after the war, didn't they?'

Alice leans over the metal railings and Marnie grasps her grandmother's forearm. Green water laps against the pilings below. There's a thick smell of seaweed permeating the air, and large seagulls hover above the water. Somewhere out there, the English Channel meets the Atlantic Ocean, connecting eventually to the same water Marnie has been swimming in her entire life.

When they walk along the promenade that runs parallel to the beach, Alice points out various landmarks. The cinema they used to sneak into, the bus station they cut through on the way to the shops, the Italian cafe whose owner was arrested at the beginning of the war, suspected of being a spy.

They pass overturned wooden boats and a fishmonger's, and when the promenade ends, Alice suddenly stops and takes off her shoes, pointing. 'Marnie! This is it! This is Sea Place Beach. This is our beach, Marnie, love. Ours!'

She makes her way over the pebbles until she reaches the water's edge. It's a hot, windless day, the sea mostly flat with gentle swells. Alice begins to pull down her trousers and unbutton her blouse, until she has stripped right down to her underwear, all in one fast movement, leaving her clothes behind in a heap. She wades out until the water is above her waist and dunks under, before swimming out into deeper water.

'Nanny! Oh my God, what is she doing?' Marnie puts her hand to her mouth.

'I think she's going for a swim, love,' Lou says.

'Oh my God!' Marnie says again.

'Come on, then, you lot.' Alice waves to Marnie and Lou. 'The water is glorious.'

'Your nan looks quite mad out there by herself. And we can't have that, now, can we? She's only just arrived. Think we'd better do as she says, don't you think? Pretty sure I've got some towels in my boot.'

Marnie looks away as Lou begins to disrobe before tiptoeing over the stones. She slowly makes her way into the water, shrieking every time a wave splashes over her. Then she puts her arms out in front of her and jumps in. Keeping her head above the water, she swims out towards

Alice. The two women laugh and call out for Marnie to join them. Marnie rolls up her jeans and begins to wade.

'No one is about,' Alice says. 'Just come in, love. You'll love it.'

Oh, fuck it, Marnie thinks. She takes off her clothes and runs into the water. She swims out to where her grandmother is floating on the waves, holding Lou's hand and sobbing yet again.

The following weeks are filled with country walks and pub lunches, trips to Brighton, Bosham, Littlehampton, Chichester, the castle in Arundel, the National Trust house in Petworth. They take the train up to London for a long day of walking, to show Marnie the sights. Alice had never been before, either. The meandering route from Victoria Station includes Buckingham Palace, Big Ben, the Houses of Parliament, Downing Street, Trafalgar Square and all the way to Tower Bridge and back.

Alice doesn't have any actual blood relations left in Spithandle, yet still she seems to know everyone. There are long dinners with bottles of wine, bonfires in back gardens that last late into the evening because the sun doesn't set until nearly ten o'clock, endless cups of tea in people's front rooms. Pearl, who lives over in Hove, is a common presence at the nighttime get-togethers.

The last day Lou takes Alice and Marnie to a country village and they walk along a pathway by the side of a sixteenth-century church, past a duck pond, through thistles and brambles and thorns, and over the railway tracks. An occasional commuter train hurtles by, carrying office workers and day-trippers to and from London. They carry on through the kissing gate, where the path widens out on to fields of grazing cattle until it dead-ends by a canal.

On the way home, they make a stop to show Marnie the Miller's Tomb. When they reach it, Lou explains to her how you are supposed to walk around it three times for good luck. 'And if you make a wish, it will come true,' Lou says. 'If you believe in that nonsense.'

'Well, I believe in that nonsense,' Alice says, taking the lead. Lou follows behind her, then Marnie. They each circle the grave three times. The sun is strong, but it's a windy day and everyone's hair blows wildly as they walk. After Alice and Lou are done, they take a seat on a bench by a plaque explaining who the miller was and how he had built the grave himself before he died. Marnie takes some pictures of her grandmother and Lou – the view of the town centre with the English Channel sparkling in the distance. Then she takes a seat.

'Isn't this where you saw the German pilot get shot down?' Lou asks. 'With Danny?'

'Yes, it is,' Alice says. 'Haven't thought of that for ages.' She stares ahead as if she is focusing on some distant point along the horizon.

'Well, I think of it every time I come up here. Which is about once a week.'

'Who's Danny?' Marnie asks. 'Have I met him?'

'No, you haven't,' Lou says. 'He was your nan's fellow. Wasn't he?'

'He was.' Alice tears up.

'Oh, Nanny. I'm sorry.' Marnie hugs her grandmother. 'Did he die in the war?'

'Oh no, love, he's fine. Lives just over in Guildford,' Lou tells her.

'Does he?' Alice turns to Lou. 'Guildford,' she repeats.

'Yes. I never told you, but his daughter worked in the home where my mother-in-law was. Betty, she is. Lovely person, really, really lovely.'

Alice swallows. 'Betty,' she whispers.

Lou goes on to explain that during her visits with her mother-in-law, Betty told her a bit about her father's life. When the war ended, Danny took a while to settle down. First, he went back to Ireland to look after his mother who wasn't well and died a year or so later. He drifted around for several years before ending up in London, where he met Betty's mother, but they'd split up when Betty left home. He'd moved down to Guildford to be near Betty and her family – she had four children – and was an excellent grandfather.

'Four grandchildren,' says Alice. 'That really is something. We're both lucky, then, aren't we?' Alice squeezes Marnie's legs and kisses her. 'The both of us.'

On the way to Heathrow, they make one last stop at the seafront so Lou can take some photos of Alice and Marnie at the very end of the pier. They put their arms around each other and Marnie smiles hard while Lou focuses the camera. Then they get back in the car and head for the motorway.

JUNCTION OF EARTH AND SKY

Alice and Lou talk nonstop the whole drive to Heathrow, reviewing the past three weeks and making plans for their next trip. Marnie contents herself with looking out the window in the back seat, a glowing feeling inside her. She got to be with her grandmother for her first trip back to Spithandle. She has never seen her grandmother this happy before, and Marnie's wish at the Miller's Tomb was for her grandmother to be able to come back here again and again and again. Maybe someday, when Marnie leaves home, her grandmother would come back to live here permanently. Maybe they both would. Marnie looks out the window, trying to memorise every detail they are speeding past: every pasture, every hill, every last thing.

25

Someday

1989

'SOMEDAY' WAS A GAME Marnie used to play with her grandmother when she was little. During their frequent trips to the library, Marnie would hunt down the world atlas and the US road atlas while Alice gathered up the children's encyclopedia and any books that had photographs of animals. They would spread them all out on a table and make up expeditions they were going to take, imagining all the places they would travel to, all the things they were going to do, just the two of them. Someday.

The 'someday' list grew longer as they discovered more and more amazing things to see around the world. Someday, they would travel to Japan to see the cherry blossom, to India and Nepal for the tigers and snow leopards and climb Mount Everest, and while they were in the general vicinity, maybe they would pop over to Tibet. They would walk along the Great Wall of China, see kangaroos and koalas in Australia, and go snorkelling along the Great Barrier Reef. They would see gorillas in Rwanda, hippos and lions and giraffes and zebras in Kenya, pyramids in Egypt. Someday they would cross the Atlantic by boat, take a train from Beijing to Moscow, and then all through Europe. They would dogsled across Alaska, travel the Amazon River. As they imagined and plotted and planned, their voices would rise with excitement, enough to be shushed by the librarian on a regular basis.

The place that Marnie wanted to go more than anywhere else was England. When she was very little, she imagined it to be filled with princesses and queens and kings and castles. Someday, she hoped, someday they would go there.

When Marnie first got her allowance, she never spent it. Instead she put it straight into the piggy bank her aunt and uncle had given her for her eighth birthday. All the money she made feeding Mrs Pearson's cat went in there, as well. She was saving for their trip to England. Someday, she would ask her grandmother, could they go see Spithandle, swim in the sea over there, on the other side of the Atlantic?

And then they did.

On the airplane home, Alice told Marnie that she thought this could be the beginning of their world travels together. They were crossing things off their someday list, she said.

But the most important things on the someday list were Alice's hopes and dreams for Marnie. She was just about to start her junior year, but well on her way to being the first person in the family to finish high school. Alice confessed to Marnie that she and Uncle Mike were already planning the big party they would have to celebrate this momentous occasion, even though it was almost two years away. And someday after that, surely Marnie would go on to college. She would do something important, her grandmother told her. 'More than what I've done, love,' she said. 'Someday, I know you will, because you are special.'

The following spring, Marnie comes home from school one day to find Alice sitting on the couch with Dolly. An opened wine bottle is on the coffee table next to balled-up wads of Kleenex, and both women are in tears.

'Sit down, love,' her grandmother says. 'I'm afraid I've got some bad news.'

Her stomach had been bothering her, and she'd been taking antacids but nothing would make it feel better. Although she always brought Marnie for her yearly check-ups throughout her childhood, and kept up with all her required immunisations, Alice was never one for doctors, but finally, she'd gone.

'It's cancer,' she tells Marnie, and goes on to explain that the doctor said it had spread so much that it was too late for treatment. She only has a few months left.

Marnie doesn't want to cry in front of her grandmother, so she excuses herself and rushes to her room, where she sobs into her pillow. Life without her grandmother is impossible to imagine. Last week, they had a meeting with Ms Fabian, the guidance counsellor, who said Marnie's grades were good enough for academic scholarships to college. But now, what is the point of even going to college, if her grandmother wouldn't be here to see her through it? What is the point of anything without her grandmother?

Over the next few months, her grandmother declines quickly, just as the doctor predicted, and eventually she goes into hospice care. During her final week, she drifts in and out of consciousness. But instead of lying still, she struggles under her oxygen mask and seems agitated, as if she wants to get up, as if there's something she still needs to do.

On her last night, the nurse explains to Marnie that her grandmother is 'transitioning' – that it won't be much longer. Marnie holds her grandmother's hand, trying to stay awake all night so she can be with her right up until the end. At one point, Alice opens her eyes and squeezes Marnie's hand.

'Nanny!' Marnie cries out.

Her grandmother manages a slight smile and gazes at her granddaughter for a long time. Then her lips start moving, but she's speaking so quietly, Marnie can't hear her, even when she puts her ear up close to her mouth. Finally, her grandmother's voice picks up.

'It's . . . you.' Her grandmother struggles to get her words out. 'It's . . . you . . . I held. When . . . you . . . were born. My son . . . never . . . but you . . . I held.' Her grandmother closes her eyes and smiles even wider. 'Do . . . the . . . somedays.'

She doesn't say anything else. An hour later, Alice is gone.

26

Route Two Citgo Station

1993

MARNIE HAS ONLY A few minutes to find Jimmy's secret stash, which is somewhere here in the car, while he goes inside the Citgo station for a pack of Marlboros. She might have a little longer if he's also getting a Yoo-hoo, his preferred brand of chocolate milk. Her boyfriend, she's realised, has been siphoning off some of the heroin they are supposed to be selling and keeping it all for himself.

She reaches over to the driver's side, searching the compartment along the door, picking through the wads of hamburger wrappers and dirty napkins. But it's not there. She grabs his bag from the back, unzips the front pocket, but there's only a lighter, pens, a bent spoon they use for cooking up dope, some loose change and condoms. Then she hears the jingling on the gas station door. It turns out to be a woman with big round sunglasses and her little girl. Not Jimmy. She keeps searching his bag and finds dirty underwear and socks and T-shirts, a packet of clean syringes they got from a needle exchange, and a notebook. But not the secret stash.

Next, she checks the glove compartment and that's where she finds the bag of heroin, hidden inside a folded-over envelope underneath the car registration, road maps and the gun. She grabs it and heads towards the bathroom.

Marnie walks across the puddled asphalt edged with remnants of grey snow, shivering and shaking her way to the side of the gas station, where the customer restroom is located.

She passes the woman with the big sunglasses, who is helping her little girl wash the windscreen of their station wagon. 'Mommy, look. Something's wrong with that girl.' She points at Marnie with the squeegee, and liquid soap drips onto the hood of their car.

'Don't point, it's rude!' Her mother slaps the little girl's hand down. She looks over at Marnie and gasps.

Marnie is so pale, her face almost ghost-like, and she has dark half-circles under her eyes, her coat wrapped tightly around her tiny frame. These days, she is so thin her ribcage is visible underneath her skin, which has become translucent and delicate, resembling moth wings that might crumble away.

Once inside the bathroom, Marnie locks the door and sits down on the filthy black and white linoleum floor littered with toilet paper, hair, crumpled-up paper towels, bloodied tampons. The toilet seat is missing, the rim of the bowl covered in pubic hair. First, she uses her lighter to cook up the white powder in the spoon with some water. She soaks it up with a cotton ball and squeezes the dope into the syringe. Then, using her belt for a tourniquet, she ties it on and searches for a viable vein on her right arm. There are track marks and scars from old infections, and when she finds a vein, she thumps it three times. She pulls back the plunger and injects herself, pushing the plunger halfway, takes off the tourniquet, and then plunges in the rest.

The familiar feeling of warm numbness comes over her, followed by a brief moment of euphoria. She lays her head back against the wall as the sense of relief spreads throughout her entire body. But then she is overcome and has to lie down on the filthy floor, curling into herself. Her breath becomes shallower, and she struggles to stay conscious. The noises coming from outside the bathroom are muffled, as if there is a pillow taped around her head. She can hear knocking on the door, the doorknob rattling, and more knocking, which turns into pounding and faraway voices yelling to open up. But she is too weak to move or call out.

'Come on, man,' someone shouts outside the metal door. 'This isn't like your own private bathroom.'

Marnie hears the jangling of keys and someone calling out, *holy shit, holy fucking shit*.

Marnie hears voices talking above her, but everything still sounds muffled, as if she's underwater, and the words are warped, like an album playing on too slow a speed and she can't seem to fully wake up. The voices are saying *overdose* and *almost died* and *shame, such a pretty face*, and numbers that she doesn't understand. Something about blood pressure and heart rate and blood oxygen levels, and how lucky she is that someone found her in time.

Her eyes are forced open and a tiny flashlight is shining into her pupils. There are hands on her right arm, wiping something cold along it. She hears more words: infection, AIDS test, and, *what's your name, hon, what's your name?*

'Marnie,' she says, but it feels like her tongue is too thick, and it comes out sounding funny.

'Sorry, sweetheart, what was that? Maya?'

She says it again but her words are even more garbled. She manages to open her eyes and tries one more time to tell them her name. There are so many faces hovering over her, but no one seems to be able to understand what she's saying. It feels like they are way too close, and Marnie starts to get the panicky feeling – the desperate, anxious feeling when she's in need of a fix. Soon, it will be too late. She needs to get out of here, wherever she is, and score. Where is Jimmy, where is he?

She tries to sit up, but that makes all the faces agitated. 'Whoa there, hold on, hon. You just lie back and let us take care of you, OK?'

There are hands all over her body, on her arms, her stomach, her legs – dozens and dozens of hands pushing her, holding her down. All she wants is to get away from the hands, to not be touched anymore. She tries to roll away from the hands and then she is writhing, thrashing around, screaming and crying, *get off me, get off me, don't touch me.* A sudden urgent need for her grandmother comes over her, and she calls out for Alice, even though she is aware somewhere in the back of her mind that she has been dead for almost four years. 'Nanny,' she yells. 'Nanny, Nanny, help me. Make them stop, Nanny. Make them stop.'

Then there is just one face, one angry face, telling her that she needs to calm down, that they are just trying to help her, but they can't if she keeps yelling and moving around. 'Try to just relax, OK, and let us take care of you,' the angry face says to her.

Marnie swallows. She is frightened and closes her eyes, hoping, somehow, they will disappear. All of the faces and voices. She hears the words *detox bed* and *rehab* and *can we at least get her name?*

She feels so sleepy, and tries one last time to say Marnie, but her tongue is even thicker than before. 'Mffff,' she says before passing out again.

When Marnie opens her eyes again, she is in a hospital bed with a plastic curtain pulled all the way around. She squints in the bright fluorescent light. It smells of ammonia and urine and the noises are no longer muffled. Instead, the whoosh and beep of machines seems extra loud and she covers her ears. But still, the sounds are overwhelming, and she can hear someone screaming, a baby crying, a little girl calling out frantically for '*Mommy*'. It's as though thousands of people are all talking at once.

All Marnie wants is a fix. She has no idea where exactly she is, what time it is, if it's day or night. Even though she barely has enough energy to sit up, she manages to get herself out of the bed. The large windowless emergency room is filled with people lying in beds, some with plastic curtains around them and some without. Someone throws up on the floor. She has to get out of here. If she felt stronger, she would run, but instead she can only hobble, grabbing hold of bed frames and chairs and the wall to keep herself from falling over. Finally, she makes it to the sliding glass doors that lead to the outside world. She keeps walking and walking, even though it's so bright and loud. Then she sees a payphone and sits in front of it, begging for change, until she has enough to make some calls. Her hands tremble as she starts dialling. Finally, she finds him. 'Come get me. Quick. I need you,' she says to Jimmy. 'I need to get out of here.' Even though she has no idea where *here* is.

27

Month of Mondays

1993

THE BRIEF MOMENT WHEN Sonny first wakes up is the only good moment of his entire day. That very beginning of coming into consciousness, yet still remaining in a dream state when his thoughts are free, loose, and he's able to wander around the few happy times in his life. It's then that his memories are the most vivid – so much so that it seems all he has to do is open his eyes and he will be transported back in time.

This morning, Sonny awakens thinking of Davie in Alaska. As if he saw the little boy just yesterday, instead of ten years ago. Davie, still eight, still in his footsie pyjamas, slurping Lucky Charms out of his Tony the Tiger cereal bowl at the end of the pull-out couch, watching television. Exactly how he was when Sonny met him that very first morning on Geena's houseboat.

Sonny keeps his eyes closed to linger in the memory a little longer, marinate in it, hoping to draw it out as long as possible. He can almost smell the mix of gasoline, salt water and fish that permeates the docks, see the orangey haze of the sun rising, like it was coming out of the bay.

It was a July morning when he first met Davie. Sonny had woken sprawled out on his stomach, completely naked, unsure at first where he was and how he had come to be on this pull-out couch, in a tangle of blankets and sheets.

'Do you like Pat Sajak?' A little boy was sitting cross-legged at the end of the mattress, watching television. He was thin, so thin, almost sickly-looking, with light brown hair matted on the left side of his head as if it had been a long time since it had been anywhere near shampoo, water or a comb.

Startled by the presence of the boy, Sonny grabbed one of the blankets and covered himself with it. His head felt like it would split open, and his stomach lurched as the tiny room tilted slightly. It was only then that he realised he was on a houseboat, floating on water.

The last thing he remembered from the night before was being at a bar with a woman. He thought for a minute before her name came to him.

'Where's Geena?' Sonny asked the boy.

'Mom's at the grocery store. She's going to make us pancakes. Neal doesn't like him.'

'Doesn't like who?'

'Pat Sajak. Says he's a phony.' The boy stared at the television.

'Who's Neal?' Sonny scanned the place for signs of another man who might suddenly explode into the room.

'Mom's friend. Neal sleeps over too, sometimes, but he doesn't snore as much as you do. Mom only makes pancakes when Neal is here. So do you like Pat Sajak?'

Sonny squinted in the bright morning sunshine. The mattress took up most of the room. There was a narrow passageway that led down to the galley kitchen on one side of the room, and on the other was a ladder to the below deck area, where Sonny could see another mattress. He just wanted to take a leak, have a drink of water, and get out of there as quickly as possible. Certainly before Geena returned. Even though he didn't really have anywhere to go – he was living in his car at the time. There was nothing Sonny hated more at that point in his life than the awkward morning-after routine with women, and he always made a point to avoid it, mumbling excuses if he ended up falling asleep with them. The last thing he felt capable of doing right then was eating pancakes with this Geena and her son.

But the kid was blocking the way to his jeans, which were in a heap on the floor, as if he had vaulted out of them. It had been a while since he last got laid.

'Hey, could you give me a sec?' he said to the kid.

The kid looked at Sonny, as if taking him in for the first time. 'What do you mean?'

'Can I, like, have some privacy so I can get dressed? Would that be OK with you?'

'But my show is on.' The kid looked back over at the television and resumed his slurping. 'And besides, I'm too tired to move. And besides, you never answered my question. Do you like Pat Sajak? Or do you think he's a phony?'

'Seems kinda phony, I suppose.'

'He's not a phony!' The kid stood up on the mattress and turned to face Sonny. 'That's what stupid Neal always says. I was hoping you'd be better!'

'That's what everyone hopes,' Sonny said. There was a pack of Camels on a shelf behind the couch. He lit one up and tried to piece together the previous evening while the boy fiddled with the antenna on top of the TV, trying to fix the signal, before resuming his position at the end of the mattress.

Sonny had only been in town for a few weeks, but already he was a fixture in the bar by the harbour, the Month of Mondays, which everyone just called Mondays. When the fishing boats returned after being out at sea for weeks at a time, the place filled up with fishermen flush with cash and the need to get drunk and have sex. As soon as possible. The previous night, Sonny happened to be sitting on a bar stool next to Geena when someone bought a round of tequila shots for everyone. They clinked glasses before downing them.

'I don't even know how long I've been here.' Geena giggled after introducing herself. Her black mascara and purple eyeliner were already streaked, and a gold cross pointed towards cleavage. Red lipstick highlighted a full mouth.

'I've never left,' Sonny said, which made her laugh so hard she started coughing and had to spit into a cocktail napkin.

They settled into a conversation while Geena kept pulling her long curly hair back and tying and re-tying it into a bun on top of her head. They soon discovered they were both recent arrivals. Geena had come up from Portland for the summer because her friends needed someone to look after their houseboat. She had just split up with her husband and was trying a new scene, she explained, which seemed like what she and her little boy needed before Davie went back to school in September.

Sonny provided her with a slightly amended version of his recent history, leaving out prison stints in Colorado and Nebraska for assault and drunk driving. He also didn't see the need to mention that he had nowhere to live. Instead, he told Geena that he'd been travelling around for a while, working on shrimp fishing boats in Louisiana, picking fruit with migrants in the San Joaquin Valley, helping out on a marijuana farm in La Honda just west of San José. Then he landed a job in a cardboard box factory in Seattle. It was there that he'd heard about the canneries in Alaska and how much money you could make – serious money, in the summer months when the sun hardly set.

'I'm still waiting to see the serious money,' Sonny said. 'Still waiting.'

'Oh God, yeah,' Geena agreed.

Sonny was just finishing his cigarette and thinking about leaving the houseboat when Geena came back from the grocery store, balancing brown paper bags in her arms. She ordered Sonny and the kid around while she made pancakes with bananas. The kid – Davie – liked his with peanut butter spread thickly on top, and it turned out Geena was pretty fun, even in daylight. Breakfast quickly turned into afternoon beers on the dock with her neighbours joining in. It was a beautiful day, and at one point during the long afternoon a whale swam into the harbour. Sonny ended up staying on into the next morning, and then the next one, and the one after that.

Before long, he was at Geena's houseboat most nights, after lengthy sessions at Mondays or partying on the docks. He found an unused hunting cabin on the edge of town where he could keep his stuff, but he hardly ever stayed there.

They settled into a routine. Most mornings, Geena got up at five to wait tables at the greasy spoon by the harbour, and when she returned in the early afternoon, Sonny would make the rounds along the wharf, looking to see if anyone needed a handyman for a small, easy job. He painted a tugboat, cleaned and gutted fish, filled in for the maintenance guys when someone was off sick? Davie hung out with the other kids who lived along the docks after a morning spent in his footsie pyjamas with Sonny watching *Wheel of Fortune*, slurping his Lucky Charms. Now, though, instead of sitting at the edge of the mattress, he was right next to Sonny, in the place Geena had been, and they both leaned back against the pillows. Sonny smoked and Davie drank 'coffee', heated-up milk with a sprinkling of Sanka, which he fixed the boy each morning while they chatted and watched TV together.

Davie often talked about all the places his father was going to take him: the Grand Canyon, a World Series game, Washington, D.C. to see the White House, the NASA space camp. Geena said they didn't even have a working phone number for Davie's dad, he was late on his child support payment, and that he'd only called Davie once the whole time they'd been up here.

'My dad says he's going to take me to Disney World,' Davie said one morning. 'In the winter.'

'Well, how about that?' Sonny replied. He had told his daughter the same thing, but he never did take her.

'Did your dad ever take you to Disney?' Davie asked.

'Nope. He sure didn't. You're pretty lucky.'

'How about your mom? Did she take you there?'

Sonny shook his head, and Davie thought this was one of the worst things he'd ever heard. 'How come she didn't take you, if your dad wouldn't?'

'Well, for one thing ...' Sonny thought for a minute. He didn't like talking about personal things with anyone, especially a young boy. 'She was from England.' He hoped that would be enough of an explanation to end the questioning about his parents.

Davie turned away from the television. Geena's aunt was tracing their family history, and sending letters to her and Davie with regular updates. He was fascinated by trying to figure out how his family ended up in Portland. 'How did your parents get to America? Did they come on the *Mayflower*?'

'Come on, I'm not that old.'

'So, how did they get here?'

'My mom took a boat, but not the *Mayflower*.'

'What about your dad?'

'He died before I was born. In England.' This is what Alice had told him when he was little. But as he got older, he wasn't sure if it was true or not. She hated talking about him. The most trivial questions – even what his name was – would send her into a foul mood for hours. He learned to avoid the subject, but it meant he really knew nothing about his father.

'Wow.' Davie thought about this for a minute. 'Do you miss him?'

'I never met him, so, no. You can't miss what you don't know.'

'I'd miss my dad if he died,' Davie said. 'I miss him now.'

The boy looked so sad all of a sudden, and Sonny knew he should say something comforting, but what, he didn't know. When Geena came home, Davie reported everything about Sonny's parents. He had even more questions about the boat that his mother came on. Was it big? Was it the *Titanic*, if it wasn't the *Mayflower*? How long did it take? The questions came faster and faster until Geena shouted at him to *cut it out, just cut it out, Davie.*

A few days later another letter from Geena's aunt arrived. 'Davie, check it out. Aunt Joyce says we're related to the people who found dinosaur bones in Utah. And now those bones are in a museum in New York City. How about that?'

'I need to see the dinosaur!' Davie jumped up and down. 'Will you take me, please, please, please? We could all go. All three of us.'

Sonny was really falling for the kid, even more than Geena. So when she asked him, one night towards the end of the summer, if he wanted to go with them back to Portland, he quickly agreed.

But a few days before they were supposed to leave, Sonny and Geena had a fight early one morning. And then he did something he hadn't done in a long time: he hit her. As soon as his fist made contact with her face, he wished more than anything he could take it back. At least Davie was still asleep in his bed down in the lower level of the boat. Geena held her cheek and told him that when she got back from work, he needed to be gone.

'Look, I'm sorry,' he said. 'I didn't mean to do that. I just—'

'Well, you did. We're leaving anyway. So let's just call it what it is – a summer thing. Nobody hits me.'

After she left, Sonny drifted off and when he woke up, Davie was staring at him.

'What is it?' Sonny asked him.

'I was wondering if I could tell.' The boy looked like he was concentrating especially hard.

'Tell what?'

'What you dream about?'

Later on in the morning, as Sonny was getting ready to leave, he couldn't figure out how to tell the kid that he wasn't going with them to Portland after all, that they probably wouldn't see each other again. Instead, he mumbled a vague excuse about needing to go take care of some things, and that was it. When he turned around to have one last look at Davie, he was sitting on the pull-out bed, in the same place he'd been on that first morning.

Maybe Sonny could still be with Davie. If only he knew how to control his anger, keep his hands from turning into weapons. But he never learned how to do those things. Instead, he went on to do even worse.

Soon, he'll have to leave his memories of Davie, and hope that maybe more will return tomorrow morning, or the next one. The only good ones he has left of anyone. When he thinks of his own daughter, who he has not seen or even spoken to in years and years, his chest constricts and he feels sick to his stomach, so he tries to push the image of her away.

There is only a small window of time left to linger with Davie. Any minute now, the guards will shout 'movement' and he'll have to get out of his narrow bunk, put on his orange jumpsuit, blend into the long line of men as they are marched along the hallway. His past, his regrets, his dreams, his stories invisible, and his only unique characteristic, the only thing that sets him apart from all the other men, is the serial number on his right front pocket.

28

Apparent Junction of Earth and Sky

1996

THICK GREY CLOUDS HOVER on the horizon and snow seems possible later on as Marnie and Uncle Mike head east on the Mass Pike. She has been on this stretch of the highway so many times, every part of it is familiar: every rest stop and landmark and exit. Except this raw feeling. She has just finished yet another stint in rehab; three months of in-patient care followed by another four months in a sober living home. It's dark by the time they arrive at Uncle Mike's house, and he warns her to be careful when she gets out of the car because the driveway is slick with ice. He carries her duffel bag, and she follows behind.

When they get inside, her uncle flips on the kitchen lights. The sink is full of dirty dishes. Empty pizza boxes are stacked on the stove, and the table in the breakfast nook is covered with McDonald's and Burger King bags, empty French fry boxes and soda cups. Plastic two-litre bottles of Diet Cokes, Dunkin' Donuts coffee cups and Budweiser cans are on top of all the counters. The Mr. Coffee is filled halfway with green sludge.

'I know, I know,' Uncle Mike says. 'This is really bad. I was going to clean before I came to pick you up, but I just . . . I don't know how to explain it. I just never have the energy. I'm sorry.' His neighbours dropped off frozen dinners in the weeks following Cath's funeral, which was in the fall, but he had no appetite, he tells Marnie. And he knew they meant well, but it was too painful when they kept checking up on him. Eventually, he asked his son, Sean, if he could please let everyone know how much he appreciated their concerns, but he wanted to be left alone. Since then, no one has been over. Sean and his wife live less than an hour away, but Mike makes excuses every time he offers to drop by. And Teresa is all the way out in San Francisco, busy with her residency programme in family and community medicine. Although Patrick did come to the funeral, he still isn't speaking to his father. 'You're the first person to set foot in here in like . . . I don't even know how long.'

Lucky me, Marnie thinks as she looks around. The rest of the house is no better. The dining room table is covered in unopened mail and stacks of newspapers and magazines and flyers. Tumbleweeds of dust swirl around on the floor. There are yet more Budweiser cans and Diet Coke bottles and empty coffee cups on either side of Mike's orange easy chair in the living room. Every single one of Cath's plants is dead, and there are brown rotting leaves in piles on the floor underneath them.

Uncle Mike asks if Marnie is hungry, but all she wants to do is lie down. She thanks him for the ride and goes straight up to Sean and Patrick's old room and climbs, fully clothed, into bed. She concentrates on her breathing, like she has been practising for months now, trying to quiet her rising panic. How will she be able to stay sober in this disgusting house with her depressed uncle? In addition to losing Cath in the fall, her uncle was also made redundant. After working as a general contractor for most of his career, he had taken an office job with a large construction company a few years ago, as a project manager. But his department was downsized last year and most of the project managers were let go, including Mike. He insists he prefers working for himself and that he still has plenty of customers, but Teresa is worried about him, she tells Marnie whenever they talk on the phone. Her cousin has made it a point to call her more often, ever since Marnie started trying to get sober yet again at the end of last summer.

After a while, Marnie manages to fall asleep, but only briefly. She jolts awake, her body slick with sweat. Downstairs, she can hear the television. She brushes her teeth, changes into a T-shirt and gets back into bed. But the rest of the night isn't much better, and once it's finally morning, she isn't certain if she has slept at all.

The house is quiet and still. Uncle Mike has slipped a note under the bedroom door explaining that he'll be back at nine. In an hour. Then he is going to take her to an NA meeting and, after that, to a therapy appointment. The next few days will be the same, and on Monday, she starts working in the front office at Evergreen Way Veterinarians, which Mike arranged through friends.

Marnie has not been alone, unsupervised, in a very long time. Cath's car is in the garage, the keys on the hook in the kitchen. Marnie could drive to the payphones by the commuter rail station, where the dealers hang out, and score before her uncle has even returned.

He was the one who found a good lawyer for Marnie when she'd been arrested after Jimmy shot the cashier at Sinclair's Pharmacy. Although it was a minor leg wound and all Marnie had done was wait in the car, she was facing significant charges for being an accomplice to an armed robbery. But Jimmy already had a record, and Marnie agreed to provide evidence against him in exchange for rehab instead of prison. She relapsed as soon as she finished court-ordered treatment and cycled in and out of facilities. After Jimmy died of an overdose in prison, she knew if she didn't find a way to stay sober, she wouldn't survive either. This last time, she had checked herself into a treatment centre for longer and then made sure to follow it up with outpatient care.

Marnie pads down the stairs, past all the family photographs lining the wall, and stops by the portrait of Aunt Cath. It was taken before she got cancer and lost all her hair. She is smiling in the picture, her piercing grey-blue eyes looking directly at the camera. Marnie runs her fingertips along the glass, over the image of Cath's thick hair.

She wanders through the house, feeling the remnants of her past and the different stages of her life. In Teresa's attic bedroom, she finds the two Sasha dolls they used to play with when they were little in a plastic box in her closet, along with the red trunk with a mirror on the inside filled with doll clothing that Cath and her sisters made for Teresa, and the wooden dollhouse. Her bedroom walls look the same as they did when she was in high school; the photo collage of her friends is still above the desk along with the posters of Van Halen, Madonna, Led Zeppelin and U2 on the walls. The main bathroom on the second floor has the same rug she got blood on when she lost her first tooth, and some red stains on the tiles left over from when she and her cousins dyed their hair. Despite the clutter in the living room, she can still picture it at Christmas time, with a tree in the far corner and stockings hung by the fireplace. She remembers sitting on her mother's lap when she must have been about seven and opening up a paint set.

Her mother sent her a plane ticket to come down to Florida for Christmas one year, back when she was with Jimmy. But she'd sold it and used the money for drugs instead. Denise had flown up with Charlie when she'd been arrested, but Marnie wouldn't talk to her. She was still angry with her mother for moving away just a few months after Alice died, for leaving her with nowhere to go except Dolly's motel, for everything. When she was in treatment, her therapist urged her to work on forgiveness, explaining that it was hard to ever truly feel OK when you were holding on to that much anger. And Uncle Mike always passes on messages from her mother, saying yet again, how much she'd love to hear from Marnie.

She walks a circle around the oval dining room table, stands for a while in the middle of the basement rec room. In the backyard, the tyre swing is still hanging, as well as the now partially rotted swing set, but the tree house is long gone.

Her grandmother rarely came up here. She said the house was too cold, too busy, and besides, she didn't want to impose. Marnie is certain they must have both been in this house at the same time, but she can't come up with a memory of it.

Her grandmother had carefully put away money year after year for Marnie's college education, she'd explained to Uncle Mike when she was dying. She had transferred her savings account to him, but he had to dip into it to pay for his niece's lawyer and rehab. But there is still some money left, he'd told Marnie, and while it's hers to do with whatever she wants, she should know that Alice had intended it for college. It had been Alice's dream, he reminds her now and then. It was once Marnie's dream, too. What would her grandmother think of her now – of what she's done, what she's become? Alice always told Marnie that the most important thing was to at least try your hardest. If she gets in Cath's car and drives to the commuter rail station and scores, she'll be letting her grandmother down even more, and she won't be able to face herself later on. Marnie waits for Uncle Mike to come home and goes to her appointments instead. She guesses that's progress of some sort.

Once she starts at the vet's office, the days are a little easier to get through. Her time is organised around the same specific tasks at work, which she finds reassuring. In the mornings, Marnie gets the patient charts ready, and then files them away after each appointment. She helps Veronica, the receptionist, deal with the mounds of paperwork that dominate the front desk, answers the phone when Veronica has her lunch break or uses the bathroom.

Veronica listens intently when people talk to her about their pets, and never says anything snarky about them after the conversation is over. Even the woman who came in, crying hysterically, with her cat after he'd swallowed a Q-Tip. When she's not on the phone or dealing with people waiting in the reception area, Veronica talks to Marnie about her thirteen-year-old daughter who just got her period and has a crush on a boy, or her ex and the details of their divorce and the custody arrangements. She ends each of her sentences with a giggle.

After work, Marnie goes to meetings, and then straight home to watch television and eat takeout in the living room with Uncle Mike. He cries quietly to himself throughout the evening and usually falls asleep right there, in his chair. Marnie covers him with a blanket before going up to bed. He hardly ever seems to make it upstairs.

One night, Uncle Mike reminds Marnie that it's her mother's birthday in a few days' time. 'Hate to sound like a broken record here, but you know your mom would love a phone call more than anything, Marn.'

Marnie closes her eyes and doesn't say anything.

'I'm sorry,' he says. 'I shouldn't have said that. I should stay out of it.'

It's OK, she tells him, but maybe they should make a deal: she'll call her mother if he calls Patrick.

'Touché, Marn.' He tears up and wipes at his face.

'Now it's my turn,' Marnie says. 'Sorry.'

'Wow, we're having a little moment here, aren't we? But you're right. You're absolutely right. I just don't know what to say to him, I really don't. So how 'bout it, then? If I call him, you'll call her?' He reaches a hand towards her. 'Pinkie swear?'

'Pinkie swear,' she repeats, and they intertwine fingers.

When the weather is warmer, Marnie goes for a run before work. She crosses off the passing weeks on her calendar. As long as nothing new or unexpected happens, she can get through the days. But even a slight deviation makes her feel panicked, and any change in the routine is overwhelming. When her uncle mentions that Sean might come by with his wife and kids over the weekend, she feels all the blood drain from her face. But he can tell without her having to say anything. 'No, you're right. We're not ready for that.'

One Friday afternoon in June, just as the last patient is leaving with their pet, and Marnie is preparing to go home, Veronica takes a call from a woman whose family dog is failing.

'I hate ending the week like this,' Veronica says when she hangs up, then pages the vet to tell him. She asks Marnie if she wouldn't mind staying a little later to help her close up after the vet has put the dog to sleep.

When the family arrive – an older couple with their two adult daughters, carrying a cocker spaniel – Veronica gets up from behind the reception desk and embraces the three women, who are all crying. The father has his hands placed gently on his daughters' backs as he ushers them towards the examination room.

'This is the worst part of the job,' Veronica says once the vet is in with them. 'Makes me so sad. I know it's just part of having a pet, part of life, but I hate it. Just hate it. Now what was I just doing?' She turns her attention back to putting stamps on a stack of appointment reminders.

Marnie is overcome with sadness and starts to weep, hoping Veronica doesn't notice. She tries to stifle her sobs, but it makes her cough, and Veronica asks if she's OK.

'I'm fine,' she says, before getting up and going into the bathroom. She sits on the lid of the toilet and tries all her relaxation techniques – deep breathing, visualisations, repeating positive mantras – but none of it works. If anything, it makes her cry even harder – so hard, in fact, that she starts to hyperventilate. She tries splashing water on her face, which helps for a moment, and she thinks she is calm enough to go back out. But then she just starts crying all over again. Five minutes turn into ten, and then almost twenty, until Veronica is knocking on the door, telling her that she's about to leave.

Once she's in her car, Marnie cries so hard that it's impossible to get through the late afternoon commuter traffic, so she pulls into a shopping centre. She should go to a meeting, but she doesn't want to listen to other people's struggles right now. She cries and cries, trying to think of where she can go to feel better. Is there anything she can do to get rid of this ugliness that has settled inside her? She just knows that there is no way she can endure another night of takeout and watching television with Uncle Mike in the filthy living room. And then it comes to her.

There's a Star Market in the shopping centre and Marnie parks her car and goes inside, heading straight for the cleaning supplies aisle. Then she goes to the CVS next door and buys a drawing pad and a package of coloured pencils.

When she gets home, Marnie rifles through the pile of CDs by the stereo until she comes across *Purple Rain*, turns it up loud and gets to work. First, she opens all the downstairs windows before tackling the living room. She fills several garbage bags with the takeout containers and coffee cups, dead plants, crumpled napkins and Kleenex. She rinses out all the Diet Cokes and Budweiser cans lined up by Uncle Mike's easy chair, clears out the pizza boxes of crusts and greasy waxed paper and puts everything in the recycling bin. She sorts through the mail, taking out the catalogues and flyers and junk mail, and puts the bills in a neat pile. She drags the vacuum cleaner into the living room and hoovers the rug, the floor, the corners, the couch, underneath the cushions and Mike's chair. Next up is the kitchen. She takes all the dirty dishes and cups and silverware that are in the sink and on the counter and puts them in the dishwasher, washes the pots and knives by hand, and arranges them to dry on the dish rack. She dumps the green sludge in the coffee pot into the garbage, before washing it out three times. She goes through the refrigerator and throws out all the mouldy food, pours out expired milk, which thunks when it hits the drain. She gets a bucket and fills it with hot soapy water and wipes down the inside of the refrigerator, the kitchen counters, the stove top, the microwave, the table in the breakfast nook and the dining room table. Then she sweeps the kitchen and sponges the floors on her hands and knees. She goes through the upstairs and downstairs bathrooms, collecting the dirty towels and the bath mat, and takes them down to the washing machine in the basement. She scrubs the bathtub in the upstairs bathroom, the sinks, and closes her eyes while she swirls a brush around the toilet basins.

She cuts some flowers from the backyard and puts them in a vase, and sits down to sketch them until Uncle Mike gets home.

That night, they feel like celebrating the clean house, so Uncle Mike grills some fish and they eat on the patio. When they are finished with dinner, they stay outside instead of heading straight for the television.

There is an almost full moon and it's such a clear night, both the Big Dipper and the Milky Way are visible. At one point, they see a shooting star. A tiny speck from the 200 billion stars inside a barred spiral galaxy, constantly rotating, always changing and shifting, in perpetual motion since time itself began. Unable to remain the same.

The following week, Uncle Mike calls Patrick. He tells Marnie that they talked for an hour, and he's going down to New York to see him and finally meet Devin. 'No way I would have had the courage to have done this without you, Marn. Would have been too scared. I might have missed my chance, without you. Don't miss yours. Your mother, Marn. She's right there, waiting for you.'

29

The Aftermath

1997

MARNIE IS IN THE back of the bar, cradling her left wrist. The man who just threw her onto the floor is being escorted out by the bartender. Two guys from the bar are helping him. They had been watching a NCAA Final Four game until the man started slapping his girlfriend around and Marnie tried to intervene.

'Oh, honey, thank you,' the girlfriend now says to Marnie. 'I can't believe you did that for me.' She is picking up the chairs that got knocked over during the altercation.

They had been just a drunk couple in a quiet bar on a Saturday afternoon, kidding around and pawing at each other, when Marnie passed them on her way to the toilets. But something happened between them in the few minutes she was in there, because by the time Marnie came out, the man was screaming at his girlfriend. He slapped her and she pushed him. He took a swing at her face and she lost her balance, ended up sprawled out on the floor. That's when Marnie got involved, trying to pull him away before he started kicking his girlfriend. He pushed Marnie hard and she went flying backwards onto a chair, and then fell right on her wrist. There had been a crunching sound when she landed on it.

'I was going to marry him,' the woman says to Marnie. 'Can you believe it?'

Marnie smiles at her. 'You should see some of the guys I used to go out with.'

The woman laughs and offers to buy Marnie a drink.

'I'm good, thanks, though,' Marnie says.

She had been reluctant when Veronica insisted Marnie come to her birthday party in a bar. When Marnie discussed the invitation with her therapist, she suggested that Marnie only go briefly. She could always leave if she felt uncomfortable, or tempted by all the booze. She thought Marnie was ready, though; she was making steady progress – so much so that she had moved into her own apartment. And besides, this was part of the goal: to be able to attend social gatherings without drugs or alcohol. Veronica said they'd be at the bar only until four because her mother was hosting a family party afterwards. So Marnie figured she could handle about half an hour, made up an excuse about something she had to do and could only stop by towards the end of the gathering. Veronica and her friends had left before the fight happened.

'Rosie, you want me to call your sister for you?' The bartender comes to help the woman pick up the overturned table. Then he puts his arm around her and helps her to a seat at the bar.

One of the guys who had been watching the basketball game returns to his stool and resumes his focus on the TV. But the other one heads towards Marnie and asks her if she's OK.

'Not sure,' Marnie says. 'My wrist hurts.' She rolls up her sleeve to have a look.

'Shots on the house. Kevin, you want one, right, dude?' the bartender says to the man by Marnie's side. 'And, miss, can I get you a shot? Or something?'

'I'm good, thank you,' Marnie says to the bartender. 'Fuck, this better not be broken. That's the last thing I need.'

'My mom's a nurse,' Kevin tells her. 'I was like a skateboarding freak when I was a kid and I was always getting hurt and she used to say, "If you can move it, it's not broken." Try squeezing my arm.' He offers her his left forearm.

Marnie grasps hold of it, and when she lets go, he shakes it in mock pain. 'Whoa, you got a killer grip there.' He smiles at her. 'Think you're OK. You should put ice on it, though. Stay here and I'll go get you some. And that shot.'

'Thanks, but not the shot. I can't do a shot.'

'Sure you can, you were just in a bar fight. Shots are in definite order.'

'No, I mean, I don't drink. I can't drink.'

Something passes across Kevin's face as he registers what she has just said. 'Got it.' When he returns with a bag of ice wrapped in a dish towel and carefully arranges it on Marnie's wrist, his touch sends a shiver right through her.

Rosie's sister arrives shortly after and consoles her in a corner of the bar. It's the last ten minutes of the game, and the bartender and Kevin's friend are shouting at the TV. Kevin tells Marnie that he and his buddy, Robbie, only came to this bar because it was one of the few in the area that wouldn't be crowded even when a Final Four game was on. 'And for some reason, it's Robbie's favourite bar. I don't know why. Every time we come here, there is this kind of shit going on. I hate this place,' he says quietly. 'But I don't want to hurt the guy's feelings. He's my best friend, so let's just keep that between us.'

'We're good as long as you don't tell anyone I was in a bar fight.' Marnie smiles at him.

'Deal.'

'I don't usually do that, by the way,' she says.

'I wouldn't have thought so.'

Marnie wants to keep talking to this nice, good-looking man, but she feels the clock embedded in her head ticking down and doesn't want to push things. So she excuses herself, says she'd better get home, and is relieved when he looks disappointed and asks for her number.

'I know you,' Marnie says when Kevin calls her the next morning.

She had woken up, made coffee and looked out the window for a while. Her wrist still hurt, but what was bothering her more was Kevin. She'd met him before, she was certain of it. Then she figured it out.

'You grew up on Wilson Street, right?' she says to him. 'Weren't you friends with Patrick and Sean? I'm their cousin.'

'Holy shit!' he says after a long pause. 'You're that Marnie?'

'I'm that Marnie.'

'Wow, that's crazy,' he says. 'So, how you been? Since then?' They both laugh. 'How are they all, anyway? My parents split up and we moved away with my mom when I was in high school and I kinda lost track of them. Wow, that house! I can like smell that house right now. Maple syrup and bacon mixed together.'

'Right?' Marnie is lying on the couch with her wrist propped up on a pillow while they reminisce about sledding in Elm Park, watching Red Sox games with her uncle and how crazy insane they made him, the Thanksgiving Leftovers Open House that one of the neighbours used to have, which seemed to always give someone food poisoning. It turns out Kevin's family went to the Cape with Marnie's cousins the first time she went along with them.

An hour goes by. Then another and another. She tells him about her grandmother dying and Jimmy and rehab. He tells her how his father left when he was fourteen and his mother started drinking heavily, got fired and they went to live with her sister. His mother got sober after she had a heart attack.

Over the next months, they will introduce each other to their friends and family. Marnie will meet Kevin's entire extended family at a wedding in June. Over the 4th of July holiday weekend, they'll go with his buddy, Robbie, to western Massachusetts to help out at the sheriff's picnic that Robbie's family always hosts. In August, it will be a camping trip in upstate New York, where they climb several mountains and see a bear and bald eagles.

It's getting dark by the time Marnie and Kevin notice that they should probably try to do something with what is left of their Sunday. After they hang up, Marnie sits for a minute and she knows. She knows something new is happening. Something good.

30

Descending Lines

1999

MARNIE SITS ON THE floor in her uncle's living room, her back against the wall. The room is filled with cardboard boxes that Gentle Giant Movers will take tomorrow, along with the rest of Uncle Mike's belongings, to his new home on the North Shore. The past month, Marnie and Kevin have been helping Uncle Mike sort through everything he and Cath accumulated during the thirty years they lived in the house.

Teresa is beside Marnie on the floor, packing up old children's books. Marnie and Kevin's baby is due in six weeks, so Marnie isn't supposed to do anything except make decisions and hold masking tape in place on the packing boxes, her doctor says.

Last week, Marnie kept Teresa company while she took down everything on her bedroom walls – the posters and the photo collages – before scrubbing off the marks they left behind, and vacuumed and mopped the floors. When she was done, there was nothing left, no trace of anything to indicate the years of Teresa's life spent in her attic bedroom. She said Marnie could keep hold of her dollhouse, 'for now. Until it's my turn.' She moved to Boston with her boyfriend after she got a job at Mass General last year. Teresa took all the board games from the basement rec room, as well as the fraying orange couch and the beanbag chairs, the entire collection of juice glasses with cartoon characters on them, and the upright piano.

Sean's wife carefully monitored all his choices, after he suggested dismantling the swing set and putting it back up in their yard. That idea was quickly vetoed. She did allow some toys, including the Big Wheel that had been in the garage for almost two decades, but only after cleaning it with bleach and boiling water. He could take his sports trophies, his Little League glove, but not the fondue set or an old popcorn maker. Patrick came up from New York with Devin to claim the family pictures lining the staircase, the photo albums, slides, old letters, and anything else related to family history. Uncle Mike is keeping most of the furniture from his bedroom, including the stuff from his home office, the sofa from the living room and his orange easy chair and the ottoman, as well as the kitchen table.

Marnie and Kevin took the dining room table and the chairs, a crib, a high chair, a changing table and a rocking chair. They moved to Dartmouth last year after Kevin got a job teaching science at a middle school, and he's spent his summer break fixing up the small second bedroom for the baby. Marnie is volunteering at a drug treatment facility in Fall River, going to college and training to be an art therapist.

It's been a hot summer, and Kevin makes sure to have the AC on in the car before Marnie gets in. Whenever they go anywhere, he brings along the small cooler bag filled with ice-cold water, sliced fruit, crackers, plus a cold cloth in case she feels too hot. 'Think Kev's even more excited about this baby than anyone I've ever known,' his mother keeps saying. His mother is his first call after every monthly check-up with the obstetrician, keeping her updated on how the foetus is developing. She's already booked time off work to help them out after the baby is born.

Denise sent Marnie a package with a strange knitted object. She'd been trying to make a blanket, but she was pretty hopeless at it. Maybe they could use it as a baby scarf, she suggested. 'You know I'm crap with crafts,' she wrote in her note. 'Kevin's mom is probably good at all that kind of stuff.' She is hoping to come up to meet the baby sometime in the fall with Charlie, she's just not sure exactly when.

Uncle Mike is on his hands and knees around the back of the TV, untangling all the wires and cable cords. It's the last of his things that needs to be packed. Otherwise, everything else is ready.

'Oh, you're not going to believe what I just found,' he announces, holding up a piece of glass. 'Look at this,' he says to Marnie and Teresa.

'A broken piece of glass?' Teresa says. 'Yeah? And?'

'This is no ordinary piece of glass. You see what it says there?' He brings it closer to them so they can read the lettering etched into the glass.

'Sip?' Teresa says. She glances at Marnie, as if to say, *see, he is losing his shit.* She's been worrying to Marnie that although she thinks the move is a good idea, it's making him act a little crazy.

'It's from Cath's favourite wine glass. See how this piece is tinted blue and thick?' He goes on to explain how it had *Sip Happens* written on it. 'You know how she liked a pun and corny sayings,' he says. She had thrown the glass against the wall during the '86 World Series, when the ball went between Bill Buckner's legs in Game Six. 'This is from that glass. I know it. What are the chances that I would find it? And today, of all days.'

'Dad, is there anything that happens to you that's not somehow connected to the Red Sox?' Teresa smiles at him and then gives Marnie another look – one of relief. That wasn't *so* crazy, she seems to be saying.

'Very funny.' Uncle Mike shakes his head. 'I'm definitely keeping this though.' Teresa tells him to at least wrap the piece of glass in something so he doesn't cut himself.

'Can you help me with this TV, or should I ask one of the boys?' her father says to Teresa. Her boyfriend and Kevin are emptying the kitchen of all the dishes and cookware that Uncle Mike isn't taking with him, and a truck from Goodwill is scheduled to arrive soon to take away the last of the unclaimed items: four beds, a desk, bookshelves, a small sofa, boxes of dishes, ice skates, sleds, an air conditioner, a chainsaw, sleeping bags and a tent, beach chairs, a desk, two bicycles and a lawn mower.

'Oh, please.' Teresa gets up from the floor to help her father. They each take one side and lift the television off the console, carry it over to a cardboard box and ease it in. They pack the box with rolled-up balls of newspaper before sealing it. Then Teresa finishes packing up the last of the children's books for Marnie.

Uncle Mike looks around the room, takes a seat on the sofa, and starts stroking his chin.

'Dad, you OK?' Teresa asks.

'Did you guys have fun last night?' he says. 'I really wanted to have one last good party.'

Teresa's boyfriend and Kevin had helped him grill hamburgers and hot dogs. Teresa and Marnie prepared a bunch of salads. Sean and his wife took care of the corn on the cob and made pitchers of vodka lemonade. Patrick and Devin brought dessert. Neighbours drifted in and out throughout the evening, and several stayed on to help clean it all up.

'It was perfect, Dad. It really was,' Teresa says and Marnie hums in agreement. 'The perfect last party.'

The Goodwill truck pulls up in front of the house. Uncle Mike has been dreading seeing his possessions being taken away, and Teresa offers to go deal with it. 'Look after him,' she mouths to Marnie.

Marnie sits next to her uncle on the sofa and rests her head on his shoulder. He holds up the piece of glass and the sun hits it, sparkling light across the wood floor. 'Someone else would have just thrown this out. Lucky I found it. Cath would have got such a kick out of this, she really would have.'

'She would have made you throw it away.'

'That is true.' He laughs. 'Anyway, this feels like a sign or something from her. She's telling me it's OK to leave, I think. Or else she's pissed. One or the other.'

Marnie puts her hands on her stomach. The baby has been wedged way over to the left, and she shifts around to try to find a comfortable position.

'How you feeling, then?' Uncle Mike takes her hand.

'Pretty good. Baby's just in a weird position today.'

Mike starts tearing up.

'You OK?'

'Yeah, I'm fine. You know me. Sometimes I cry.' He wipes at his face. 'I'm just remembering when you were born. Me and Cath came down to meet you. And when we got there, Alice was holding you, and she was just weeping. You must have been only a couple of hours old or something. She kept saying, over and over, how beautiful you were. And then she told us that she had thought of her life as a kind of tragedy. Until that moment. She said – and I'll never forget this. She said, "*I was wrong, it isn't a tragedy at all.*" You were the love of her life, Marn. And now you'll see. In a few more weeks. You'll know what I'm talking about. It's the greatest thing ever. To get to love someone so much.' His voice cracks and tears are rolling down his face. 'Jesus, will you look at me? Like the old days, huh, Marn?'

'No, it's not like the old days. We came a long way, didn't we?'

'We really hung in there.' Mike squeezes her hand. 'Six more weeks, Marn. Six more weeks.'

Once they are finished, Marnie and Kevin will take their things and go back down to Dartmouth. Teresa will help her father finish up, and that will be it. Marnie will never sit in the living room, never spend the night here again.

Tomorrow, Kevin and Marnie are driving to Crane's Beach for the day. When Marnie was in rehab, the counsellors taught her visualisation techniques to counter panic attacks, urging her to imagine herself in a favourite place any time the bad thoughts became overwhelming. Marnie never found it useful. She could never picture being at Crane's Beach without also thinking of her grandmother, which would cause a deep spiral of grief and longing. And yet here she is, living an hour away, and she hasn't taken Kevin to see her favourite place in the world. In fact, Marnie hasn't gone there, not even once, since Alice died.

Tomorrow, Marnie will float on her back in the Block Island Sound with Kevin looping his arms underneath her, cradling her body, her large belly popped up out of the water. They will drift with their eyes closed in the gentle waves at Crane's Beach. The same water where she spent countless afternoons wading and swimming with her grandmother. The same water that connects further up the coast and out to the beaches at the very end of the Cape and stretches across the Atlantic, to the English Channel and to Sea Place Beach, where her grandmother swam throughout her own childhood.

Marnie still has the photo album that her grandmother made from their trip to Spithandle. On the last page, there's a picture of the two of them with their arms around each other, smiling at the end of the pier on their last morning. Marnie managed to hold on to the album all these years, and a manila envelope of Danny's letters to Alice that he continued to write to her, even after she finished with him, pleading with her to reconsider. His love for her lasted so much longer than their time together, stretching across decades, and maybe even still exists today, right now, at the very end of this century. Just like her grandmother's legacy, spanning two continents and all the miles she travelled. She will always be more than just pictures Marnie has held on to. Alice was here, and everything is different because of it.

  Marnie places her hand over her belly, feels the dull thud against the wall of her uterus, small, gentle kicks. As if the baby is saying, *I'm coming, I'm coming, hold on, just hold on. I'm almost here.*

Acknowledgements

I AM EXTREMELY GRATEFUL to everyone who not only made it possible for me to write this novel but also to get it published. First, I want to thank Pat and Ernie Blackman, my extraordinary in-laws, whose stories of their childhoods during World War Two were a huge source of inspiration for this novel. They provided numerous oral histories, answered many, many questions, helped find resources as well as being the king and queen of grandparents and have always been incredibly supportive of my writing. Meg and Jack Ansell, Ann and Bill Gardner, and Pete Lock also took time to share their childhood wartime experiences.

This novel would never have been published without my amazing agent, Millie Hoskins, who I have been so lucky to have in my corner, supporting and advocating for me. A huge, enormous thank you to Amy Blackman for introducing us, and for being so supportive. I could not have dreamed of a better editor than Arzu Tahsin, and a huge thank you to Zoe Yang. I feel so incredibly grateful that my novel has found such a good home with Manilla Press and also want to thank Sophie Orme and everyone else.

For years of support and encouragement of my writing as well as friendship: Richard Arthur, Moira Brennan,

Steve Brown, José Carlos Casado, Barbara Findlen, Meredith Fuchs, Jay Gardner, Anne Gisleson, Kristen Golden, Judy Goldschmidt, Catherine Gund, Jeanne Koenig, Jeff Magness, Colleen McCabe, Justin Morreale, Billy Morrissette, Sujean Rim, Filemon Rodriguez, Dean and Allison Sprankling, Keith Summa, Richard Shepard, Maura Tierney, Megan Tingley, and Dan Zevin.

I benefitted greatly from the opportunity to work with amazing teachers and writing mentors. Thank you to Elizabeth Gaffney for invaluable feedback and support and A Public Space for providing high-calibre writing workshops. Thanks also to co-teacher Andrea Chapin and the other writers in the 2018 and 2019 workshops, especially Megan Cummins, Alanna Schubach, Anisa Rahim, and Ibby Reilly Sollors. Thank you to John Reed, Katie Rogin, Jason Lees, Bernard Lumpkin, Carolyn Goldhush, Jennifer Cooke, Alice Naude, Jody Winer, and Abigail Hastings for encouragement and feedback when I was getting started. Thank you to the Writers Room in New York City and the Virginia Center for the Creative Arts for providing a quiet oasis where drafts of this novel were written.

I want to thank my students at the Bedford Hills Correctional Facility, the Queens, Brooklyn and Westchester public libraries, and the schools in the Bronx and Queens where I taught during the writing of this novel for sharing their stories with me. And thank you to my teaching colleagues, especially David Ciminello, Ellen Hagan, Elizabeth Hamilton, Abigail Hastings, and Renée Watson.

Thank you for love and support and fun during the writing of this novel to my siblings and their partners, my nieces and nephews and their partners, my god-daughter, Petra, and my entire extended family, spanning three continents, including Australia. A special thank you to my parents who instilled from a young age a life-long passion for the written word and, despite losses during their own childhoods, went on to provide me and my siblings with such a loving, supportive and stable one, and made us the center of their lives. They are also amazing and devoted grandparents, which has been invaluable for everyone.

To my daughters, Rae and Lola, thank you for everything, for always inspiring me in so many ways, and making me feel hopeful. And for Andy, what would my life be if we never ended up talking that night at that pub in August, 1987?

For my life-long friend, Marsh McCall, who is gone much too soon. I almost abandoned this project, but you motivated me to pick it back up and see it through to the end.

Finally, this story centres around the bond between a grandmother and her granddaughter, a bond I had the good fortune to experience myself. My grandmother, Helen, was an extraordinary, brave, amazing person, who has inspired me my whole life. She always believed in me and this book is for her and also in honour of grandmothers and the unique love between them and their grandchildren.

Portions of the book were previously published, in different formats, in the following publications: the *Atticus Review* and *Liars League NYC*.